Dear Reader,

Have you ever wondered what it would be like to find
yourself seduced by a tall, dark stranger from a foreign land?
A man so infuriatingly arrogant, yet so achingly irresistible?
Well, wonder no more. Silhouette is proud to bring you
Sheiks of Summer, a powerful and passionate anthology
featuring the most famous of the fantasy heroes, the sheik.

The collection starts off with "The Sheik's Virgin" by
Susan Mallery. Who better to tell the story of an innocent
beauty chaperoned through exotic lands by a seductive
stranger than Susan, author of the bestselling sheik miniseries
DESERT ROGUES? You won't want to miss this sensual new
story!

Next up, visit the SONS OF THE DESERT in Alexandra Sellers'
captivating new romance, "Sheikh of Ice." For this spirited
heroine, a coolly arrogant sheikh is not exactly a fantasy
man—until she finds beneath that hard-bodied exterior
the heat that sets her soul on fire.

And in Fiona Brand's mesmerizing tale "Kismet," past lives
and heartrending passion bring together a seemingly plain
woman and a drop-dead-gorgeous prince. Will fate keep these
star-crossed lovers together forever?

We hope you enjoy this brand-new collection of fantasy sheik
heroes!

Happy reading!

The Editors
Silhouette Books

SUSAN MALLERY

"If you haven't read Susan Mallery, you must!"
—*New York Times* bestselling author Suzanne Forster

Susan Mallery is the bestselling author of nearly fifty books for Silhouette Books & Harlequin Books. She makes her home in the Pacific Northwest with her handsome prince of a husband and her two adorable-but-not-bright cats.

ALEXANDRA SELLERS

"Alexandra Sellers' sheikhs are overwhelmingly sexy and always fascinating."
—Award-winning author Leigh Michaels

Alexandra Sellers is the author of over twenty-five novels and a feline language text published in 1997 and still selling. Born and raised in Canada, Alexandra first came to London as a drama student. Now she lives near Hampstead Heath with her husband, Nick. They share housekeeping with Monsieur, who jumped through the window one day and announced, as cats do, that he was moving in. What she would miss most on a desert island is shared laughter. Readers can write to Alexandra at P.O. Box 9449, London NW3 2WH, England.

FIONA BRAND

"Fiona Brand has become one of my favorite writers. She has that magic touch with heroes that gets me every time."
—*New York Times* bestselling author Linda Howard

Fiona Brand has always wanted to write. After working eight years for the New Zealand forest service as a clerk, she decided she could spend at least that much time trying to get a romance novel published. Luckily, it took only five years, not eight. Fiona lives in a subtropical fishing and diving paradise called the Bay of Islands with her two children.

Sheiks of Summer

Susan Mallery
Alexandra Sellers
Fiona Brand

Published by Silhouette Books
America's Publisher of Contemporary Romance

SILHOUETTE BOOKS

ISBN 0-373-48470-4

SHEIKS OF SUMMER

Copyright © 2002 by Harlequin Books S.A.

The publisher acknowledges the copyright holders
of the individual works as follows:

THE SHEIK'S VIRGIN
Copyright © 2002 by Susan Macias Redmond

SHEIKH OF ICE
Copyright © 2002 by Alexandra Sellers

KISMET
Copyright © 2002 by Fiona Walker

CONTENTS

THE SHEIK'S VIRGIN
Susan Mallery

Dear Reader,

One of the best parts of writing for Silhouette Books is the opportunity to spend my day writing about fabulous men. I'm not talking about the cute guy at the water cooler, or the everyday hero who takes the time to (gasp) pick up his socks. I mean really amazing fantasy men.

To me, that's what sheik stories have always been. Tales about incredibly rich strangers who desperately need the love of a good woman…even if they haven't quite figured that out yet.

Sheik books are often variations on a theme. Some are intense, dark stories that deal with some of life's reality. Some are more of a cross between *Cinderella* and *Arabian Nights*. I tend to write the latter. Sexy, funny, oh-my-gosh-did-he-really-say-that kind of books that will (I hope) make you shiver, make you smile and make you appreciate your real-life hero, whomever he may be.

Here's to the heroes in our lives, be they husbands, fathers, brothers or simply good friends. And here's to a little time spent with a fantasy!

All the best,

Susan Mallery

Chapter 1

The island of Lucia-Serrat glittered like an emerald in a bed of sapphires. Phoebe Carson pressed her forehead against the window of the small commuter plane and stared at the lush landscape below. As they circled in preparation for landing, she saw a snow-white beach, a rain forest, a crescent of blue, blue ocean, then a small city perched on a cliff. Her heart pounded in her chest and her ears popped.

The flight attendant announced that it was time to return seat backs and tray tables to their upright positions. What had seemed so strange when her journey had begun was second nature to her now. Phoebe tightened her seat belt and checked her tray table. She'd been too busy staring out the window to bother putting her seat back. She'd wanted to see everything as they approached Lucia-Serrat.

"Just as you promised, Ayanna," she whispered to herself. "So beautiful. Thank you for allowing me to spend this time here."

Phoebe returned her attention to the view out the window. The ground seemed to rush up to meet them, then she felt the gentle bump of the airplane wheels on the runway. She could see lush trees and bushes, tropical flowers and brightly colored birds. Then the plane turned to taxi toward the terminal and her view of paradise was lost.

Thirty minutes later Phoebe had collected her small suitcase and passed through customs and immigration. The official-looking young man had greeted her, stamped her passport and had asked if she had anything to declare. When she said she did not, he waved her through.

As easy as that, Phoebe thought, tucking her crisp new passport into her handbag.

All around her families greeted each other, while young couples, obviously on their honeymoon, strolled slowly arm in arm. Phoebe felt a little alone, but she refused to be lonely. Not at the beginning of her adventure. She found the courtesy phone and called her hotel. The hotel clerk promised that the driver would arrive to pick her up within fifteen minutes.

Phoebe had started for the glass doors leading out of the airport when a small store window caught her eye. She didn't usually shop very much, but the display drew her. Bottles of French perfume sat in nests of satin. Designer handbags and shoes hung on barely visible wires from the ceiling of the display case. Everything looked beautiful and very expensive, yet she knew there was no harm in looking while she waited for her ride to the hotel.

Phoebe stepped into the coolness of the store and inhaled a cloud of perfume-scented air. Different fragrances blended together perfectly. Although she was intrigued by the bottles on display, the tall, chicly dressed woman behind the counter made her nervous, so she turned in the opposite direction, only to find herself in front of a case of jewelry.

Rings, earrings, bracelets and necklaces appeared to have been casually tossed into the velvet-lined case. Yet Phoebe suspected it took a long time to make everything look so artless. She bent to get a closer look. One of the center diamonds in a cocktail ring was larger than the nail on her little finger. Phoebe figured she could probably live well for a couple of years on what that one piece cost. If this was an example of shopping in Lucia-Serrat, she would restrict hers to looking in windows.

"I think that is too large for you."

The unexpected comment caught her off guard. She straightened immediately, pressing her hand to her chest.

"I was just looking," she said breathlessly. "I didn't touch anything."

A man stood in front of her. While she was tall— nearly five-ten—he was several inches taller. Dark hair had been brushed back from his handsome face. There were tiny lines by the corners of his amazing brown-black eyes, and a hint of a smile teasing at the corners of his mouth. She told herself to look away— that it was rude to stare—but something about his expression, or maybe it was the sculptured lines of his cheekbones and jaw, compelled her.

He looked like a male model in an expensive liquor ad, only a little older. Phoebe instantly felt out of place and foolish. Her dress had cost less than twenty dollars at a discount outlet, and that had been last year, while the man's suit looked really expensive. Not that she had a lot of experience with things like men's suits.

"The bracelet," he said.

She blinked at him. "Excuse me?"

"I thought you were looking at the sapphire bracelet. While it's lovely and the color of the stones matches your eyes, it is too large for your delicate wrist. Several links would have to be removed."

She forced herself to tear her gaze from his face, and looked at the jewelry case. Right in the center was a sapphire bracelet. Oval blue stones surrounded by diamonds. It probably cost more than a beachfront hotel back home in Florida.

"It's very nice," she said politely.

"Ah, you do not like it."

"No. I mean yes, of course I like it. It's beautiful." But wishing after something like that was about as realistic as expecting to buy a 747.

"Perhaps there was something else you were shopping for?"

"No. Just looking."

She risked glancing at him again. There was something about his dark eyes, something almost…kind. Which made no sense. Handsome gentlemen didn't notice women like her. Actually no one noticed women like her. She was too tall, too thin and much too plain. Nor had anyone ever made her stomach flutter as it was doing right now.

"Is this your first visit to Lucia-Serrat?" he asked.

Phoebe thought of the blank pages in her new passport. "It's my first trip anywhere," she confessed. "I'd never been on a plane until this morning." She frowned as she thought about the time zones she'd crossed. "Or maybe it was yesterday. I flew from Miami to New York, then to Bahania, then to here."

He raised one eyebrow. "I see. Forgive me for saying this, but Lucia-Serrat seems an unusual place to begin one's travels. Many people are not familiar with the island. Although it is very beautiful."

"Very," she agreed. "I haven't seen very much. I mean, I just arrived, but I saw it from the plane window. I thought it looked like an emerald. So green and glittering in the middle of the ocean." She inhaled deeply. "It even smells different. Florida is sort of tropical, but nothing like this. Everyone seems so cosmopolitan and sure of themselves. I don't even know what—"

She pressed her lips together and ducked her head.

"Sorry," she murmured, wondering if she could have sounded more like a schoolgirl. "I didn't mean to blurt all that out."

"Do not apologize. I am enjoying your enthusiasm."

There was something about the cadence of his speech, Phoebe thought dreamily. His English was perfect, but had a more formal quality. There was also a trace of an accent, not that she could place it.

He lightly touched her chin, as if requesting she raise her head. The contact was fleeting at best, and yet she felt the impact all the way down to her toes.

"What brings you to my island?" he asked gently.

"You live here?"

"All of my life." He hesitated, then shrugged. "My family has been in residence for over five hundred years. We came for the spices and stayed for the oil."

"Oh, my." That sounded so romantic. "I, um, wanted to visit because of a family member. My great-aunt was born here. She always talked about the island and how she hated to leave. She passed away a few months ago." Some of Phoebe's happiness bled away as a pang of loneliness shot through her. "She wanted me to see the world, but it was her request that I begin here, where she was born."

"You and your great-aunt were close?"

Phoebe leaned against the jewelry case. From the corner of her eye she saw two store clerks talking frantically in the corner. They gestured wildly, but didn't approach either her or the stranger.

"She raised me," she said, returning her attention to the kind man in front of her. "I never knew my father, and my mother died when I was eight. Great-Aunt Ayanna took me in." She smiled at the memory. "I'd been raised in Colorado, so moving to Florida was pretty exciting. Ayanna said it was the closest place to Lucia-Serrat she could find. I think she missed the island very much."

"So you honor her memory by visiting the island."

Phoebe hadn't thought of it that way. She smiled. "That's exactly right. I want to visit the places she liked to go. She even gave me a list."

The tall stranger held out his hand. Obviously he wanted to read the list. Phoebe reached into the outside pocket of her purse and handed it to him.

He unfolded the single sheet of paper and read silently. She took the opportunity to study his thick hair and the length of his lashes, the powerful build of his body. They weren't standing very close at all, yet she would swear she felt the heat of his body. A crazy thing to be thinking, she told herself. But true. A warmth seeped through her as she watched him.

As he returned the list to her, he said, "All excellent choices. Are you familiar with the legend of Lucia's Point?"

Phoebe had long since memorized Ayanna's list. Lucia's Point was second from the bottom. "Not at all."

"They say that only lovers may visit. If they make love in the shade of the waterfall, they will be blessed all the days of their lives. So have you brought your lover with you?"

Phoebe suspected he was teasing her, but she couldn't stop herself from blushing. A lover? Couldn't the man tell from looking at her that she'd never even had a boyfriend, let alone a lover?

Before she could think of something to say—preferably something witty and charming and sophisticated—a uniformed man appeared at her side.

"Ms. Phoebe Carson? I am here to take you to your hotel." He bowed slightly and took her luggage. "At your convenience," he said, and backed out of the store.

Phoebe glanced out the window and saw a green van sitting at the curb. Gold lettering spelled out Parrot Bay Inn, where she would be staying for the next month.

"My ride is here," she told the stranger who had lingered to chat with her.

"I can see. I hope you will enjoy your time in Lucia-Serrat."

His dark eyes seemed to see inside her. Could he read her mind? She hoped not—if he could, he would figure out that she was an inexperienced fool who was completely out of her element with him.

"You've been very kind," she murmured when nothing more charming occurred to her.

"My pleasure."

Before she could turn away, he reached out and took her hand in his, then raised it to chest level. He bent his head and lightly kissed her fingers. The old-world gesture took her breath away, as did the tingling that instantly shot up her arm.

''Perhaps we will be lucky enough to run into each other again,'' he said.

Phoebe was incapable of speech. Fortunately he left before she did something really embarrassing like stutter or babble. After a couple of seconds she was able to draw in a breath. Then she forced herself to start walking. She left the store and stepped out into the warm afternoon. It was only when she was settled in the hotel van that she thought to look for the man she'd met in the store. She didn't even know his name.

But look as she might, she couldn't spot him. The driver climbed in and started the engine. Five minutes later they had left the airport behind them and were on a two-lane road that hugged a cliff above the sea.

The ocean stretched out to the horizon on her right, while on her left, lush foliage crept down to the side of the road. Flashes of color fluttered from branch to branch, proof of the wild parrots that made their home on the tropical island. Phoebe could smell that salty air and the rich, dark earth dampened by a recent shower. Excitement coursed through her—she was really here, she thought as the van arrived at the hotel.

The Parrot Bay Inn had been built nearly two hundred years before. The white building soared up several stories, with red and pink bougainvilleas covering the bottom two floors. The foyer was an open atrium, the reception desk hand carved with an elegance from an older time. Phoebe registered and was shown to her room.

Ayanna had made her niece promise to visit the island of Lucia-Serrat for a month, and to stay only at the Parrot Bay Inn. Phoebe refused to consider the expense as she was shown to a lovely corner mini-suite complete with a view of the ocean and a balcony worthy of Romeo and Juliet. She felt as if she were floating as she stepped out to watch the sun sink toward the west.

A reddish-orange bath colored the sky. The water turned from blue to dark green. She breathed in the scents of the island as she leaned against her balcony railing and savored the moment.

When it was dark, she moved back into her room to unpack and settle in for her stay. The four-poster bed looked comfortable and the bathroom, while old-fashioned, was large and contained every amenity. If the silence made her a little sad, she refused to dwell on her loneliness. She was used to making her own way. Here, on the island of her great-aunt's birth, she would connect with all that Ayanna had spoken of. She would feel her aunt's presence. She would begin to live her life.

Just before she went down to dinner there was a knock on her door. When she opened it, a bellman carried in a large spray of tropical flowers, touched his cap and left before Phoebe could tell him there must be some mistake. No one would be sending her flowers.

Even though she knew it was foolish, she couldn't help imagining the handsome stranger she'd met at the duty-free shop at the airport. No. Not him. He had to be at least thirty-three or thirty-four. He would think of her as a child, nothing more. Yet her fingers trembled as she opened the white envelope tucked among the blossoms.

"May your stay on the island be delightful."

No signature. Which meant that while they weren't from the man at the store, she could pretend they were. She could imagine that instead of awkward, she'd been funny and charming. Instead of dressed in something old and out of style, she'd been elegant and sophisticated and that he couldn't stop thinking about her. Much as she couldn't stop thinking about him.

The next morning Phoebe took the stairs instead of the elevator. She wore loose cotton trousers and sandals, a tank top covered by a matching short-sleeved shirt. While Lucia-Serrat was more forward thinking than many Arab countries, she didn't want to cause offense by dressing too immodestly. In her oversize straw bag she'd packed sunscreen, a few pieces of fruit from the bowl in her room, a bottle of water and a map. Today she would begin to tackle Ayanna's list, beginning with what was closest to the hotel.

When she grew more familiar with her way, she would rent a car and explore the outlying areas. As for visiting Lucia's Point, well, she would deal with that problem when she had to.

Phoebe skipped down the last two steps and stepped into the foyer of the hotel.

"Good morning. I trust you slept well?"

She skittered to a stop, unable to believe what she was seeing. It was him—the man from the store the previous day. Oh, the suit was gone, replaced by casual trousers and a crisp white shirt. But she recognized his handsome features and the odd fluttering in her stomach. His teeth flashed white as he smiled at her.

"I see by your expression of surprise that you remember me. I hope the memory is pleasant."

She thought of how she'd gone to sleep remembering his light kiss on her fingers, and her dreams of a dark-haired stranger promising to show her the delights of Lucia's Point. A blush crawled up her face.

"Good morning," she whispered, thinking that response was a whole lot safer than discussing her memories of him.

"So you begin your tour of my island today. I remember—your aunt's list. What did you wish to explore first?"

Phoebe didn't know what to say. "I thought I would start with the Parrot Cove beach," she said hesitantly, not sure what brought him to the hotel, or why he bothered to speak with her. While thoughts of him had kept her occupied for hours last night, she couldn't have been a very interesting encounter for him.

"Not the beach," he said with a flick of his wrist. "While we have the most beautiful beaches in the world on the island, there is nothing extraordinary about sand. I have decided we will start with the banyan tree."

Phoebe resisted the urge to stick her finger in her ear to see if something was stuck there. She couldn't possibly have heard the man correctly. "I, um…" She took a deep breath. "I don't understand."

"Then I need to be more clear. I was charmed by what you told me yesterday and I have decided to assist you in fulfilling your late aunt's last request. Therefore I shall escort you to all the places on the list." He gave her a rakish smile. "Well, perhaps not *all* the places."

She instantly thought of Lucia's Point, which was no doubt what he wanted her to do. She thought the man might actually be teasing her. Was it possible? No one ever took the time to kid around with her.

And as tempting as his offer might be, there were a couple of things she couldn't forget. "I wouldn't want to be a bother, and even if you were willing to share your time with me, we've only just met. I don't even know your name."

He touched his fingertips lightly to his chest. "I am most remiss," he said, and swept her a low bow. He should have looked silly, but somehow he managed to look very elegant. "I am Mazin, a resident of the island, and your servant for as long as you command me to serve."

Phoebe couldn't believe this was happening—maybe in a movie, but not in real life and certainly not to her. She glanced around and realized that everyone in the lobby was watching them. She hesitated, torn between what she wanted to do and what she knew she *must* do.

"Miss Carson?" A man approached. The brass name tag said he was Mr. Eldon, the hotel manager. "I want to assure you that, ah…" He glanced at the stranger. "That Mazin is a most honorable gentleman. No harm will come to you while you are in his presence."

"You see," Mazin said. "I have those who are willing to vouch for my character. Come, Phoebe. See the wonders of Lucia-Serrat with me."

She was about to refuse—because she prided herself on being sensible—when Ayanna's words came back to her. Her aunt had wanted her to live life to the fullest and never have regrets. Phoebe knew she would regret refusing Mazin's invitation, regardless of how foolish it might be to accept.

"The banyan tree sounds very nice," she said softly, and allowed Mazin to lead her out to his waiting car.

Chapter 2

The young woman cast one last tentative glance over her shoulder before slipping into the front seat of his Mercedes. Mazin closed the door and circled to the driver's side, all the while trying to figure out what he was doing.

He didn't have time to play games with children—and that's exactly what Phoebe Carson was. A child of twenty or so. Far too young and inexperienced to succeed at his kind of game. Why was he bothering? Worse, why was he wasting his time?

He slid onto the driver's seat and glanced at her.

She stared at him, her eyes wide—as if she were a cornered rabbit and he were some deadly predator. A perfect metaphor, he thought wryly. He should walk away—tell her that he was too busy to take her on a tour of the island. If he wanted a woman—*a woman,* not a child—there were dozens who would fly to his side at the first hint of his interest. They knew him and his world. They knew what was expected. They understood the rules.

Phoebe understood nothing. Even as he put the car in gear, he knew he was making a mistake. Because he was acting against his good sense—something he never allowed himself to do. His nature didn't allow him to take advantage of those who were not his equal. So why was he here with her?

Yesterday he had seen her going through customs. She had seemed both brave and terrified...and very much an innocent. At first he had kept track of her because he had been sure she was being met and he wanted to make sure she found her way. Later, when he had realized she was alone, he had found himself compelled to approach her for reasons he could not explain.

He had just returned from his own trip abroad. He should have been eager to go home. And yet he had taken the time to speak with Phoebe. Having spoken with her, he could not forget her.

Madness, he told himself. Simple madness.

"The weather seems very nice," she said, interrupting his thoughts.

Mazin glanced out the front windshield. The sky was blue and cloudless. "With only the occasional sprinkle, this is our dry season," he told her. "In the fall we have a rainy season, followed by several weeks of monsoons. Sometimes I am surprised that all of Lucia-Serrat doesn't wash away into the sea. But we survive and after the rains, everything grows.''

Maybe it was her eyes, he thought as he turned onto the main road. So wide and blue. Trusting, he thought grimly. She was far too trusting. No one could be that innocent. He gritted his teeth. Was that the problem? Did he think she was pretending?

He wasn't sure. Did women like her really exist, or was this all an elaborate plot to get close to him? He glanced at her, taking in the long blond hair pulled back in a thick braid and her simple, inexpensive clothing. Was she trying to put him at his ease by appearing so far out of his league as to be beneath notice? Yet he had noticed. For reasons he could not explain, she intrigued him.

So he would play her game—whatever that might be—until he learned the truth, or grew tired of her. Because he would grow tired…he always did.

"You said your family had been here five hundred years," she said, glancing at him quickly, then returning her attention to the window. "I can't imagine having that much personal history."

"The island was first discovered by explorers setting out from Bahania nearly a thousand years ago," he told her. "It was uninhabited and considered sacred ground. The royal family claimed it for their own. As European sailors set out to conquer the New World, the king of Bahania grew concerned that his private paradise would be taken for Portugal, Spain or England. So he sent relatives to live here. Eventually the island became populated. A sovereignty was established. To this day, the crown prince of the island is a cousin of the king of Bahania."

Phoebe looked at him, her eyes wide. "I guess I knew about there being a prince, because that's how my great-aunt got in trouble, but I never thought about there being one right this minute. Does he live on the island?"

"Yes, he is a permanent resident."

She looked as if she were about to ask another question, when they drove past a break in the trees. Phoebe stared at the view of the ocean and caught her breath.

"It's so beautiful."

"Do you not see the ocean where you live?"

"Sometimes." She gave him a quick smile before returning her attention to the view. "Ayanna's house is a few miles inland. I used to spend a lot of time by the water when I was in school, but after she became ill, I never had the time."

She pressed her fingers against the window. Her hands were as delicate as the rest of her. Mazin eyed her clothes. They were worn, although well cared for. In the right designer gown, with a little makeup and her hair styled, she would be a beauty. Like this, she was a plain gray dove.

While the fantasy of Phoebe as a femme fatale appealed to him, he found himself equally attracted to the little dove sitting next to him.

A dove who had no idea of his identity. Perhaps that was part of her appeal. He so rarely spent time with women who were not clear on who he was and what he could give them.

"There is a grove of spice trees," he said, pointing to his left. "People assume that spices come from seeds, but often they are found in the tree bark."

She turned to look. As she leaned toward his side of the car, he caught the scent of her body. Soap, he thought, nearly smiling. She smelled of the rose soap left for guests at the Parrot Bay Inn.

"Dozens of different kinds of spice are grown here," he said.

"What are those flowers?" she asked. "Are they growing out of the tree bark?"

"No. They're orchids. They're grafted into the branches of the trees and grown for use in flower arrangements. Some are used in perfume. Mango trees are the best hosts, but you will find orchids growing everywhere on the island."

"I haven't seen any oil pumps. You said there was oil on the island. Or is it out at sea?"

"Both."

He waited, wondering if this was where she would tip her hand. Interest in oil meant interest in money...specifically his. But Phoebe didn't even blink. She turned her attention to the passenger window, almost as if the oil didn't matter.

Now that he thought about it he realized that her
enthusiasm for the island was far greater than her enthusiasm for him accompanying her. Was she really
the shy tourist she claimed to be?

He couldn't remember the last time a woman
hadn't hung on to his every word. It was almost as if
she wasn't overly interested in what he had to say. If
true, it was a unique experience.

They rounded a bend. The main bazaar stretched
out on a flat stretch of stone-covered earth.

"The Lucia-Serrat marketplace has been in exis-
tence for nearly five hundred years," he said. "These
outer walls are part of the original walls that surrounded the area."

Phoebe clapped her hands together in delight. "Oh,
Mazin, we must stop. Look at everything they're selling. Those little copper pots and flowers and oh, is
that a monkey?"

She laughed as a small monkey climbed across several open-air booths to snatch a particularly ripe slice
of mango from a display. The owner of the monkey
handed over a coin before the owner of the fruit stall
could complain.

Mazin shook his head. "Not today, Phoebe. We
will save the bazaar for another day. After all, you
have a list and to see everything, we must proceed in
an orderly fashion."

"Of course. Your way makes sense." She leaned
back in her seat. "I've always been in favor of being
orderly." She sighed softly. "Except something about

this island makes me want to be reckless.'' She smiled at him. ''I am not, by nature, a reckless person.''

''I see.''

Her innocent words, the light in her eyes and the way her smile lingered on her full mouth sent a jolt of desire through him. The arousal was so unexpected, Mazin almost didn't recognize it at first.

He wanted her. He *wanted* her. How long had it been since he had done little more than go through the motions of making love? His desire had faded until he could barely remember what it was like to ache with passion. He had bedded the most skilled, the most beautiful women of his acquaintance and none of them had stirred him beyond the desire necessary to perform. Yet here, with this plain gray dove, he felt heat for the first time in years.

The fates that determined his life were once again having a great laugh at his expense.

''What do you know of present-day Lucia-Serrat?'' he asked.

''Not very much. Ayanna mostly talked about the past. What it was like when she was my age.'' Her expression softened with obvious affection. ''She would describe glittering parties she attended. Apparently she was invited to the prince's private residence for several events. She talked about meeting visiting dignitaries from other countries. She even met the Prince of Wales—the one who became King Edward

and then abdicated the throne for Mrs. Simpson.
Ayanna said he was an elegant dancer.''

She talked about other parties her great-aunt had
attended. Mazin wasn't sure if her lack of knowledge
about current events on Lucia-Serrat was real or pre-
tense. If she played a game, she played it well. If
not—

He didn't want to think about that. If Phoebe
Carson was exactly what she appeared to be, he had
no business involving himself with her. He was jaded
and far too old. Unfortunately, with his body unexpectedly hard with desire, he doubted he was noble
enough to walk away.

"Look," Mazin said, pointing out the window.
"There are parrots in the trees."

Phoebe strained to see, then rolled down her window. The tall trees were alive with the colorful birds.
Reds, greens, blues all blended together into a fluttering rainbow of activity. She breathed in the sweet
air of the island and thought how it was a miracle that
she was here at all.

Mazin turned left, heading inland. Mazin. Phoebe
still couldn't believe that he'd actually come to her
hotel that morning simply to show her around the
island and help her with Ayanna's list. Men never
noticed her. It was amazing enough that he'd bothered
to speak with her yesterday, but to have remembered
her through the night—who would have thought it
possible?

She brushed her hands against her slacks. Her

palms were damp. Nerves, she thought. She'd never met anyone like Mazin. He was so sophisticated and worldly. He made her nervous.

A sign up ahead caught her attention. A carving of a small creature standing on its back feet and staring toward the sky sat on top of the sign.

"Meerkats," she breathed. "Oh, look. It's the reserve."

"I suppose you're going to ask me to stop there, as well."

She wanted to, but thought the banyan tree was a better outing to share with her companion. At least staring at a tree wouldn't make her babble like an idiot. Being around adorable meerkats with their funny faces and charming antics would make her gush in a very embarrassing way.

"I'm determined to abide by the schedule," she said, trying to sound mature. "I'll see the meerkats another day."

"Quite sensible," Mazin murmured.

His tone of voice caught her attention. She glanced at him, taking in his strong profile and the air of confidence and power that surrounded him. She didn't know why he bothered with her, but she knew that whatever his expectations, he was destined to be disappointed. She had never been good at fitting in. She had no experience with the opposite sex—not that he was interested in her that way.

"You probably think of me as a child," she said before she could stop herself. Heat instantly flared on her cheeks and she had to resist the need to bury her face in her hands. Instead she pretended to be engrossed in the view out the passenger window.

"A child," he repeated. "Not that. A young woman. How old are you, Phoebe?"

She thought about lying, making herself sound older, but what was the point? People already thought she was much younger than her actual age.

"I'm twenty-three."

"So very grown-up," he teased.

She glanced at him. Their eyes met and she was relieved when she saw his expression was kind. "I'm not all that grown-up. I've seen little of the world, but what I have seen has taught me to depend on myself." She swallowed, then risked asking a question of her own. "How old are you?"

"Thirty-seven."

She did the math instantly. Fourteen years. Not such an impossible distance, although she didn't know what Mazin would think of it. No doubt his world was incredibly different from hers. They would have no experiences in common—which might make the age difference seem even larger.

Not that it mattered, she reminded herself. She didn't know why he'd taken time out of his day to show her around the island, but she doubted he had any *personal* interest in her.

She briefly wondered if he'd ever been married, but before she could gather the courage to ask, he turned down a narrow road. Trees and shrubs grew on both sides, their bright green leaves nearly brushing against the sides of the car.

"The banyan tree is protected by royal decree," Mazin said as he pulled into an empty parking lot. "It is considered a national treasure."

"A tree?"

"We value that which is unique to our island."

His low voice seemed to brush across her skin. Phoebe shivered slightly as she stepped out of his car. She glanced back once, noticing for the first time that he drove a *large* Mercedes. She recognized the symbol on the hood, but had no idea about the type of car, save that it was big and a silvery gray. Back home she drove a nine-year-old Honda.

Different worlds, she thought again.

"Is the park open?" she asked as they headed for a path leading to a covered patio with an information booth at the far end. She glanced both left and right. "There isn't anyone else around."

"This is not our busy season for tourists," Mazin told her as he lightly touched the back of her arm to guide her up the stairs toward the information booth. "Plus it is early in the day for visitors. However, the park is open."

Phoebe studied the plants they passed. She didn't know any of them on sight. There were brightly colored blossoms everywhere. Lavender star-shaped flowers hung from spindly trees. Spine-covered pods in vivid red reached for the sun. A wild and sultry perfume filled the air as if the flowers conspired to

intoxicate her. Even the air brushed against her body
like a sensual caress. Lucia-Serrat was like no place
she had ever been.

Mazin reached the information booth. He spoke
quietly with the person inside. Phoebe glanced up and
saw that the price of admission was three local dollars. She reached for the purse she'd slung over her
shoulder, then hesitated. What was she supposed to
do? It hadn't occurred to her that Mazin would pay,
but would he be mad if she said anything?

She had barely fumbled with the zipper on her
purse when he turned and looked at her. His dark eyes
narrowed.

"Do not even consider insulting me, my dove."

There was steel behind his words. Phoebe nodded
and dropped her hands to her side. Then she replayed
his sentence, pausing at the very end. *My dove.* It
didn't mean anything, she told herself as she mentally
stumbled over the two words. No man had ever called
her by anything other than her name. But it wasn't
significant. He probably used flowery language with
everyone.

She would store this memory away, she told herself. Later, when she was alone, she would pull it out
and pretend that he had meant something wonderful.
It would be a harmless game, something to hold the
loneliness at bay.

He collected two tickets and they walked through
an arch covered with blossoming bougainvillea.

"People think the pink and red on bougainvillea

are the flowers," Phoebe said inanely before she could stop herself. "Actually those are just leaves. The flowers are very small and often white."

"You know horticulture?" Mazin asked.

"Uh, not really. Just that. I read about it somewhere. I read a lot of things. I guess my head is full of obscure facts. I could probably do well on a game show."

She consciously pressed her lips together to keep from talking. Could she sound more stupid? The fact that Mazin made her nervous was of interest to no one save herself. If she continued to act like an idiot, he wasn't going to want to spend any more time with her.

The stone path had been worn smooth by years of use. They stepped from bright sun into shade provided by large trees. There were several formal gardens all around them. As they turned a corner, Phoebe caught her breath. In front of them stood the famous Lucia-Serrat banyan tree.

From where they were standing, they couldn't see the center of the tree. Branches spread out in all directions, some slender, some as thick around as a man. Sturdy roots grew down from the branches, anchoring the tree to the ground in hundreds of places. The tree itself stretched out for what seemed like miles. A small sign said that the circumference of the aerial roots was nearly ten acres.

"Is it the biggest in the world?" she asked.

"No. There is a larger tree in India. There is also a large one in Hawaii, although this one is bigger."

The leaves were huge and oval, tapering on each end. She stepped forward, ducking under several branches. There were paths through the aerial root system. She could see where others had walked. Reverently she touched the surprisingly smooth bark. This tree had been alive for hundreds of years.

"It feels like it's a living part of the structure of the island," she said, glancing back at Mazin.

He shrugged. "There is strength in the tree. Once it gets established, it can survive most any kind of storm. Even if one part is destroyed, the rest survives."

"I wouldn't mind being that strong," she said as she crouched down and picked up a fallen leaf.

"Why would you think you are not?"

She glanced at him. He stood within the shade of the tree. His dark eyes were unreadable. Phoebe suddenly realized she knew nothing about this man, that she was on a strange island and for all she knew, he made a habit of abducting female tourists traveling alone. She should be cautious and wary.

Yet she didn't want to be. Whatever had drawn her to Mazin continued to pull her to him today. She was foolish to trust him, and yet trust him she did.

"Strength requires experience and knowledge," she said. "I haven't lived very much. I never made it to college." She rose to her feet, still clutching the leaf in her hand. "My aunt got sick the summer after

I graduated from high school. She wanted me to go live my life, but I stayed home to take care of her.''

She rubbed the leaf between her fingers, then dropped it to the ground. "I'm not complaining. I don't have any regrets. I loved Ayanna and would give up everything to have her with me again. I would rather be with her now than be here or—''

Phoebe broke off when she realized what she'd said. Embarrassment gripped her. "I'm sorry. I didn't mean to imply that I wasn't enjoying your company.''

Mazin dismissed her apology with a wave of his hand. "It is of no concern. I am not insulted. Your affection for your aunt does you credit.''

He stared at her as if she were some strange creature he'd never seen before. Phoebe touched her cheek with the back of her hand and hoped the shadows of the tree kept him from seeing how she blushed. No doubt he found her silly and boring.

"Are you hungry?'' he asked abruptly. "There is a café nearby. I thought we could have lunch.''

Her heart fluttered, her embarrassment fled and it was as if the sun brightened the sky a little more than it had. Mazin held out his hand in invitation. Phoebe hesitated only a second before placing her trembling fingers in his hand.

Chapter 3

The café sat on the edge of the ocean. Phoebe felt as if she could stretch out her foot and touch the blue water. A soft breeze carried the scent of salt and island flowers, perfuming the air. The sun was hot, yet a large umbrella shielded them so that they felt only pleasantly warm.

She had the strongest urge to bounce up and down with excitement. She couldn't believe she was really here, on the island, having lunch with a very handsome man. If this was a dream, she didn't ever want to wake up.

Mazin was being so very kind. Her fingers still tingled from his touch when he'd held her hand as they'd walked to his car. She knew he hadn't intended the gesture to have meaning. There was no way he could have known how the heat from his hand had burned into her skin or made her heart race so delightfully.

"Have you decided?" he asked.

She glanced at the menu she held and realized she hadn't read it. She'd been too busy admiring the view.

"Maybe there's a local dish you would like to recommend," she said.

"The fresh fish. The chef here prides himself on his preparation. You won't be disappointed."

As she knew she wouldn't be able to taste anything, she didn't doubt that he was right. He could feed her ground-up cardboard and she would be content.

Their waiter appeared and Mazin gave him their orders. Phoebe picked up her iced tea and took a sip.

"This is such a beautiful spot," she said as she put down her glass. "I'm surprised it's not crowded for lunch."

Mazin seemed to hesitate. "Sometimes it is, but we're a little early."

Phoebe glanced at her watch. It was nearly noon, but she wasn't about to contradict her host. Besides, it might be fashionable to dine late on the island.

They sat on a patio that held about a dozen tables, all protected by umbrellas. In the distance she could see a grove of trees filled with parrots. Small lizards sunned themselves on the stone wall across from their table.

"What do you think of my island?" Mazin asked.

She smiled with contentment. "It's beautiful.

Ayanna always talked about Lucia-Serrat being paradise, but I'm not sure I ever believed her. Everything is so clean. It's not just the absence of trash on the road, but the fact that plant life grows everywhere. Are there really other people on this island?"

He smiled. "I assure you, my dove, we are not alone."

Too bad, she thought wistfully.

"There has been much debate about the future of the island. We require certain resources to survive, yet we do not want to destroy the beauty that brightens our world."

"There's a lot of that kind of talk in Florida," Phoebe said, leaning forward slightly. "Developers want to build apartment buildings and hotels. They impact the infrastructure. Growth is good for the economy, but irresponsible growth can be bad for the land itself. It's a delicate balance. I worry about things like the rain forest. Part of me wants to come firmly on the side of whatever tree or animal is in need, but I know that people need to eat and heat their homes."

"I would have assumed you were a rabid conservationist," he said, his voice teasing.

She smiled. "I'm not the rabid type. I care and I do what I can. I don't think there are any easy answers."

"I agree. Here on Lucia-Serrat we seek to find a balance. We live in harmony with nature. Yes, we must dig for oil, but all precautions are taken to protect the sea and those creatures who live there. That adds to the cost. There are those who protest, who want more oil and less worry about the birds and the fish.'' His brows drew together. ''There are those who would influence policy, but so far I have been—''

He broke off in midsentence, then shrugged. ''So far I have been happy with the choices the prince has made.''

Phoebe rested her elbows on the table. ''Do you know the prince?''

''I am familiar with the royal family.''

She turned that over in her mind. It was hard to imagine. ''I've never even met the mayor where I live,'' she said, more to herself than to him. ''Don't you like him?''

Mazin's eyebrows rose in surprise. ''Why do you ask me that?''

''I don't know. The way you said you've been happy with his choices. There was something in your voice. I thought maybe you didn't like him.''

''I assure you, that is not the case.''

She sipped her iced tea. ''Is there a parliament or something to keep the prince in line? I mean, what if he started making unfair rules? Could anyone stop him?''

''Prince Nasri is a wise and honorable ruler. To answer your questions, there is a form of parliament. They handle much of the government, but the prince is the true leader of the people.''

''Is he well liked?''

''I believe so. He is considered just. Two days a

month anyone may come to see him and discuss a grievance.''

"What about you? What do you do?" she asked.

Mazin leaned back in his chair. "I am in the government. I coordinate oil production."

She had no idea what that might involve. If he was in the government and knew the royal family then he had to be a pretty important man. "Is it all right that you're here with me now?" she asked. "I wouldn't want you to get in trouble for taking the day off."

"Do not worry yourself," he told her with a slow smile. "I have plenty of vacation days available to me."

They walked along the beach after lunch. Mazin couldn't remember the last time he'd simply gone for a walk by the sea. Although he could see the ocean from nearly every window in his house, the view had ceased to be beautiful. He doubt he even saw it anymore.

Yet with Phoebe, all was new. She laughed with delight as waves rolled close and lapped at her feet. She'd rolled up the legs of her slacks, exposing her slender ankles. He studied the naked skin, amazed that he felt aroused gazing at her. She was completely dressed except for her bare feet and he *wanted* her.

Twenty-three, he reminded himself. She was only twenty-three. No younger than he had suspected, but younger than he had hoped.

"Is there a coral reef?" Phoebe asked.

"Not on this side of the island, but on the north end. The area is more protected there. Do you dive?"

She wrinkled her nose. "I'm assuming you mean skin diving. I've never done it. I don't know that I could. Just the thought of being trapped underwater makes me nervous."

As she spoke, she pulled her braid over her shoulder so the length of blond hair lay against her chest. She unfastened the ribbon, then finger-combed her hair so it fluttered loose around her face.

Sunlight illuminated the side of her face, highlighting her perfect bone structure. If she were any other woman of his acquaintance, he would have assumed she was going for an effect, but with Phoebe, he wasn't so sure. While he still thought she might be playing a game with him, several hours in her company had made him stop wondering about the sincerity of her innocence. She blushed too easily for someone at home in the world. And if she was as inexperienced as he suspected, then she was in danger of being taken advantage of by someone....

Someone like himself, he thought grimly. Someone who could easily pluck the flower of her womanhood, savor its sweetness, then discard it.

He did not consider himself a bad person. Perhaps Phoebe had been sent into his life as a test of that theory. Perhaps he was taking this too seriously. He should simply enjoy her company for the day, return her to her hotel that afternoon and forget he'd ever met her. That would be the wisest course of action.

''The ocean is very different here,'' Phoebe said as they continued to walk along the beach. ''I don't have a lot of experience, but I know the color of the water is different than it is in Florida. Of course, the color is often a reflection of how shallow the water is. Around the gulf coast there are places you can wade out forever. Is it deeper here around the island?''

''Three sides are deep. The north end of the island is quite shallow.''

Phoebe sighed softly to herself. Why couldn't she talk about something more interesting? Here she was strolling along a beautiful beach next to a charming man and she babbled on about ocean depth. *Be brilliant,* she ordered herself. Unfortunately she didn't have a lot of experience in the brilliant department.

''Would you like to have a seat?'' he asked when they reached a cluster of rocks sticking out of the white sand.

She nodded and followed him to a flat rock warm from the sun. She dumped her shoes and purse on the sand, then slid next to him, careful to make sure they didn't touch. A light breeze teased at her hair and made goose bumps break out on her wet feet.

''Tell me about your great-aunt,'' he said. ''What was her life like here on the island?''

Phoebe drew one knee to her chest and wrapped her arms around her leg. ''Her mother owned a beauty shop in town and Ayanna learned to be a hairdresser there. When she was eighteen she went to work in the Parrot Bay Inn. Apparently back then it was an international hot spot.''

Mazin grinned. ''I have heard many stories about 'the old days,' as my father would call them. When people flew in from all over the world to spend a week or two in the Lucia-Serrat sun.''

''Ayanna said the same thing. She was young and beautiful, and she wanted a great romantic adventure.''

''Did she find it?''

Phoebe hesitated. ''Well, sort of. There were several men who wanted to marry her. She became engaged to one or two, always breaking it off. One of the men insisted she keep the ring. It was a lovely ruby ring. She wore it often.'' She smiled at the memory.

''If she broke the engagements, then they weren't romantic adventures,'' he said.

''You're right. I know the great love of her life was the crown prince. Apparently they were in love with each other, even though he was married. Eventually people found out and there was a great scandal. In the end, Ayanna had to leave.''

Mazin gazed out toward the ocean. ''I remember hearing something about that. Despite being such an old man, I was not alive then.''

''You're not so very old.''

He nodded regally. ''I'm pleased you think so.''

She wasn't sure if he was teasing or not. ''I don't think Ayanna ever heard from the prince again. She never admitted anything to me, but I have always suspected that in her heart of hearts she thought he would come find her. So her romance has an unhappy ending.''

''She lived in your country for many years. Didn't she marry?''

Phoebe shook her head. ''There were always men who wanted her, right up until she died. But although she enjoyed their company, she never loved any of them.''

''Did they love her?''

''Absolutely. She was wonderful. Charming, intelligent, funny and so lovely in every respect.''

He turned toward her, then placed his index finger under her chin. ''I would imagine you look much like her.''

Phoebe's eyes widened in surprise. ''Not at all. Ayanna was a great beauty. I don't look anything like her.''

How could he pretend to think she could even compare to Ayanna?

''You have a lovely face,'' he murmured, more to himself than her. ''Your eyes are the color of the sea on a cloudless day, your skin is as soft as silk.''

Phoebe felt heat flaring on her cheeks. Telling herself he wasn't really complimenting her didn't stop her from being embarrassed. She felt like some hick straight off the farm, with hay in her hair.

She pulled back slightly so that he wasn't touching her. ''Yes, well, you're very kind, but it's hard to ignore facts. I'm too tall and too skinny. Half the time I think I look like a boy more than a grown woman. It's fairly disheartening.''

Mazin gazed at her. His dark eyes seemed able to see into her soul. ''I would never mistake you for a boy.''

She couldn't look away. Her skin prickled as if she'd been in the sun too long. Maybe she had. Or maybe it was the island itself, weaving a magic spell around her.

''Men don't find me attractive,'' she said bluntly, because she couldn't think of anything else to say. ''Or interesting.''

''Not all men.''

Was it her imagination, or had he just moved a little closer? And was it suddenly really hot?

''Some men find you very attractive.''

She would have sworn he didn't actually say that last sentence, because his lips were too close to hers to be speaking. But she couldn't ask, because she was in shock. Tremendous shock. She even stopped breathing, because at that moment he kissed her.

Phoebe didn't know what to think or do. One minute she'd been sitting on a rock by the ocean trying not to babble, and the next a very handsome, very sophisticated older man was kissing her. On the lips. Which, she supposed, was where most people kissed. Just not her. Not ever. In fact—

Stop thinking!

Her mind obeyed, going blank. It was only then

that she realized his mouth was still on hers, which meant they were kissing. Which left her in the awkward position of having no clue as to what was expected of her.

The contact teased, making her want to lean into him. She liked the feel of his lips against hers and the way he placed one hand on her shoulder. She felt the heat of his fingers and the way his breath brushed across her cheek. She could see the dark fan of his lashes and the hint of stubble on his cheek. He smelled like sunshine, only more masculine.

Every part of her felt extrasensitive and her mouth trembled slightly.

He broke the kiss and opened his eyes, making her think perhaps hers should have been closed.

"You did not want me to do that," he said quietly.

She blinked several times. Not want her first kiss? Was he crazy? "No, it was great."

"But you didn't respond."

Humiliation washed over her. Phoebe slid off the rock onto the sand, then reached for her shoes. Before she could grab them, Mazin was at her side. He took her hands in his and somehow compelled her to look at him.

"What aren't you telling me?" he asked.

"Nothing." Everything, she thought.

"Phoebe."

He spoke in a warning tone that made her toes curl into the sand. She swallowed, then blurted the truth out all at once, or at least as much of it as she was willing to confess.

"I don't have a lot of experience with men. I never dated in high school, because I didn't fit in. Then Ayanna got sick and I spent the four years nursing her. That didn't leave time for a social life—not that I wanted one. The past six months I've been sad. So I'm not really good at the whole kissing thing."

She stopped talking and hoped he would buy her explanation without figuring out that no man had ever kissed her before.

She waited for him to say something. And waited. A smile teased at the corners of his mouth. His dark expression softened slightly. Then he cupped her face in his large, strong hands.

"I see," he murmured before once again touching his lips to hers.

It should have been the same kiss she'd just experienced. Weren't they all the same? But somehow this felt different. More intense. Her eyes fluttered closed before she realized what had happened. Oddly, the darkness comforted her. Her brain shut down as well, which was nice because in the quiet she could actually feel the contact of skin on skin.

He kissed her gently, yet with a hint of fire that left her breathless. Somehow she found the courage to kiss him back. Tiny electric tingles raced up and down her arms and legs, making her shiver. Mazin moved closer, until they were practically touching. He swept his thumbs across her cheeks, which made her

want to part her lips. When she did, she felt the light
brush of his tongue against hers.

The contact was as delightful as it was unexpected.
The tingles in her arms and legs turned into ripples
and she found it difficult to stand. She had to hold on
to him, so she rested her hands lightly on his shoulders. They were kissing. Really kissing.

He stroked her lightly, circling her, exciting her.
After a minute or so, she found the courage to do the
same to him. Every aspect of the experience was
amazing.

Of course, she'd read about this in books and seen
passionate kissing in the movies, but she'd never experienced it herself. It was glorious. No wonder teen-
agers were willing to do it for hours. She found herself wanting to do the same.

She liked everything about it—the way he tasted,
the scent of him, the heat flaring between them. Her
body felt light, as if she could float away. When he
released her face and wrapped his arms around her,
pulling her close, she knew there was nowhere else
on earth she wanted to be.

Their bodies touched. From shoulder to knee, they
pressed together. She'd never been so close to a man,
and was stunned to find every part of him was muscled and hard. She felt positively delicate by com-
parison.

At last he drew back and rested his forehead
against hers.

"That was a surprise," he said, his voice low and husky.

"Did I do it wrong?" she asked before she could stop herself.

He laughed. "No, my dove. You kissed exactly right. Perhaps too right."

Their breath mingled. Phoebe felt all squishy inside. She wanted to stay close to him forever, kissing until the world ended.

Instead of reading her mind, Mazin straightened, then glanced at his watch.

"Unfortunately, duty calls," he said, then put his arm around her. "Come. I will see you back to your hotel."

She wanted to protest, but he'd already given her so much. In a single day she'd experienced more than she could ever have imagined.

"You've been very kind," she said, savoring the weight of his arm around her waist. He waited while she picked up her purse and shoes, then drew her close again.

"The pleasure was mine."

Oh, please let him want to see me again.

They walked to the car in silence. Once there, Mazin held open the passenger door.

Phoebe told herself not to be disappointed. One day was enough. She could survive on these memories for a long time. But before she slid into the car, he caught her hand and brought it to his lips.

"Tomorrow?" he asked in a whisper.

"Yes," she breathed in relief. "Tomorrow."

Chapter 4

Phoebe stepped carefully along the stone path through the center of the botanical garden. A light rain had fallen early that morning, leaving all the plants clean and sweet smelling. Overhead tall trees blocked out most of the heat from the midday sun. It was a pretty darned perfect moment.

"There are legends about ancient pirates coming to the island," Mazin was saying. "Archaeologists haven't found any evidence of raiders on the island, but the stories persist." He smiled. "Children are warned that if they don't behave, they'll be taken from their beds in the middle of the night."

Phoebe laughed. "That should scare them into doing what they're supposed to."

"I'm not sure they actually believe in the ancient pirates."

"Did you?"

He hesitated, then grinned. "Perhaps when I was very small."

She tried to imagine him as a little boy and could not. She glanced at his strong profile, wondering if his features had ever looked childish and soft. Her gaze lingered on his mouth. Had he really kissed her yesterday? It seemed more like a dream than something that had actually happened.

The hem of her dress brushed against a bush growing out onto the path. Drops of water trickled onto her bare leg. She tugged on her short-sleeved jacket and knew that, dream or not, she had been foolish to put on a dress that morning. Slacks would have been more sensible.

Only, she hadn't been feeling very sensible. She'd wanted to look special for Mazin—pretty. As she didn't wear makeup or know how to do anything fancy with her hair, a dress had been her only option. Now that she was with him, she hoped he didn't realize she'd gone to any effort. Yesterday he had said kind things about her appearance, but she wasn't sure she believed the compliments. Of course she'd had plenty of time to relive them last night, when she'd barely slept at all.

"Are there other stories about the island?" she asked.

"Several. Legend has it that when there is a lunar eclipse visible from Lucia-Serrat, there is magic in the air. Mysterious creatures are said to appear, and animals can talk.''

"Really?"

He shrugged. "I have no personal experience with talking animals.''

A branch stretched across part of the path. Mazin took her arm and led her around the obstruction.

His fingers were warm against her bare skin. Some time before dawn it had crossed her mind that he might be trying to seduce her. As she had no experience with the process, she couldn't be sure. If he was, should she mind? Phoebe couldn't decide.

Her plan had always been to go to college and become a nurse. She knew little of love and less of marriage. For years she'd had the feeling both were going to pass her by—hence her education-career plan. She wanted to be prepared to take care of herself.

But an affair was not marriage. She was on the island for only a few weeks. If Mazin offered to teach her the mysteries between a man and a woman, why on earth would she say no?

They turned left at the next opportunity. Tall bamboo shared space with different kinds of bananas. Some were small, some large. Many were unfamiliar.

"I've never seen anything like this," she said as they paused next to a cluster of red bananas.

"Florida is tropical," he reminded her.

"I know, but where I live it's more suburban. There are some exotic plants, but nothing like this."

"You moved there when you were young, I believe?"

She hesitated. "Yes."

"You do not have to speak of your past if you do not wish to."

"I appreciate that. I don't have anything to hide." They began walking again. Phoebe folded her arms over her chest. She didn't mind talking about her life—she just didn't want him to think she was some backwater hick.

"I was born in Colorado. I never knew my father, and my mother didn't speak of him. Her parents died before I was born. She did…" Phoebe hesitated, her gaze firmly fixed on the ground. "She didn't like people very much. We lived in a small cabin in the middle of the woods. There weren't any other people around and we never had contact with the outside world. There was no electricity or indoor plumbing. We got all of our water from a well."

She cast a quick glance at Mazin. He seemed interested. "I did not know there were parts of your country without such amenities."

"There are some. My mother taught me to read, but didn't discuss much of the outside world with me. We were happy, I guess. I know she cared about me, but I was often lonely. One day when I was eight, we were out collecting berries. There was a lot of water from the spring snow runoff higher in the mountain. She slipped on some wet leaves, fell and hit her head. I found out later that she died instantly, but at the time I didn't know why she wouldn't wake up. After a few hours, I knew I had to go get help, even though she had always forbidden me to have anything to do with other people. There was a town about ten miles away. I'd stumbled across it a couple of times when I'd been out exploring.''

Mazin stopped walking and grabbed her by her upper arms. ''You had never been into the town before?''

She shook her head.

''You must have been terrified.''

''I was more scared that there was something wrong with my mother, or that she was going to be mad when she woke up.'' She sighed, remembering how she'd been trying so hard not to cry as she explained what had happened to several strangers before one of them finally took her to the sheriff's office.

''They went and got her,'' she said. Mazin released her arms and she started walking. It seemed easier to keep moving as she talked. ''Then they told me she was dead. I didn't know what it meant for a long time.''

''Where did you go?''

''Into a temporary foster home until they could locate a relative. It took about six months, because I didn't know anything about my family. They had to go through all of her personal effects to get leads. In the meantime I had to adjust to a life that everyone else took for granted. It was hard.''

Those three words couldn't possibly explain what

it had been like, Phoebe thought. She still remembered her shock the first time she'd seen an indoor bathroom. The toilet had stunned her, while the idea of *hot* running water on demand had been a taste of heaven.

"I started school, of course," she said.

"You must have had difficulties."

"Just a couple. I knew how to read, but I'd had no education. Math was a mystery to me. I knew my numbers, but nothing else. Plus I'd missed all the socialization that most children undergo. I didn't know how to make friends, and I'd never seen a television, let alone a movie."

"Your mother had no right to do that to you."

She glanced at him, surprised by the fierceness in his voice. "She did what she thought was best. Sometimes I think I understand, other times I'm angry."

They stepped into the sun and Phoebe was grateful for the warmth.

They walked in silence for several minutes. There were things about her past that she'd never admitted to anyone, not even Ayanna. Her aunt had been so kind and supportive from the first that she hadn't wanted to trouble her.

"I didn't make friends easily," Phoebe whispered. "I didn't know how. The other children knew I was different and they stayed away from me. I was grateful when they found my aunt, not only to have a home, but to get away from the loneliness."

Mazin led her to a bench on the side of the path.

She settled in a corner, her hands clasped tightly together, the memories growing larger in her mind.

"Ayanna drove out to get me. Later she told me it was because she thought the car trip would give us time to get to know each other." She smiled sadly. "Her plan worked. By the time we reached Florida, I was comfortable with her. And I did a little better making friends. I'd learned from previous mistakes. Unfortunately, I had more trouble in school. For a while the teachers were convinced I was retarded. I couldn't even score well on the IQ tests because I didn't have the frame of reference to answer the questions."

"Yet you were successful."

She nodded. "It took a long time. Ayanna took me to the library every week and helped me pick out different books so that I could learn about things. It's the little things, like knowing that the word *pipe* has two meanings."

She suddenly realized how long she'd been talking, and groaned. "I'm sorry. I don't even remember what you asked me. I know you couldn't have wanted this long answer."

"I'm happy to hear about your past," Mazin told her, lightly touching the back of her hand. "I am impressed by your ability to overcome a disadvantage."

She supposed his answer should have pleased her, but it didn't. She wanted him to see her as someone he could find exciting, not as an example of a job well done. She wanted him to take her in his arms again and kiss her thoroughly.

With a fierceness that both shocked and frightened her, she found herself wishing that he *did* want to seduce her.

But instead of kissing her or even holding her close, he rose.

Reluctantly she got to her feet.

They continued to walk through the garden. Mazin was a most attentive host, pointing out plants of interest, inquiring about her state of well-being in the hot morning. As the sun rose in the sky, her spirits plummeted. She shouldn't have told him about her strange upbringing. She shouldn't have spilled her secrets. How could he think of her as anything but odd?

"You have grown silent," Mazin said when he realized Phoebe had stopped talking.

She shrugged.

He took in the slump of her shoulders and the way her fingers endlessly pleated her skirt. "Why are you sad?"

"I'm not. I just feel…" She pressed her lips together. "I don't want you to think I'm stupid."

"Why would I think that?"

"Because of what I told you."

She had told him about her past. From his perspective, the information had only made her more dangerous. Yesterday she had been a pretty woman who attracted him sexually. Their kiss had shown him the possibilities and the accompanying arousal had disturbed his sleep. Today he knew that she was more than an appealing body. He knew that she had a strong spirit and that she had succeeded against impossible odds. Why would that make him think she was stupid?

Women were complex creatures.

"Put it from your mind, my dove," he told her, taking her hand in his. "I admire your ability to overcome your past. Come, I will show your our English rose garden. Some of the rosebushes are very ancient, and still annoyed to find themselves so far from home."

The next morning Phoebe had almost convinced herself that Mazin meant what he said—that he admired her for her past. However, she couldn't quite embrace the concept, mostly because he hadn't kissed her goodbye. He'd kissed her on the first day, but not on the second. Didn't that mean they were moving in the wrong direction?

She stood in front of the bathroom mirror and pulled her hair back into a ponytail. As the dress hadn't created any magic the day before, she was back in slacks and a T-shirt. Maybe now he would want to kiss her.

She finished with her hair and dropped her hands to her side. After only two days in the company of a handsome man, her brain was spinning. It was probably for the best that there hadn't been any kissing.

Except she'd really enjoyed how she'd felt in his arms.

"At least I'm having an adventure, Ayanna," she said as she smoothed sunscreen on her arms. "That should make you happy."

She was still smiling at the thought of her aunt's pleasure when the phone rang. Phoebe turned to look at it, her stomach clenching. There was only one person who would be calling her, and she already knew the reason.

"Hello?"

"Phoebe, this is Mazin. Something has come up and I will not be able to join you today."

She was sure he said more, that he kept talking, but she couldn't hear anything. She sank onto the bed and closed her eyes.

He wasn't coming. He was bored with her. He thought she was a child, or maybe he'd been lying when he'd said he appreciated her past. It doesn't matter, she told herself, squeezing in the pain. This trip wasn't about him—it never had been. How could she have forgotten?

"I appreciate you letting me know," she said brightly, interrupting him. "I'll let you get back to your day and I must begin mine. There is so much to see on this beautiful island. Thank you, Mazin. Goodbye."

Then she hung up before she did something stupid like cry.

It took her fifteen minutes to fight back tears and

another ten to figure out what she was going to do.
Her aunt had specifically left her the money to visit
Lucia-Serrat. Phoebe couldn't repay her by wasting
time sulking. She read Ayanna's list and then studied
the guidebook. The church of St. Mary was within
walking distance. Next to that was a dog park. If the
beauty of the architecture and stained glass didn't
ease the disappointment in her heart, then the antics
of the dogs would make her laugh.

That decided, Phoebe headed out on her own. She
found the church, a stunning structure with high
arches and cool interiors. She admired the carvings
and let the silence and peace ease her pain.

She'd known Mazin only a little over two days, she
told herself as she sat in a rear pew. He had been
more than kind. It was wrong and foolish of her to
expect more of him. As for the kiss and her fantasies
that he might want to seduce her, well, at least she
had been kissed. The next time, with the next man,
she would do better. Eventually she would figure out
how to be normal.

She left the church and walked to the dog park. As
she'd hoped, there were dozens of dogs playing, running and barking. She laughed over the antics of several small dalmatian puppies and helped an older
woman put her Irish setter in the back of her car.

By the time she stopped for lunch her spirits had
risen to the point where she could chat with the wait-
ress about the menu and not think about Mazin.

While waiting for her entrée, she made friends with

the older English couple at the next table, and they recommended she try the boat tour that went around the island. The trip took all day and offered impressive views of Lucia-Serrat. As they were all staying at the Parrot Bay Inn, they walked back together and Phoebe stopped at the concierge desk to pick up a brochure on the boat trip. Then she headed up to her room, pleasantly tired and pleased that she'd gotten through the day without thinking of Mazin more than two or three dozen times.

Tomorrow she would do better, she promised herself. By next week, she would barely remember his name.

But when she entered her room, the first thing she noticed was a new, larger spray of flowers. Her fingers trembled as she opened the card.

"Something lovely for my beautiful dove. I'm sorry I could not be with you today. I will be thinking of you. Mazin."

Her throat tightened and her eyes burned as she read the card. She didn't have to compare the handwriting with that on the first card she'd received—she knew they were the same. The fact that he had just been trying to be nice didn't lessen her pain. Perhaps she was being foolish and acting like a child, but she missed him.

The phone rang, interrupting her thoughts. Phoebe cleared her throat, then picked up the receiver.

"Hello?"

"Here I had imagined you spending the day pining

for me when in truth you were out having a good time.''

Her heart jumped into her throat. She could barely breathe. "Mazin?"

"Of course. What other man would call you?"

Despite her loneliness, she couldn't help smiling. "Maybe there are dozens."

"I wouldn't be surprised." He sighed. "Aren't you going to ask me how I knew you weren't alone in your room, pining for me?"

"How did you know?"

"I've been calling and you have not been there."

Her heart returned to her chest and began to flutter, even though she knew she was a fool. "I went to the church and the dog park. Then I had lunch. A lovely couple told me about the boat tour around the island. I thought I might do that tomorrow."

"I see."

She plowed ahead. "You've been more than kind, but I know you have your own life and your own responsibilities."

"What if I wish to see you? Are you telling me no?"

She clutched the receiver so hard, her fingers hurt. Tears pooled in her eyes. "I don't understand."

"Nor do I."

She wiped away her tears. "Th-thank you for the flowers."

"You are welcome. I am sorry about today." He

sighed. "Phoebe, if you would rather not spend time with me, I will abide by your wishes."

Tears flowed faster. The odd thing was she couldn't say exactly *why* she was crying. "It's not that."

"Why is your voice shaking?"

"It's n-not."

"You're crying."

"Maybe."

"Why?"

"I don't know."

"Would it help if I said I was disappointed, as well? That I would rather be with you than reading boring reports and spending my day in endless meetings?"

"Yes, that would help a lot."

"Then know that it is true. Tell me you'll see me tomorrow."

A sensible woman would refuse, she thought, knowing Mazin would not only distract her from her plans for her future, but that he would also likely break her heart.

"I'll see you tomorrow."

"Good. I will see you then."

She nodded. "Goodbye, Mazin."

"Goodbye, my dove. Until tomorrow. I promise to make the day special."

He hung up. She carefully replaced the phone, knowing that he didn't have to try to make the day special. Just by showing up he would brighten her world.

Chapter 5

"Where are we going?" Phoebe asked for the third time since Mazin had picked her up that morning. They'd already toured the marketplace, after which he had promised a surprise.

"You will see when we arrive," he said with a smile. "Be patient, my dove."

"You're driving me crazy," she told him. "I think you're doing it on purpose."

"Perhaps."

She tried to work up a case of righteous indignation, but it was not possible. Not with the sun shining in the sky and the beauty of Lucia-Serrat all around them. Not with Mazin sitting next to her in his car, spending yet another day with her.

She had known him little more than two weeks.

They had spent a part of nearly every day together, although not any evenings. So far they'd worked their way through a good portion of Ayanna's list. Phoebe had seen much of the island, including a view from the ocean on the tour boat.

"Is it a big place, or a small place?" she asked.

"A big place."

"But it is not on my list."

"No."

She sighed. "Did my aunt visit there?"

"I would think so."

They drove toward the north end of the island, heading inland. Gradually the road began to rise. Phoebe tried to picture the map of the island in her mind. What was in this direction? Then she reminded herself it didn't really matter. She had memories stored up for her return home. When she was deep in her studies, she would remind herself of her time on Lucia-Serrat, when a handsome man had made her feel special.

She glanced at him out of the corner of her eye. He was concentrating on his driving and did not notice her attention. Although he was unfailingly polite, he had yet to kiss her again. She wasn't sure why, and her lack of experience with men kept her from speculating. She thought it might have something to do with the fact that she *was* inexperienced, but couldn't confirm the information. Asking was out of the question.

They rounded a corner. Up ahead, through a grove of trees, a tall house reached up toward the sky. She squinted. Actually it was more of a castle than a house, or maybe a palace.

A palace?

Mazin inclined his head. "The official residence of the prince. He has a private home, but that is not open to the public. Although this is not on your Ayanna's list, I thought you might enjoy strolling through the grounds and exploring the public rooms."

She turned to him and smiled with delight. "I would love to see it. Thank you for thinking of this, Mazin. My aunt came here often to attend the famous parties. She danced with the prince in the grand ballroom."

"Then we will make sure we see that part of the castle."

They drove around to a small parking lot close to the building. Phoebe glanced at the larger public lot they had passed on their way in.

"You forget I have a position of some importance in the government," he said, reading her mind as he opened his car door. "Parking here is one of the perks."

He climbed out of the car, then came around to her side and opened the door. Phoebe appreciated the polite gesture. Sometimes she even let herself fantasize that he was being more than polite, that his actions had significance. Then she remembered she was a nobody from Florida and that he was a successful, older man simply being kind. Besides, she had her life already planned. Okay, maybe her plan wasn't as exciting as her imaginings about Mazin, but it was far more real.

"This way," he said, taking her hand in his and heading for the palace. "The original structure was built at the time of the spice trade."

"You told me that the crown prince is always a relative of the king of Bahania. He was probably used to really nice houses."

Mazin flashed her a grin. "Exactly. Originally the prince lived in the palace, but as you can see, while it is a beautiful palace, it is not especially large. Quarters were cramped with the prince's family, his children and their children, various officials, servants, visiting dignitaries. So in the late 1800s the prince had a private residence constructed."

Mazin paused on the tree-lined path and pointed. "You can see a bit of it through there."

Phoebe tilted her head. She caught a glimpse of a corner of a building and several windows. "It looks nearly as big as the palace."

"Apparently the building project grew a little."

She returned her attention to the graceful stone palace in front of them. "So official business occurs here? At least the prince doesn't have much of a commute."

"I'm sure he appreciates that."

They crossed the ground around to the front of the palace. Phoebe still felt a little uneasy about trespassing, but as Mazin wasn't worried, she did her best to enjoy the moment. He was a knowledgeable host, explaining the different styles of architecture and telling her amusing stories from the past.

"Now we will go inside," he said. "Our first stop will be the ballroom."

They headed for the main gates overlooking the ocean. As they crossed the open drawbridge, a distant call caught Phoebe's attention. She looked toward the sound. A small boy raced toward them, down the length of the drawbridge. Dark hair flopped in his face, while his short, sturdy legs pumped furiously.

"Papa, Papa, wait for me!"

Phoebe didn't remember stopping, but suddenly she wasn't moving. She stared at the boy, then slowly turned her attention to Mazin. Her host watched the child with a combination of affection and exasperation.

"My son," he said unnecessarily.

Phoebe was saved from speaking by the arrival of the boy. He flew at his father. Mazin caught him easily, pulling him close into an embrace that was both loving and comfortable. They obviously did this a lot.

A tightness in her chest told her that she'd stopped breathing. Phoebe gasped once, then wondered if she looked as shocked as she felt. She knew Mazin was older. Of course he would have lived a full life, and it made sense that his life might include children. But intellectualizing about a possibility and actually meeting a child were two very different things.

Mazin shifted his son so that the boy sat on his left forearm. One small arm encircled his neck. They both turned to her.

"This is my son, Dabir. Dabir, this is Miss Carson."

"Hello," the boy said, regarding her with friendly curiosity.

"Hi." Phoebe wasn't sure if she was expected to shake hands.

He appeared to be five or six, with thick dark hair and eyes just like his father. She had been unable to picture Mazin as a child, but now, looking at Dabir, she saw the possibilities.

Mazin settled his free hand at Dabir's waist. "So tell us what you're doing here at the castle. Don't you have lessons today?"

"I learned all my numbers and got every question right, so I got a reward." He grinned at Phoebe. "I told Nana I wanted to see the swords, so she brought me here. Have you seen them? They're long and scary."

He practically glowed as he spoke. Obviously viewing the swords was a favorite treat.

Phoebe tried to answer, but her lips didn't seem to be working. Mazin spoke for her.

"We were just about to walk into the castle. We haven't seen anything yet. Miss Carson is visiting Lucia-Serrat for the first time."

"Do you like it?" Dabir asked.

"Um, yes. It's lovely."

The boy beamed. "I'm six. I have three older brothers. They're all much bigger than me, but I'm the favorite."

Mazin set the boy on the ground and ruffled his hair. "You are not the favorite, Dabir. I love all my sons equally."

Dabir didn't seem the least bit upset by the announcement. He giggled and leaned against his father, while studying her.

"Do you have any children?" he asked.

"No. I'm not married."

Dabir's eyes widened. "Do you like children?"

Phoebe hadn't thought the situation could get more uncomfortable, yet it just had. "I, ah, like them very much."

"Enough," Mazin said, his voice a low growl. "Go find Nana."

Dabir hesitated, as if he would disobey, then he waved once and raced back into the castle. Phoebe watched him go. Children. Mazin had children. Four of them. All boys.

"He's very charming," she forced herself to say when they were alone.

Mazin turned toward her and cupped her face. "I could read your mind. You must never try to play poker, my dove. Your thoughts are clearly visible to anyone who takes the time to look."

There was a humiliating thought. She sighed. "You have lived a very full life," she said. "Of course you would have children."

"Children, but no wife."

Relief filled her. She hadn't actually allowed herself to think the question, but she was happy to hear the answer.

"Come," he said, taking her hand in his. "I will show you the ballroom where your Ayanna danced. As we walk, I will tell you all about my sordid past."

"Is it so very bad?"

"I'm not sure. Your standards will be higher than most. You will have to tell me."

They walked into the castle. She tried to catch a glimpse of Dabir and his Nana, but they seemed to have disappeared.

"Some of the tapestries date back to the twelfth century," he said, motioning to the delicate wall hangings.

She dutifully raised her gaze to study them. "They're very nice."

Mazin sighed, then pulled her toward a bench by the stone wall. "Perhaps we should deal with first things first, as you Americans like to say."

He sat on the bench and pulled her next to him. She had the brief thought that actually sitting on furniture in the royal castle might be punishable by imprisonment, or worse, but then Mazin took her hands in his and she couldn't think at all.

"I am a widower," he told her, staring into her eyes. "My wife died giving birth to Dabir. We have three boys. And I have another son from a brief liaison when I was a young man."

That last bit of news nearly sent her over the edge, but all she said was "Oh."

Four sons. It seemed like a large number of children for one man. No wonder he hadn't been spending his evenings with her; he had a family waiting at home. If they were all as charming as Dabir, he must hate being away from them.

"I've been keeping you from them," she said

softly. "I've told you that you don't have to keep me company."

"I choose to be here."

She wanted to ask why, but didn't have the courage. "You must have help with them. Dabir mentioned Nana."

He smiled. "Yes. She is a governess of sorts for my youngest. The two middle boys are in a private boarding school. My oldest is at university in England."

She tried not to show her shock. "How old is he?"

"Nearly twenty. I am much older than you, Phoebe. Did you forget?"

"No, it's just…" She did the math. He'd had a child when he'd been seventeen? She was twenty-three and had been kissed only once. Could they be more different?

"I know you say you choose to be here," she said, "but you have a family and work obligations. I must be a distraction. Please don't be concerned. I'm very capable of entertaining myself. How could I not enjoy my time on this beautiful island?"

"Ah, but if you remain alone, you will never be able to visit Lucia's Point."

She ducked her head as heat flared on her cheeks. Lucia's Point—the place for lovers. It seemed unlikely that she would be visiting that particular spot on this trip.

A horrifying thought occurred to her. She tried to push it away, but it refused to budge. Then she found herself actually voicing it aloud as she risked looking at him.

"You have four sons, Mazin. Do you see me as the daughter you never had?"

He released her hands at once. She didn't know what that meant, but she was aware of his dark eyes brightening with many emotions. None of them seemed paternal.

"Do you see me as the father you never had?"

Her blush deepened. "No," she whispered. "I never thought of that."

"I do not think of you as a child, especially not my own. On the contrary. I see you very much as a woman."

"Do you? I want to believe you, but I've lived such a small life."

"It is the quality of one's life that matters."

"Easy to say when you had your first affair at seventeen," she blurted before she could stop herself. She pressed her fingers to her mouth, horrified, but Mazin only laughed.

"An interesting point. Come. We will walk to the ballroom. When we are there, I will tell you all about my affair with the ever-beautiful Carnie."

"She was an actress," Mazin said ten minutes later as they strolled through a vast open area.

Tall, slender windows let in light. Dozens of candelabras hung from an arched ceiling. There was a stage in one corner, probably for an orchestra, and enough space to hold a football game.

Phoebe tried to imagine the room filled with people dressed in their finest, dancing the night away, but she was still caught up in his description of his first mistress as "ever beautiful."

"*Was* she very lovely?" she asked before she could stop herself.

"Yes. Her face and body were perfection. However, she had a cold heart. I learned very quickly that I was more interested in a woman's inner beauty than her outside perfection."

His statement made her feel better. Phoebe knew that in a competition of straight looks, she wouldn't have a chance, but she thought her heart would stand up all right.

"We met when the film company came here to shoot part of a movie. She was an older woman— nearly twenty-two. I was very impressed with myself at the time and determined to have her."

She didn't doubt he'd achieved his goal. "What happened when you found out she was pregnant?"

He took her hand in his. The pressure of his palm against her, the feel of their fingers laced together nearly distracted her from his words.

"She was upset. I don't know if she'd hoped for marriage, but it was out of the question. My father…" He hesitated. "The family did not approve. We had money, so an offer was made. She accepted."

Phoebe stared at him. "Didn't you love her?"

"Perhaps for the first few weeks, but it faded. When I found out about the child, I wanted my son, but I didn't think Carnie and I had much chance at happiness. She stayed long enough to have the baby, then left.''

"I could never do that,'' Phoebe said, completely shocked by Carnie's behavior. "I would never give up my child. I don't care how much money was involved.''

Mazin shrugged. "I don't think my father gave her much choice.''

"That wouldn't matter. I would stand up against anyone. I'd go into hiding.''

"Carnie preferred the cash.''

Mazin heard the harshness in his voice. Most of the time he was at peace with his former lover, but occasionally he despised her for what she had done, even though it had made his life simpler.

"Is she still alive?''

"Yes, but she rarely sees her son. It is better that way.''

He watched the play of emotions across Phoebe's face. She was so easy to read. She was outraged by Carnie's decision, yet it went against her nature to judge anyone negatively. Her wide mouth trembled slightly at the corners and her delicate brows drew together as she tried to reconcile harsh facts with her gentle nature.

She was a good person. He couldn't say that very often, not with certainty. She wanted nothing from him, save his company. Their time was a balm and he found himself in need of the healing only she could provide. Being with her made him quiet and content. Two very rare commodities in his life.

She had been startled by Dabir's sudden appearance. Mazin had been, as well, but for different reasons. He had seen something as he'd watched her. Over the past six years he had become an expert at judging a woman's reaction to his children. Some pretended to like them because they wanted to be his wife. Some genuinely enjoyed the company of children. He put Phoebe in the latter category.

He liked her. Mazin couldn't remember the last time he had simply liked a woman. He also wanted her. The combination caused more than a little discomfort. Because he cared about her, he refused to push her into his bed, which was exactly where he wanted her to be. Holding back was not his style, yet this time it felt right.

She was different from anyone he'd ever known. He suspected she would say the same about him.

"Phoebe, you must know I'm a rich man," he said.

She bit her bottom lip. "I sort of figured that out."

"Does that bother you?"

"A little."

She glanced at him. Her long blond hair fell down her back. He wanted to capture it in his hands and feel the warm silk of the honeyed strands. He wanted many things.

"I don't understand why you spend time with me," she said in a rush. "I like being with *you*, but I worry that you're bored."

He smiled. "Never. Do you remember yesterday when we went to see the meerkats?"

"Yes?"

"You fed them their lunch of fruits and vegetables. You were patient, feeding each in its turn, never tired."

She sighed. "They were wonderful. So cute and funny. I could watch them for hours. I love how they stand guard, watching out for each other."

"You told me you'd seen a show about African meerkats and how one was burned in a fire."

She stopped walking. He moved to stand in front of her. As they had the previous day, her eyes filled up with tears.

"It tried to stand guard, but couldn't," she whispered. "They all huddled around it. Then a couple of days later, it left the group and went off to die."

A single tear rolled down her cheek. Mazin touched it with his finger. "Tears for a meerkat. What would you give to a child in need?"

"I don't understand the question."

"I know, but these tears are why I am not bored with you."

She sniffed. "You're making absolutely no sense."

He laughed. "You would find others to agree with you. So tell me, what do you want from your life?"

Her blue eyes widened slightly. "Me? Nothing special. I'd like children. Three or four, at least. And a house. But before any of that, I want to get my degree."

"In what?"

"Nursing. I like taking care of people."

He remembered her dying aunt. Yes, Phoebe would do well with the sick.

"I would like—" She shook her head. "Sorry.

This can't be interesting. My dreams are very small and ordinary. Like I said, a small life. I'm not sure there's all that much quality there.''

"On the contrary. You have much to recommend you."

Then, against his better judgment, he pulled her close.

She came willingly into his arms, as he had known she would. Her body pressed against him, her arms wrapped around him. She raised her head in a silent offering, and he did not have the strength of will to deny her.

He touched his mouth to hers. This time she responded eagerly, kissing him back. He kept the contact light, because if he took what he really wanted, they would make love here in the public rooms of the castle. So he nipped at her lower lip and trailed kisses along her jaw. He slid his hands up and down her back, careful to avoid the tempting curves of her rear.

Her breathing accelerated as he licked the hollow of her throat. She wore a dress with a slightly scooped neck. The thrust of her small breasts called to him. It would be so easy to move lower. He could see the outline of her tight nipples straining against the fabric of her clothing. Desire filled him with an intensity that made him ache.

Good sense won. He returned his attentions to her mouth. She parted in invitation. He might be able to resist her other temptations, but not that one. He had to taste her sweetness one more time.

He plunged into her. She accepted his conquest and

began an assault of her own. Just once, he thought hazily, and slipped his hand onto the curve of her hip. She responded by drawing closer, pressing her breasts against his chest and breathing his name.

Mazin swore. Phoebe was very much an innocent, and she didn't know what she was offering.

He wanted her and he couldn't have her. Not only because she was a virgin, but because he hadn't told her the truth about everything. At first he'd withheld the information because it had amused him. Now he found he didn't want her to know.

He forced himself to pull back. They were both breathing heavily. Phoebe smiled at him.

"You've probably heard this a thousand times before," she said, "but you're a really good kisser."

He laughed. "As are you."

"If I am, it's because of you."

The blush of arousal stained her cheeks; her lips were swollen. Her beauty touched him deep in his soul. He wanted to see her in diamonds and satin.

He wanted to see her in nothing at all.

"What are you thinking?" she asked.

"That you are an unexpected delight in my life."

Her blue eyes darkened with emotion that he didn't want to read. Slowly, tentatively she touched his mouth with her fingertip. Her breath caught in her throat.

"What do you want from me, Mazin?"

He found himself compelled to speak the truth. "I don't know."

Chapter 6

Phoebe pulled a chair close to the balcony and stared out at the stars. The balmy night air brushed against her bare arms, making her tremble slightly, although she couldn't say why. It wasn't that she was cold or even fearful. She knew in her heart that nothing bad could happen while she was on the island.

Perhaps it was the memory of Mazin's kiss that made her unable to keep still. Something had happened that afternoon when he'd taken her in his arms. She'd seen something in his eyes, something that had made her think this might not just be a game to him. His inability to tell her what he wanted from her made her both happy and nervous. One of them had to know what was going on, and she didn't have a clue. Which left Mazin.

She pulled her knees to her chest and wrapped her arms around her legs. Her long white cotton nightgown fluttered in the breeze.

There had been a difference in his kiss today. An intensity that had shaken her to her core. Did he want her that way? Did he want to make love with her? Did she want to make love with him?

He was not the man she had fantasized about. In her mind, Mazin had no life, save that time he spent with her. Now she knew that he had been a husband. He was a father, with four sons. He had a life that didn't include her, and when she was gone, he would return to it as if she'd never been here at all.

Were all his sons like Dabir? She smiled at the memory of the bright, loving little boy. Spending time with him would be a joy.

Several years of baby-sitting had taught her to assess a child very quickly. Dabir would no doubt get into plenty of trouble, but he had a generous heart and a sense of fun. She bit her lower lip. One child would be easy, but four? Worse, Mazin's oldest was only a few years younger than she was. The thought made her shiver. Not that Mazin's children were going to be an issue, she reminded herself.

Phoebe stared up at the stars, but the night skies didn't hint at how long until Mazin grew tired of her, nor did they whisper his intent. Instead of meeting her during the day tomorrow, Mazin had arranged for them to spend the evening together. Somehow the change of time made her both excited and nervous.

No matter what, she told herself, she would never have regrets. Just as Ayanna had made her promise.

Moonlight sparkled on the ever-shifting ocean. Phoebe breathed in the scent of sea spray and nearby flowers. Whatever else might happen in her life, she would remember this night forever.

Mazin sat across from her, handsome as always. Tonight he wore a suit, making her glad she'd spent more than she should have for a pretty blouse in the hotel boutique. Her slim black skirt had seen better days, but it was serviceable enough. After nearly an hour of fussing with her hair, she'd managed to pin it up into a French twist. She felt almost sophisticated. Something she would need to counteract the effect of Mazin's attraction by moonlight.

"I feel a little guilty," she said as the waiter poured from the wine bottle.

"Why?" Mazin asked when the waiter had left and they were alone. "Have you done something you should not have done?"

"No." She smiled. "But it's evening. You should be home with your family."

"Ah. You are thinking of my children."

Among other things, she thought, hoping he couldn't read her mind and know how many times she had relived their kisses.

"Dabir, especially," she murmured. "Wouldn't you rather be home, tucking him in bed?"

Mazin dismissed her with a shake of his head. "He is six. Far too old to be tucked in bed by his father."

"He's practically a baby, not a teenager."

Mazin frowned. "I had not thought he would still need that sort of attention. He has Nana to take care of him."

"That's not the same as having you around."

"Are you trying to get rid of me?"

"Not at all. I just don't want you to take time away from them to be with me. I know if I had children, I would want to be with them always."

One corner of his mouth turned up. "What of your husband's needs for you? Would they not come first?"

"I think he'd have to learn to compromise."

Mazin's humor turned to surprise. "It is the children and the wife who must compromise." He shrugged. "Most of the time. I was married long enough to have learned that on rare occasions the man does not come first."

"I should think not." She leaned toward him. "Tell me about your sons."

"Why do I sense you are more interested in them than in me?"

"I'm not. It's just…" She hesitated, then decided there was no point in avoiding the truth. "I find the subject of your children very safe."

"Because I am unsafe?"

Rather than answer, she took a sip of her wine.

He chuckled and reached forward, capturing her

free hand in his. "I know you, my dove. I have
learned to read you when you avoid my eyes and busy
yourself with a task. You do not wish to respond to
my question. Now my job is to learn why."

He studied her, his dark eyes unreadable. She
wished she could know him as well as he seemed to
know her.

"Why do you fear me?" he asked unexpectedly.

Phoebe was so surprised that she straightened, pulling her hand free of his. She clutched her fingers together on her lap.

"I'm not afraid." She bit her lower lip. "Well, not
too afraid," she added, because she'd never been
much of a liar. "It's just that you're different from
anyone I've ever met. You're very charming, but also
intimidating. I'm out of my element with you."

"Not so very far." He patted the table. "Put your
hand here so that I may touch you."

He spoke matter-of-factly, but his words made her
whole body shiver. She managed to slide her hand
over to his, where he linked their fingers together. He
felt strong and warm. He made her feel safe, which
was odd because he was the reason she felt out of
sorts in the first place.

"See?" he said. "We fit together well."

"I don't think that's true. I don't know why you
spend so much time with me. I can't be anything like
the other women in your life."

Now it was his turn to stiffen. He didn't pull his
hand away, but ice crept into his gaze. "What other

women?'' he asked curtly. ''What are you talking about?''

She sensed that she had insulted him. ''Mazin, I didn't mean anything specific. Just that I can see that you're a handsome, successful man. There must be dozens of women throwing themselves at you all the time. I have this picture of you having to step over them wherever you go.''

She wanted to say more, but her throat tightened at the thought of him being with anyone else, even though it probably happened all the time.

''Do not worry, my dove,'' he said softly. ''I have forgotten them all.''

For how long?

She only thought the question. There was no point in asking. After all, Mazin might tell her the truth, and that would hurt her.

''I can see you do not believe me,'' he said, releasing her fingers. ''To prove myself, I have brought you something.''

He snapped his fingers. Their waiter appeared, but instead of bringing menus, he carried a large flat box. Mazin took it from him and handed it to her.

''Do not say you can't accept until you have opened it. Because I know in my heart that once you see my offering, you won't be able to refuse it.''

''Then I should refuse it before I see it,'' she said.

''That is not allowed.''

Phoebe lightly touched the gold paper around the box. She tried to imagine what could be inside. Not jewelry. The box was far too big—at least eighteen inches by twelve. Not clothes—the box was too slender.

"You won't be able to guess," he told her. "Open it."

She slipped off the bow, then pulled the paper from the box. When she lifted the lid and drew back the tissue, her breath caught in her throat.

Mazin had given her a framed picture of Ayanna.

Phoebe recognized the familiar face immediately. Her great-aunt looked very young, perhaps only a year or two older than Phoebe was now. She stood alone, in front of a pillar. Behind her, open archways led to the ocean. She recognized the palace at once.

Ayanna wore a formal ball gown. Diamonds glittered from her ears, wrists and throat. With her hair pulled back and her posture so straight and regal, she looked as elegant as a princess.

"I've never seen this picture before," she breathed. "Where did you find it?"

"There are photographic archives. You had mentioned that your aunt was a favorite with the crown prince. I thought there might be pictures of her, and I was right. This one was taken at a formal party at the prince's private residence. The original remains in the archives, but they allowed me to make a copy."

She didn't know what to say. That he would have gone to all this trouble for her moved her beyond words. Still, she had to make an attempt to speak. "You're right. I can't refuse this gift. It means too much. I have a few pictures of Ayanna, but not nearly enough. Thank you for being so thoughtful and kind.''

"My only motive was to make you smile.''

She didn't care what his motive had been. There was no other present in the world that could have had so much meaning. Phoebe didn't know how to explain all the feelings welling up inside her. She wanted to go to Mazin and wrap her arms around him. She wanted to try to explain her gratitude, and she wanted him to kiss her until she couldn't think or speak or do anything but respond to him. Her eyes burned with unshed tears, her heart ached and there was a hollow place inside that she couldn't explain.

"I don't understand you,'' she said at last.

"Understanding isn't necessary.''

She wondered what was.

He sipped his wine. "In two nights there is a celebration of the heritage of Lucia-Serrat,'' he said. "While we are a tropical paradise, our roots are in the desert of Bahania. Along with a special meal, there will be entertainment. Dancers and music. Although this event is not on your Ayanna's list, I suspect you would enjoy yourself. If you are available that evening, I would be honored if you would accompany me.''

As if she had other plans. As if she would rather be with anyone but him. "Thank you for asking me, Mazin. The honor of accompanying you is mine.''

He stared at her, his dark eyes seeing into her soul.

"It is probably for the best that you cannot read my mind," he murmured. "All that is between you and the death of your innocence is a thin thread of honor that even now threatens to unravel."

Once again he left her speechless. But before she could try to figure out if he really meant what he said—and deal with the sudden heat she felt in her belly—the waiter appeared with their menus. The mood was broken. Mazin made a great show of putting the picture safely back in the box. They discussed what they would have for dinner. His comment was never again mentioned.

But Phoebe didn't forget.

Two days later, a large box was delivered to her room. Phoebe knew instantly that it was from Mazin, but what could he be sending her? She unfastened the large bow and ribbon holding it in place, then lifted the cover.

Moving aside several layers of tissue revealed a dark blue evening gown that shimmered as she lifted it up to examine the style. Her breath caught in her throat. The silky fabric seemed to be covered with scatters of starlight. The low-cut bodice promised to reveal more than she ever had before, while the slender skirt would outline her hips and legs. It was a sensual garment for a sophisticated woman. Phoebe wasn't sure she had the courage to wear it.

A note fluttered to the floor. She set the dress back in the box and picked up the folded paper.

She recognized the strong, masculine handwriting instantly. Besides, who but Mazin would be sending her a dress?

"I know you will try to refuse my gift," he wrote. "You may even call me names and chide me for my boldness. I could not face your temper—for the thought of your anger leaves me trembling with fear. So I am leaving this dress in secret, like a thief in the night."

Phoebe knew she couldn't possibly accept such an extravagant gift. However, Mazin's note made her smile and then laugh. As if anything about her could ever frighten him.

She made the mistake of carrying the dress over to the mirror and holding it up in front of herself. Then she tried it on.

As she'd feared, the sensual fabric clung to every curve. Yet something about the material or the style or both made her actually look as if she *had* something worth clinging to. Her breasts seemed fuller, her waist smaller. She had a vision of herself in more dramatic makeup, with her hair cascading in curls down her back. While she'd never believed that she looked anything like Ayanna, with a little help she might come close.

Still wearing the dress, Phoebe dashed for the phone. She called the beauty salon in the hotel. Luckily they had a cancellation and would be happy to assist her in her transformation. If she would care to come downstairs in a half hour or so?

Phoebe agreed and hung up. Then she returned her attention to her reflection. Tonight she would look like the best possible version of herself. Would it be enough?

Phoebe arrived first at the restaurant. Mazin had called at the last minute, telling her that he was delayed with a small matter of work. He had sent a car to collect her and had promised to join her by seven.

She was shown to a private table upstairs. Carved screens kept the curious from knowing who sat there, while allowing her a perfect view of the stage. A cluster of musicians sat on one side of the room playing for the diners. Candlelight twinkled from every table.

The waiter lingered for several minutes, talking and staring until Phoebe realized he thought she was attractive. She'd never captured a man's attention before, and while the appreciative gleam in the young man's eyes flattered her, there was only one opinion that mattered.

The waiter disappeared for a few minutes, then returned with champagne. He poured her a glass. When he would have lingered longer, she told him she would be fine by herself. Obviously disappointed by the dismissal, he left.

Phoebe sipped the bubbly liquid. To think that after nearly three short weeks on the island a young man had actually noticed her. Much of it was the dress and the makeover, she thought, knowing she had never looked better. But she suspected there was some other reason. She was a different person than she had been when she arrived on the island.

Being with Mazin had changed her.

She leaned back in her chair. Except for the occasional afternoon when he'd had to return to work or his family, Mazin had spent most of his days with her. They had talked about everything from history to books to movies to her youth to her plans when she returned to Florida. They had shared sunsets, meals, laughter and he had been more than kind the few times she had given in to tears. They had been to every place on Ayanna's list. Every place but one. Lucia's Point.

Phoebe took a deep breath to calm her suddenly frantic nerves. She had little time left on the island, and then she would return to her small, solitary world. She knew that being with Mazin was a once-in-a-lifetime experience, but when she was home things would go on as before. She would attend college and get her degree in nursing. Perhaps she would do better at making friends, perhaps she might even meet a young man. But there, no one would ever be as much a part of her as Mazin. Wherever she went and whatever she did, he would be with her.

She knew that their time together hadn't meant the same thing to him as it did to her, and she could accept that. But she liked to think that she mattered a little. He had indicated that he found her attractive, that he enjoyed kissing her. So she had to ask.

Maybe he would laugh. Maybe he would be embarrassed and try to refuse her gently. Perhaps she had completely misunderstood his interest. But regardless of the many possibilities for rejection, she would not have regrets.

Voices in the hallway distracted her. She turned and saw Mazin slipping between the screens. He was as tall and handsome as ever. The black tuxedo he wore only emphasized his good looks. She rose to her feet and approached him. His smile turned from pleased to appreciative, and their kiss of greeting seemed as natural as breathing.

"I see you are wearing the dress I sent you. I trust you will not punish me for my boldness."

His teasing made her smile. In that moment her heart tightened in her chest, giving her a little tug. Phoebe had the sudden realization that she was in more danger than she had thought. Had she already fallen in love with Mazin?

Before she could consider the question, the pace of the music increased. Several young women took to the stage and began to dance. Phoebe and Mazin were seated and the waiter appeared with their first course.

Something about the rapid movement of the dancers captured Phoebe's attention. Part of it might have been that it was safer to look at them than gaze at Mazin. Apprehension made it impossible for her to eat.

"Some dances are for entertainment," he said, leaning close to be heard. She could inhale the masculine fragrance of him, and the appealing scent made her tremble. "Some tell a story. This is the journey of the nomads in their search for water. The life-giving force is essential."

He continued talking, but she couldn't listen to anything but the thundering of her heart. Could she do this? Could she not? Would she rather ask and know, or would she rather wonder? Hadn't Ayanna made her promise not to have regrets?

"You have yet to touch your food, and I suspect you are not listening to me."

She turned to him. The beat of the music seemed to thunder in her blood.

She studied his face, the way his dark hair had been brushed back from his forehead, the strong cut of his cheekbones, the faint bow in his top lip.

He touched her face with his knuckles. "Tell me, Phoebe. I can see the questions in your eyes, and something that looks like fear. Yet you need not fear anything from me. Surely we have spent enough hours together for you to know that."

"I *do* know," she whispered, unable to look away from his compelling gaze. "It's just…" She drew in a breath. "You have been more than kind to me. I want you to know that I appreciate all you've done."

He smiled. "Do not thank me too heartily. Kindness was not my motivation. I'm far too selfish a man for that."

"I don't believe that. Nor do I understand what you see in me. I'm young and inexperienced. But you've made everything about my time here really wonderful. So it seems wrong to ask for one more thing.''

"Ask me for anything. I suspect I will find it difficult to refuse you.''

He brushed his thumb across her lower lip. She shivered. The contact made her want so much, and it also, along with his words, gave her courage.

"Mazin, would you take me to Lucia's Point tomorrow?''

His dark eyes turned unreadable. Not by a flicker of a lash did he give away what he was thinking. She swallowed.

"I know the custom. That I may only go there with a lover. I don't have one. A lover, I mean. I've never...'' Why didn't the man say something? She could feel herself blushing. Words began to fail her. "I thought you might like to stay with me tonight. To change that. To—''

Her throat closed and she had to stop talking. Unable to meet his gaze any longer, she stared at her lap and waited for him to start laughing.

Mazin studied the young woman in front of him. He had always thought of her as a quiet beauty, but tonight she was the most beautiful creature he had ever seen. Some of her transformation came from the dress and makeup, but much of it was the result of a subtle confidence. At last Phoebe didn't doubt herself.

Until she had asked him to be her lover. He read the uncertainty in her posture, the questions in the quiver of her mouth. He knew she was unaware of how much he desired her, nor would she understand the iron control it had taken for him to keep his distance. Even as they sat there, his arousal pulsed painfully. If she had any experience, she would not question her appeal. But she did not possess that kind of worldliness.

He supposed a better man would find a way to refuse her gently. He knew he was the wrong person to take the precious gift she offered. For the first time in his life, he did not feel worthy.

Yet he could not find it in his heart to walk away. He had wanted her for too long. The need inside him burned. To be her first, to hold her and touch her and make her his own—no one had ever offered him more.

"My dove," he murmured, leaning close.

She raised her head, her eyes brimming with tears. Doubt clouded her pretty features. He brushed away a few tears that spilled over, then kissed her mouth.

"I have ached for you from the moment I first saw you," he said, speaking the absolute truth. "If I do not have you, a part of me will cease to exist."

Her mouth curved into a smile. "Is that a yes?"

He laughed. "It is."

There would be consequences. To make love with a mature woman of experience was one thing—to take a virgin to his bed was another. Honor was at stake. Perhaps in this modern time there were those who took such things lightly, but not him. Not with Phoebe.

He wondered what she would say if he told her the truth. Would she still want him in her bed? His conscience battled briefly with the notion of telling her. But he needed her too much to risk it.

He shifted so he could speak directly into her ear.

"Tell me of your appetites," he murmured. "Would you like to stay for the rest of the meal and watch the dancers? Lingering will increase the anticipation. Or do you prefer to adjourn now?"

"I don't want to wait."

Her simple words sent a bolt of desire through him. His arousal ached. Tonight would be both endless torture and ultimate pleasure. He was determined to show her all the possibilities and make her first time as perfect as possible. Assuming his need did not kill him first.

Chapter 7

They left the restaurant immediately. Phoebe tried not to be scared as they stood waiting for Mazin's car. But instead of his usual Mercedes, a black limo pulled up.

"I wanted tonight to be special," he said with a smile as he helped her into the back seat. "I thought you would enjoy the change."

She'd never been in a limo before, but saying that would make her sound even more unworldly and innocent than she was. Instead she tried to smile her thanks, even though her mouth didn't seem to want to cooperate.

Her brain was a complete blank. The drive back to the hotel would be about fifteen minutes. Obviously they had to talk about something, but she couldn't come up with a subject. What exactly was one supposed to discuss before making love for the first time?

She glanced frantically around the luxurious interior. The seats were camel color, and the softest leather she had ever touched. To the left was a complicated entertainment center with dozens of dials, levers and switches, along with a small television. To the right was a full bar. A bottle of champagne sat in an ice bucket.

"Had you already planned on us..." Her voice trailed off.

Mazin followed her gaze and touched the bottle of champagne. "I had thought we might take a walk along the beach and enjoy the moonlight," he said. "But I had not hoped to have the honor of doing more than kissing you. If I had, I would have been more prepared."

More prepared? Was that possible? Didn't the limo and the champagne spell seduction? Had her invitation simply made things easier for him?

She wanted to ask Mazin, but he was no longer paying attention to her. Instead he seemed to be searching for something. He ran his hands along the back of the seat and pressed against the wood paneling on the doors.

"What are you looking for?" she asked, bewildered.

"There is a storage compartment somewhere." He shifted to the seat behind the driver and examined the leather.

"My oldest son mentioned it to me," he said, more to himself than to her. "He joked about always keeping the car stocked."

Phoebe had no idea what he was talking about. She assumed he meant the older of his four boys, the one away at college.

"Why would your son be using a limo?"

Mazin didn't answer. He pressed against the wood panel. "At last," he said as it gave way.

The paneling opened to reveal a good-sized compartment. There was a change of clothing, more champagne and a box that she couldn't quite see. Mazin reached for the box. She shrank back into the corner of the seat when she read the labeling.

Condoms.

Phoebe's romantic images of what might happen that evening crashed in around her. Reality was not a fuzzy, slow-motion dance of kissing and touching. If they were going to make love, then there were potential consequences of the act. Protection was required. The sensible part of her brain applauded Mazin's sensible nature. Her romantic heart shriveled inside.

He glanced up and saw her. She was unable to turn away before he had a chance to see the expression on her face. She didn't know what she looked like, but whatever it was, it was enough to make him swear under his breath.

He shoved several packets into his tux pocket, closed the compartment and returned to her side.

"You do not want me to be practical?" he asked, putting an arm around her and pulling her close.

"I know it's important." She stared at the crisp edge of his collar rather than at his face. "I appreciate you taking care of me by, um, you know. Making sure you had, ah, protection."

"But it has destroyed the fantasy, yes?"

She raised her gaze to his face. "How did you know what I was thinking?"

"I know you, my dove. I promise to make this night as fantastical as I know how, but I will not compromise your health or leave you with something you did not want."

A baby. He was talking about her getting pregnant. In that second, Phoebe desperately wanted to have his child. What she would give to have a little girl with his dark, flashing eyes and easy grace. Or a sturdy little boy like Dabir, who fearlessly took on the world.

He touched her chin, forcing her to raise her head, then he bent and kissed her.

The soft pressure of his lips chased away her doubts. He kept the kiss light, but just being close to him was enough to make her body tingle all over. Before she could tempt him to deepen the contact, the car stopped.

She raised her head. "Where are we?"

"A side entrance to the hotel," he said, opening the door and stepping out into the night. "I did not think you would be comfortable walking with me to the elevator. At this time of night the lobby would be crowded.''

''Thank you,'' she said as she followed him down a flower-lined path to a glass door that led in from the garden.

Trust Mazin to be so considerate. She would have been embarrassed to have everyone know what they were going upstairs to do.

Once inside, he led her to a service elevator in the back and they arrived on her floor without being seen by anyone. She fumbled for her key until he took her small evening bag from her and removed it. Then he unlocked the door and drew her inside her room.

The balcony door stood open. A single lamp on the nightstand burned, and housekeeping had already been by to turn down the bed. Phoebe could smell the scent of the sea. She told herself to focus on that and not on her jangling nerves.

Mazin locked the door and set her purse on the table by the mirror. He crossed to stand in front of her.

''I see your tension has returned,'' he said lightly. ''Feel it if you must. But feel this as well.'' He pressed his mouth to her throat.

The warm, damp kiss made her legs go weak. She had to hold on to him to keep from sliding to the floor. He kissed her neck, and licked the sensitive skin by her ear. One of his hands rested on her shoulder, his fingers rubbing her bare skin.

"Beautiful Phoebe," he breathed before taking her earlobe into his mouth and nibbling.

Goose bumps broke out on her skin as he shifted to stand behind her. Her breasts seemed to swell as her nipples tightened. Between her legs she felt a tension and an ache that made her want to press herself against him.

He moved her hair over her shoulder and kissed his way down the back of her neck, to her shoulder blades. She hadn't thought of her back as a very erotic part of her body, but when he lightly stroked her there, and followed that contact by an openmouthed kiss, she found it difficult to breathe.

As he nibbled on her shoulder, he ran his hands up and down her arms. From there he slid his fingers to her waist. Anticipation filled her as he circled slowly, climbing higher and higher. He stood behind her and kissed her neck, even as he moved his hands up to touch her breasts.

She exhaled in wonder as he cupped her small curves, holding them in his hands as if they were most precious cargo. Even through the material of the dress she felt his warmth and the tender way he moved against her sensitized flesh.

The style of the dress was such that she couldn't wear a bra—at least, not any one that she had. At first she'd been nervous about going out that way, but now, with him stroking her, she was grateful. One less layer between his fingers and her aching body.

She loved how he explored her curves. She wanted

to beg him to slip off her dress so she could know what it was like to have him touch her bare skin. She wanted—

She gasped as he lightly touched her nipples. She'd known they were tight with desire, but she hadn't realized how sensitive that puckered skin could be. Fire shot through her, racing along her arms and legs before settling deep in her belly. He brushed against them again and again, making her groan and lean back against him as pleasure filled her.

She wasn't sure how long they stood there, him touching her, her savoring the contact. At last he turned her in his arms and kissed her. A deep, satisfying kiss that made her body melt and her toes curl. She wrapped her arms around him, wanting to be as close as possible. This was what she'd waited for all her life. Nothing could go wrong as long as Mazin continued to touch her.

She felt the slide of the zipper being pulled down in back. Cool evening air tingled against her bare skin. She wore panties, a garter belt and stockings under her dress. Nothing more. The ladies in the boutique had insisted on the latter when they'd seen her dress, telling her that regular panty hose would be a crime under such a beautiful gown. Phoebe hadn't been sure, but as Mazin pushed her dress off her shoulders and she thought of how she looked underneath, she was glad she had let them convince her.

The dress fell to the floor. She was close enough to him that she wasn't yet embarrassed about being practically naked. His large, warm hands moved up and down her back, touching her, soothing her, arousing her until she longed for him to do more. Then he slipped lower—to her hips and the garter belt there. And lower, to the high-cut panties, the bare skin of her thigh, then to the tops of the stockings. He froze.

Mazin broke the kiss and stared at her. Fire seemed to radiate from his dark eyes and tension pulled his mouth straight.

"I want you," he breathed.

There was nothing he could have said that was more perfect. The last of Phoebe's fears faded. She leaned forward and kissed him. It was the first time she had initiated any contact. She licked his lower lip, then nipped at the full flesh. He grabbed her and pulled her close, deepening the kiss with an intensity that convinced her he was a man in great need of a woman.

She felt something hard pressing against her belly. His arousal, she thought, happy to know that she could affect him so. She wanted to explore her new and wondrous power over him when he moved his hands to her waist.

The feel of them on bare skin was very different than the feel of them through her dress. She moved back so he could move higher. He didn't disappoint her. He slipped up to cup her breasts, then touched her nipples with his thumbs.

She hadn't known there was that much pleasure in the world. Her mind faded to blackness and she could only experience what he was doing to her. She wasn't even aware of pulling away from the kiss until her head sagged back and she exhaled his name.

Instead of being angry, Mazin laughed softly. He bent forward, took one of her nipples in his mouth and sucked. More fire filled her. She cupped his head, running her fingers through his hair and begging him to never stop. He moved from breast to breast, back and forth, licking, blowing, caressing. Between her legs her panties grew damp. Then without warning her legs gave way.

He caught her as she fell. With an ease that surprised her, he picked her up in his arms and carried her to the bed. Her shoes got lost along the way. After standing her next to the bed, he quickly peeled off her panties, leaving her stockings in place, then eased her onto the bed.

Phoebe had a brief flash of panic, but before it could take hold, he was next to her, holding her, kissing her. He rested his hand on her breast, which made her forget everything bad and think only of how he made her feel.

When he moved his hand lower, he kissed her so deeply, she barely noticed. But at the first brush of his fingers against her damp curls, she found herself very aware of what he was doing.

Questions filled her mind. What was she supposed to do? What would it feel like? Before she could ask, he stroked the inside of her thigh. Without her being aware of doing anything, her legs fell open. He touched her lightly, exploring her, finding wonderful places that made her breathing quicken. He found that most secret place and slipped inside. At the same time he shifted his attention from her mouth to her breasts.

He circled her nipple, licking her sensitive skin. She didn't know what to think about—his mouth or his fingers. He withdrew from her and rubbed between her curls. Without warning, his mouth closed on her nipple and his fingers found some amazingly sensitive spot.

The combination made her forget to breathe. Not that it mattered, because whatever he was doing was too good for her to live through. She was going to die. No one could survive such pleasure. It terrified her. She never wanted it to stop.

He rubbed her gently, moving faster and faster. Suddenly she was breathing again, or rather gasping. She rolled her head back and forth as pressure built.

"Mazin?"

"Hush, my dove. I am here."

And then he was kissing her and touching her and the world began to spin. There was a final push within her, a pinnacle of pressure, and then the most glorious release. She clung to him, shaking, trembling, hungry and satisfied, all at the same time.

When it was over, he drew her close, kissing her face and making her feel as if she were the most precious creature on earth.

"I didn't know," she whispered. "That's pretty amazing."

He stared into her eyes. "There is so much more I long to show you."

"I'd like that."

He sat up and pulled off his coat and shirt. Shoes and socks followed, then trousers. When he was naked, she raised herself up on one elbow to study him. The sight of his body pleased her. She watched as he slipped on the condom, then parted her legs for him.

He waited to enter her, first kissing her and touching her everywhere until that unbelievable pleasure built up to the point of nearly exploding. Just when she was about to go over the edge, he pushed inside her.

Her body stretched to take him. The pressure was uncomfortable at first, then eased. He reached between them and touched that one perfect spot. The feel of him inside her while he stroked her sent her higher and higher. She could barely hold on.

He shifted so that he could wrap his arms around her and kiss her. The change in their positions forced his arousal in deeper. She clung to him. Everything was so unfamiliar, yet so right, and she lost herself on the next thrust. She called out his name even as he shuddered and clung to her.

She opened her eyes. Mazin stared at her. Even as her climax washed over her and his ripped through him, they gazed at each other. It was a moment of intimate connection, far beyond anything she'd ever experienced. In that moment, she knew the truth. That no matter how far she traveled from this magical paradise, no matter who she met or what she experienced, she would only ever love one man.

Mazin.

Chapter 8

Phoebe awoke just before dawn. An unfamiliar weight draped around her waist and it took her a second to realize it was Mazin's arm. She smiled and snuggled closer to him.

"Good morning," he whispered in her ear. He lay behind her, his body warm and welcoming against her own. "How are you feeling?"

"Pretty darned perfect," she said happily.

Something hard poked into the back of her leg. She giggled. "I didn't realize that people could make love so often," she said.

"I assure you that four times in a night is not usual. You inspire me." He withdrew a little. "However, this is new to you, so I will restrain myself."

She thought about how one of the times he hadn't entered her at all. He'd kissed her intimately until she'd been unable to keep from losing herself in the glory of his attentions. He'd then taught her how to pleasure him that way. As he had promised, there was much to explore.

He glanced at the clock and groaned. "I must return home for a short time, my dove. I have breakfast with Dabir each morning and I would not want to explain my absence. But I will return in a few hours and we can make our way to Lucia's Point." He leaned over and kissed her. "There in the shadow of the waterfall I will make love with you."

She melted at the thought.

He rose and quickly dressed, then kissed her again before leaving. "Miss me," he said. "As I will miss you."

"Always," she promised, and knew it was the truth.

The sound of the waterfall made it nearly impossible to speak. Phoebe stood, transfixed by the sight of so much water tumbling from nearly a hundred feet in the air. A fine mist cooled her bare arms and face. She leaned back in Mazin's arms.

This was, she thought contentedly, a perfect moment. Last night she had learned what it meant to be loved by a man. Over and over Mazin had touched her, kissed her and taken her to paradise. With practice, she would learn to seduce *him*. She wanted that. She wanted to make him ache with longing. She wanted to make him tremble and hunger so that he couldn't hold back any longer.

She wanted to make him love her.

Phoebe sighed quietly. Love. Could a man like Mazin ever care about her? She was young and didn't share his life experiences. He was worldly and wealthy. She hadn't even been to college. They had very little in common. And yet…in her heart, being with him felt so very right. Now, in his embrace, she knew that she had come home. How could her feelings be so strong without him having the same reaction? Was it possible for her to love so deeply and have him completely unaffected?

"What are you thinking?" he asked, speaking the question directly in her ear.

"That the falls are very beautiful. Are we really going to make love here?"

He turned her in his arms and kissed her. She recognized the passion flaring in his eyes. "Do not doubt my desire for you, my dove," he said, taking her hand and placing it on his arousal.

He was already hard. She wrapped her arms around him. "Oh, Mazin."

"Yes. Speak my name," he murmured against her mouth. "Know only me."

He undressed her slowly, peeling away layers of clothing until she was naked on the blanket he'd brought with them. Sunlight shone through the leaves overhead, creating changing patterns of shadows on her legs and torso. Mazin undressed himself, then joined her on the ground. As he kissed her deeply and touched her breasts, she felt herself melting inside.

Heat filled her. Dampness signaled her readiness. When he stroked her intimately, she shuddered in preparation of her release.

He took her to the edge and when she would have
slipped off into paradise, he drew back enough to ease
her on top of him. The unfamiliar position felt awkward at first, but she soon saw the advantages of controlling his rhythm inside her. While she moved up
and down on his maleness, he cupped the apex of her
thighs and rubbed his thumb against her tiny place of
pleasure. Tension made her shudder. Need made her
cry out.

She lost control there in the warm sunlight, with
the thunder of the falls in the background. The soft
call of birds provided romantic music for their lovemaking. He shuddered beneath her, losing himself as
well, calling out her name, making her feel as if she'd
finally found her place to belong.

"We must talk," he said later, when they were
dressed and walking back to his car. "There is something I haven't told you."

Phoebe didn't like the sound of that. She shivered,
as if the sun had disappeared behind a cloud. Was he
going to tell her that their time together was over?

"I don't want to talk," she said quickly. "I'm leaving in a few days. Can't we keep these happy memories alive until then?"

He sighed. "Phoebe, I do not mean to frighten you.
I am not trying to end our relationship—I simply seek
to change it. But before I do that, I must tell you the
truth about myself."

She climbed into the car. Where before her flesh
had tingled with anticipation, now her skin simply felt
cold. She wanted to wrap herself in the blanket Mazin

had brought. Except it carried the sweet fragrance of their lovemaking, and if she inhaled that, she would cry. She was determined that regardless of what Mazin said, she would not cry. She would be strong and mature and brave. She owed that to herself, if not to him.

She waited until he slid behind the wheel, then stared straight out the front windshield.

"You're married."

He turned to stare at her. "I told you, my wife died six years ago. I have not remarried. For a time I had thought I would take another wife, but finding someone seemed an impossible task. I gave up the idea."

He started the engine. "I am doing this badly. Perhaps rather than telling you, I should show you. I want—" He hesitated. "Most women would be pleased, but I am not sure of your reaction."

If he was trying to make her feel better, he was doing a lousy job. Phoebe bit her bottom lip as he drove them toward the coast road, and then headed north. Part of her wanted to hear what he had to say, because if he told her to her face that their relationship was over, then eventually she would be able to stop loving him. At least, that would be her plan. But if she ran away, she might never get over him. Although the thought of disappearing back into her hotel and not coming out until it was time for her flight had a certain appeal.

She was lost in her thoughts and didn't notice they'd begun to drive up to the top of the island until she recognized the road to the palace. Her throat tightened, making it impossible to swallow.

"Mazin, why are we here?"

He didn't say anything. Her mind began to race, and not in a good way. Various possibilities occurred to her and she wasn't sure she liked any one of them.

Instead of stopping in front of the palace, he kept driving down a road that led to a large building. One he'd pointed out to her before. The private residence of the prince.

Her entire world shifted slightly. Her brain froze, her heart stopped beating for a second, then began again but this time at a thunderous pace. And before either of them could speak, a small child broke through a grove and ran toward the car.

Mazin slowed, then pulled to the edge of the road. When he parked, Dabir ran to her side of the car and pulled open her door.

"Did you ask her? Did she say yes?"

"Dabir, we have discussed nothing," Mazin growled, although his son didn't seem the least bit impressed by his temper. "We need more time."

"But you've had all morning," the boy complained. "Did you tell her that I think she's pretty? Did you tell her about being a princess?"

"Dabir!"

Mazin's voice echoed through the trees. Dabir squeaked, then grinned. "Say yes, Miss Carson. Please?" he pleaded, then took one look at his father and headed back the way he'd come. The sound of his laughter drifted to them.

Phoebe didn't know what to say or what to think. She felt as if she'd fallen into an alternative universe. "M-Mazin?"

He sighed. "This is not what I had planned. We are sitting in a car. It is not romantic." He released his seat belt and angled toward her. "Phoebe, what I have not told you is that I am more than a minister in the Lucia-Serrat government. I am Crown Prince Nasri Mazin. I rule this island. The house before us is my home. My sons are princes."

She blinked several times. C-crown p-prince Nasri Mazin? Even her thoughts stuttered. "No," she whispered. "You can't be."

He shrugged. "Yet I am."

She stared at his familiar face, at the dark eyes and firm mouth. The mouth she'd kissed and that had kissed her back in many very intimate places. Heat flared on her cheeks. "But I've seen you naked!"

He grinned. "Yes. As I have seen you."

She didn't want to think about that. "I don't understand. If you're really a prince, why didn't you tell me? And why did you want to be with me?"

He brushed a strand of hair from her face. "When I met you at the airport, I had recently returned from an extended journey. In the back of my mind had been the thought that I should find a wife. I did not expect to marry for love, but I thought I would find a woman with whom I could enjoy life. But that was not to be. The women I met bored me. I grew tired of them wanting me for my position or my money. I came home weary and discouraged."

He shrugged. "Then I saw a pretty young woman walk into the duty-free shop. She looked fresh and charming and very unlike the other women I'd been seeing. I followed her on an impulse. That same impulse caused me to speak with her. She had no idea who I was. At first I thought her innocence was a game, but in time I discovered it was as genuine as the young woman herself. I was intrigued."

She still wasn't thinking straight. In fact, she wasn't thinking at all. "But Mazin..." She swallowed. "I mean Prince Nasri—" She squeezed her eyes shut. This couldn't be happening to her.

A prince? She'd fallen in love with a prince? Which meant any teeny, tiny hopes she'd had about a happily ever after had just disappeared like so much smoke.

"Phoebe, do not look so sad."

She opened her eyes and stared at him. "I'm not. I feel foolish, which is different. I should have guessed."

"I went to great pains to see that you did not. I arranged our travels in advance, making sure there wouldn't be anyone around."

And here she'd just thought it was the slow season. She'd been a fool. "I guess no one is going to believe me if I try to tell them this when I get back home."

"Ayanna would have believed," he said softly.

She nodded. Ayanna would have understood everything, she thought with a sigh. Because the same sort of thing had happened to her aunt. And Ayanna had spent the rest of her life loving the one man she could never have.

Pain tightened her chest, making it difficult to breathe. "You should, ah, probably take me back to the hotel now," she murmured.

"But I have not answered your second question."

She wasn't sure how much longer she could sit there without crying. "W-what question is that?"

"You asked to know why I wanted to be with you."

Oh. She didn't think she wanted to hear that answer. It couldn't be good. Or at least not good enough.

He put his hands on her shoulders. "You enchanted me. I do not get the opportunity to meet many people without them knowing I am Prince Nasri of Lucia-Serrat. With you, I could be myself. When you told me about your aunt's list of places to go, I decided to show them to you. I wanted to spend time with you. To get to know you."

That wasn't so bad. She forced herself to smile. "I appreciate all you've done. You were very kind."

He shook her gently. "Do you think kindness was my sole purpose?"

Why was he asking such hard questions? "I thought, maybe, after a while, you might want to seduce me."

Mazin groaned, then leaned forward and kissed her on the mouth. "Yes, I wanted you in my bed, but it was more than that," he said between kisses. "I wanted to be with you. I could not forget you. You became very important to me. I did not plan for you to meet my son, but that turned out to be most fortuitous. Dabir thinks you are very lovely and that you would make an excellent mother."

If the world had tilted before, it positively spun now, swooping and zooming around her until she found it impossible to keep her balance. Her fingers

shook as she unfastened her seat belt, then stumbled
out of the car. She was going to faint. Worse, she
thought she might be sick.

Mazin…make that Prince Nasri…hurried around
the car to stand next to her. "Phoebe? What's
wrong?"

"You want me to take Nana's place?"

No. That wasn't possible. She couldn't stay here
and take care of Mazin's child, all the while watching
him with other women. She would be destroyed. Even
if her heart weren't a consideration, she had her own
dreams and they didn't involve her staying on Lucia-
Serrat as a nanny.

Suddenly he was in front of her, grabbing her by
her upper arms and shaking her gently. "Is that what
you believe?" He stared at her face, then shook his
head and pulled her close. "Don't you know I love
you, you little fool? What did you think? That I
wanted to hire you as a caretaker to my child? I have
that for Dabir already. What I do not have is a mother
for him and a wife for myself. I do not have a woman
to love—someone to love me in return."

She stepped back and looked at him. His words
filled her brain, but she couldn't grasp them. "I don't
understand."

"Obviously."

And then he kissed her.

His warm, tender mouth settled on hers. As he
wrapped his arms around her, she allowed herself to
believe that he might have been telling the truth.

"You love me?" she asked, breathless, but with a
little less heart pain.

"Yes, my dove. I suspect nearly from the first." He stroked her hair, then her cheek. "For many years now I have been disenchanted with my life. Everything felt wrong. I loved my sons, but they could not completely fill my heart. I have traveled everywhere and never felt at home, until I met you. When I saw my island through your eyes, it was as if I had seen it for the first time. Your gentle strength, your honest heart, your giving spirit touched me and healed me. I have searched the world only to find my heart's desire standing right in front of me."

He kissed her again. "Marry me, Phoebe. Marry me and stay here. Be mother to my sons, be princess to my people. But most of all, love me always, as I will love you."

"A p-princess?"

He smiled. "It's a very small island. Your duties would not be taxing."

"I wouldn't mind the work. I just never imagined anything like this."

"Will you say yes?"

She gazed into his dark eyes. She didn't care that he was a prince. What mattered to her was that he was the man she loved. This wasn't *her* dream...it was something much bigger and better. It was her heart's desire.

"Yes."

He drew her close and hugged her as if he would never let her go. "For always," he promised. "We will live life to the fullest, with no regrets. Just as your Ayanna would have wanted."

SHEIKH OF ICE
Alexandra Sellers

Dear Reader,

It's a great pleasure to be asked for another Cup
Companion story. I am thrilled to think that you enjoy
reading my SONS OF THE DESERT stories as much as
I love writing them. And for those of you who've never
yet visited the Barakat Emirates nor met my powerful,
handsome sheikhs—I hope you, too, will share in the
magic.

Readers familiar with my Barakati world know that my
princes each have twelve Cup Companions. In centuries
past, the Cup Companions were just that—the monarch's
drinking friends. Their role was to entertain the prince and
take his mind off affairs of state, whether by hunting with
him, discussing philosophy and wisdom, or reciting poetry
over the cups. But modern Cup Companions form a cabinet
to advise and serve their prince, in a variety of capacities,
in the joint endeavour to create a safe and happy kingdom
for their people. They are men of character, power and
influence.

And one by one, willing or unwilling, they each find
love with their perfect woman. As it happens, Hadi, my
"Sheikh of Ice," is unwilling. But Kate is the woman of his
dreams. How will he resolve that dilemma? I hope you'll
enjoy his journey of discovery as much as I did.

All the best,

Alexandra Sellers

Prologue

He stood behind the one-way glass, idly watching the arriving passengers as they filed up towards the desks of the immigration officers. There was no anxiety in his gaze—an agent would signal him when she arrived. He was only passing the time until that happened.

Even so, the habit of constant alertness was ingrained. What his gaze took in, his mind assessed.

The majority of the arrivals were young Barakatis, men and women returning from trips abroad, a reflection of the vibrant new economy that was flourishing under the young princes' rule.

The foreigners were mostly young and middle-aged European couples on holiday. As he watched, a fresh-faced pair stepped up to the desk that stood nearest to his hidden post. Their new clothes, neatly cut hair and bright smiles showed that they had high hopes of a romantic and memorable honeymoon here in the beautiful Barakat Emirates.

His jaw tightened with a bitterness so deeply embedded it was a part of his nature. The girl was painfully young and pretty, with a cap of short blond curls, a laughing, carefree mouth. Her eyes plainly showed she adored her young husband, who kept a proud, firm arm around his bride as he handed the official their passports.

So young. So full of courage. So confident of the future. Their demeanour told the world that their wedding had been attended by two happy families, who had approved wholeheartedly of the union. Whatever the future of this marriage, it had begun in hope and love.

With a discipline that was also part of his nature, he drew his eyes away from the couple, suppressing the memory they had almost called up, and went back to searching the faces of the arriving passengers.

There was a large sprinkling of foreign business people on this flight, and he amused himself by trying to guess which of them was the woman he was waiting for. There had been no photograph among the papers the office had sent, and he had no clue as to what she looked like, except that she was twenty-seven years old. So far he had seen several women travelling alone, but in the absence of a signal from any of the immigration officers, he had let them all pass.

His eyes returned to the line nearest him again as a large man stepped up to the desk in the wake of the honeymoon couple, and the people behind shuffled and shifted their hand luggage to a new position.

At the head of the line now was a woman he had not noticed before. She must have been hidden by the bulk of the passenger ahead of her, but to the man watching it was as if she had suddenly appeared out of nowhere. She was bending over her wheeled case to pull her papers out of a zipped pocket, completely unaware of his gaze.

She was just below medium height, very, very slender, and with short, elfin, black hair. For a moment he imagined she might be the foreign-educated daughter of one of the mountain tribes, who were known for producing the wand-like women said to be descendants of the ancient *Peri*. In that moment he even had a faint feeling of recognition, and he gazed at the wisps of hair against her averted cheek with a frown of curiosity, willing her to lift her head.

In unconscious obedience she straightened, giving him a view of her profile. Involuntarily he stiffened. No, he did not know her. He had never before seen the darkly lashed eyes, the curving cheek, the lips that shimmered under the stark lighting, as if she had just licked her lips to prepare for a man's kiss. Her jaw was just slightly square—an inherited determination from her father, he guessed, firmly underpinning the very feminine beauty she had doubtless got from her mother.

But still her beauty was all woman. He narrowed his eyes and blamed her as feeling stirred in him, but his self-discipline failed now: he could not turn away.

Her sunglasses on her head ruffled the short hair as she fingered through the neat travel wallet in her hand, checking her papers. She was wearing a simple, ankle-length dress in soft jade green. With cap sleeves and a plain neck, it was unwrinkled after her hours in the air, a no-nonsense travel outfit. But the fabric brushed her breast, her hip, suggestively, so that his mind involuntarily filled in the promise with an image of high, full breasts, the slenderest of waists, gently curving hips.... He curbed his thoughts with distant anger, but although he forced his eyes to move on, in another second his gaze had found her again.

With a nod the immigration agent gave the large man back his passport and signalled to the next in line. The *peri*-woman clasped the handle of her wheeled bag and approached the desk.

She passed the agent her passport with unconscious grace and a smile, and stood for a moment with the determinedly absent stare of the innocent. Abruptly, then, although it was impossible she could be aware that a watcher stood behind the wall of opaque black glass, she turned her head to stare straight at him, giving him a full, unobstructed view of her face.

It was too unexpected, too sudden; he had no time to defend himself. The dark eyes, wide and trusting, wondering, a little excited, seemed to look right into him; and for a moment, as if it were contagious, he felt a direct sense of her happy anticipation.

The gaze pierced him, hurting him, and his stomach clenched involuntarily against the blow. Sweat beaded his forehead. Like a dog who has been beaten long ago but still remembers what a stick is, he felt suddenly that he both hated and feared her.

As if his feelings reached her, the excitement in her eyes was suddenly replaced with disquiet. Her eyes grew guarded and watchful, and just under the level of consciousness, he warned her, *Yes, I am dangerous to one like you.*

A loud buzzer sounded in the room, and he closed his eyes with an involuntary plea. *Not her.* Then, calling himself a fool, he turned to the official whose office he had, for these few minutes, invaded. The man was pointing at the computer screen.

"That's your party, sir," the official said, and with a resigned lack of surprise he waited for the inevitable. "Station 1. The young woman in green straight in front, no doubt."

Chapter 1

Kate Drummond twitched nervously and gazed at the shadow images reflecting from the black panels at the side of the arrivals area. She felt unsettled without any reason. Everything was in order, as far as she knew. The Consulate of the Barakat Emirates in Vancouver had arranged everything for her, including her visa and a guide. There shouldn't be any problem.

But her skin shivered with the animal awareness of threat. She stared at the reflection of the crowd behind her, looking for any anomaly, anything out of place, but she saw nothing that might have triggered an unconscious alarm. After a moment, she turned around and looked at the room directly. Everything seemed normal, and Kate told herself to relax. Someone walking over her grave, that was all it was.

She watched the immigration official punch her data into the computer terminal. It wasn't likely that anything would go wrong with her visa, but in this business, you never knew. The immigration process was always the first hurdle in any country, and she willed it to go smoothly. She had high hopes of the Barakat Emirates, but it would be useless to plan the vacation of the year for her customers if things were going to come apart right at the get-go.

The agent, a middle-aged, keen-eyed woman, peered at the screen for a moment, hit another key, and looked up. Women immigration officials were always just that little bit tougher, a fact that someone in Barakat had apparently taken on board, since all the agents were women.

Kate was sure that smugglers and others with a dishonest motive hated nothing more than being faced with a middle-aged woman at immigration. Even she, whose motives were completely innocent, quailed a little before the assessing gaze and thanked God she had no secrets to hide.

Maybe this was the source of the strange disquiet that had gripped her, she thought, with an inward grin.

"What is the purpose of your visit to the Barakat Emirates?" the agent asked in accented but fluent English.

"I'm here on business."

A small nod. "You do business with Barakati companies?"

Kate smiled. "I'm a travel agent. I'm here to work

out an itinerary for an adventure holiday for my clients. Luckily for me, I have to travel the route myself first.''

The agent, looking interested, got a bit warmer. ''Is there a big demand in Canada for holidays here?''

Kate smiled and shook her head. The Barakat Emirates was only just opening up to tourism and certainly wasn't going to encourage mass tourism. She was sure no Barakati really liked the idea of hordes of beer-swilling sunseekers invading their beautiful country, no matter how much cash such visitors might spread around.

On the other hand, it was always flattering to think that other nationalities dreamed of visiting your country.

''My agency is a specialist one,'' she told the woman. ''We design very exclusive vacation packages for people who are looking for physical and intellectual meat in their holidays. I'm sure there are thousands of Canadians who would adore to stretch out on the beaches of Barakat in an alcohol-soaked haze if they were given a chance, but my agency certainly won't be sending them here. We create exclusive travel adventures, often including guided lecture tours of sites of historical and geographical interest given by scholars and local experts.''

''You've sold me,'' the agent said with a grin, and Kate grimaced and wrinkled her nose with pretty self-deprecation. She had sounded like a Drummond and Venables Travel Adventures brochure.

"Sorry," she murmured, smiling. "I get carried away."

"Don't apologize," the agent said firmly. "You love your work, and that is good."

"Yes, I do," Kate said softly.

"How long will you stay?"

"Three weeks."

A number of probing questions followed, but Kate had nothing to hide, and when the catechism was over, the agent relaxed into chattiness.

"You seem to be looking forward to your visit. Is it your first?"

Kate smiled broadly, her eyes lighting up with excitement. "I've been entranced by the thought of a visit to the Barakat Emirates for years—since before I went into the travel business. From the outside it looks like just a thrilling country. I can't wait to visit some of the places I've heard about."

The woman nodded and firmly stamped her passport. "I am sure you will find many places to interest your clients here."

Kate asked, more casually than she felt, "Do you know of a place in the Noor Mountains called The Valley?"

"There are many valleys in the Noor Mountains."

"I think the one I mean is just called *Al Darreh*. Doesn't that mean 'the valley'?"

The agent's smile broadened into tolerant pity. "But this is a mythical place. The one place in the Barakat Emirates which no invader, including Genghis Khan, ever conquered because they could not find it. *Darreh* is our Parvan word for 'valley,' and *al* means 'the' in Arabic. But there is no such place as *Al Darreh*. It is like the Atlantis legend."

She initialled the stamp and Kate's visa with a pen, slipped a sheet of printed paper on top of the passport and held it out to Kate. Kate clasped it, but, not letting go, the woman looked into her eyes and said firmly, "We have a beautiful country, and we are proud of it. Please read this paper. It will explain a little of our laws and customs. All visitors are expected to be familiar with them and respect them. We ask you to remember that you are a guest in our home. Please do not abuse our hospitality. We hope that you will enjoy your visit."

Kate's eyes opened wide. It was the first time she had ever heard such a speech on entering any country. "Do you say that to all tourists?"

"To all foreign visitors," the woman corrected her matter-of-factly, letting go of her passport. "*Ahlan wa sahlan.* Welcome to the Barakat Emirates."

With a brief nod of thanks, he stepped out of the official's office and, still half-hoping for a reprieve, moved over to the agent at Station 1. Not that he doubted her efficiency, merely that, in some irrational part of himself, he was hoping to discover that she was wrong. That the *peri*-woman was not the one he was waiting for.

The agent glanced up at him without surprise as he

bent over her shoulder to peer at the computer screen. She had never seen him before, but officials from the Tourism Ministry were not infrequent visitors to Immigration, and this one had an air of authority that seemed bred in the bone. He was certainly no petty official, and she wondered who Kate Drummond was to warrant his interest.

Another arrival was already handing her a passport, and she took it with one hand while with the other she tapped a key to summon up the previous arrival's data for the man.

Drummond, Kate Barbara, his eyes read, clinching the matter. The date of birth, too, matched the one he had been given with his notes. But now he did not close his eyes and plead with fate. His jaw tightened briefly, but he only nodded, straightened and turned away.

Reluctantly he followed the slim green-clad figure into the baggage claim area. Then, without conscious decision, he stopped at a distance, watching again, as if circumstance might still intervene to prevent the necessity for meeting her.

Yet at the same time he felt his heartbeat quicken, his thighs tighten, with the curiously possessive knowledge that the meeting was inevitable.

Stopping by the baggage carousel, Kate pulled out her palm pilot and keyed in some notes while she waited. So far, so good. Under *Airport, arrivals* she typed *gd AC, cln, modn.* Under *Immigration* she quickly noted *fem agts, Eng spk. Cmptrs. Thor chck, but enuf agts to kp flow. Gvn familizn broch and short lecture (!)*

Next on the chart was *Baggage handling—trolleys*, and Kate blinked and looked up. She didn't usually forget to check out the trolleys, especially when, as today, she had some checked baggage and would need one.

A glance around the area showed her a line of empty trolleys against the wall, under a large sign written in the beautiful Arabic script. Kate walked quickly over and snared a trolley. Lifting her carry-on case onto it, she turned, her eyes automatically going to the elevated conveyor belt that fed the carousel. No sign of the luggage yet. The crowd milled impatiently around the carousel's perimeter, and an alien visitor might have guessed that the group's anxious shifting was some kind of dance designed to call up their possessions from the snaggle-toothed maw above.

This unbidden thought about the human condition made her smile wryly to herself and wish there were someone with whom to share it. It was one drawback of this side of her work—the essential loneliness. Now that Michael no longer came with her, she nearly always travelled alone.

She felt another prickling of awareness, as if someone were watching her. Her eyes combed the crowd as she moved back towards the carousel.

Her breath caught with dismay as she saw him.

A man was leaning against a pillar, his arms crossed over his chest, staring at her with a gaze that first chilled, then burned her. He had a fine-featured face, with a broad forehead and wide cheekbones cradling deep-set, thoughtful eyes that she would have found attractive except for their expression of wary hostility. His hair was cut long around his head, tousled and curling; his strong chin covered with a neat black beard.

His eyes were green fire, his mouth generously formed but tight now with disapproval. Kate told herself it must be general disapproval of the world—it could not be directed at her, though that was what it felt like.

Even in the linen business suit and open-necked shirt, he could never be mistaken for anything other than what he was—one of the proud Parvans. Kate's research had informed her that Prince Omar of Central Barakat was related by blood to the royal family of neighbouring Parvan. There had always been good relations between the two nations, and there were many citizens of Parvan descent in the Barakat Emirates.

This looked like one of them. In other clothes, she thought, he would look very different, but even in the Western suit he gave off an air of contained danger.

He was a total stranger to her, but from the way he was looking at her you'd think she'd stolen his last hope. Kate wasn't normally a coward, but instinctively she refrained from challenging him with her eyes, and turned away as if she hadn't noticed the intensity of his gaze.

As she manoeuvred her trolley into the crowd around the luggage carousel, she couldn't resist throwing another glance towards the pillar, but all that met her eyes now was a poster with a sketch of a suitcase and another notice in what she assumed was Arabic, or perhaps Parvani, or both.

Shaking her head at her own foolishness, Kate pulled out her palm pilot again and under *Airport facilities: Languages* remarked *no Eng sgns.*

She was just slipping it into her bag again when a loud rumbling from the direction of the carousel, and the expectant ripple that ran through the waiting passengers, told her that the luggage had begun to appear.

He saw her straighten to attention as a distinctive, battered brown leather case appeared in the gap above, and she immediately began to shift forward.

By the time the case tumbled down from the conveyor belt onto the revolving cone of the carousel, he was there to reach for it. His hand was a few seconds faster than her own.

She was close, and now he smelled her perfume, the light scent of some flower whose name eluded him, the gentle musk of her body underneath. As his hand closed on the handle of her bag, she checked her quick forward movement and glanced up with a half smile. He sensed her shock when her eyes reached his face, and she stumbled, her hands spreading in an instinctive bid to save herself as she fell towards the carousel.

It happened too quickly for thought. He automatically let go of the bag and reached for her, his arms clasping her firmly, dragging her back from her fate. She was lighter than he had guessed, and so she was swept up against him, high on his chest, his eyes devouring her, like an impatient lover meeting his beloved after too long apart.

Chapter 2

They were frozen there for a moment, utterly disoriented, as if the unexpected turn of events had shifted them into some other world, and they were groping for their bearings in this new life where they shared both a past and a future.

How light in his hold she was, as if her bones were hollow, like a bird. He felt her heart's flutter, too, through the delicate rib cage. She might be a wood-pigeon brought to him by his falcon. His arm tightened in involuntary possession, and his eyes searched her startled, wondering face.

The stranger's emerald gaze devoured her, and there was a masculine urgency in his hold that, against her will, heated Kate's blood. Her cheeks went pink.

A woman nearby sighed audibly, and with that sound, the familiar world returned.

"What the hell do you think you're doing?" Kate cried, but even as she spoke, she was back on her feet. He snatched his hands away from her like someone who has touched a stove.

He was already furious, both with himself and with her. He never lost his self-control with women, but it was threatened now, a fact which outraged him even more.

Her challenge neatly clipped through the last threads.

"Do you not recognize assistance when it is offered?" he demanded icily. "Should I have let you fall?"

The crowd murmured its disappointment. Not a lovers' meeting, after all.

"You caused me to overbalance in the first place," Kate cried. "So I think we can agree that I'd be better off if you'd left me alone!"

"You are independent, of course!" he exclaimed, in a hot voice. "You can do without a man's help! But this is—"

"And you can't do without a woman?" Kate snapped back.

She had no idea what she was saying. Adrenaline charged through her blood, alerting all her system with a buzzing awareness that nearly deafened her.

But the sight of his face cooled her angry, self-righteous heat.

She had scored a direct hit. Never had fire burned so green as in his eyes now. She saw his mouth tighten, his nostrils flare as his chest filled with oxygen to fuel his reaction. Her heart kicked nervously, and Kate braced herself.

"What do you—" he began in a rough-edged voice.

And then, as suddenly as they had flared up, his emotions were under control. She watched in appalled fascination as the shutters came down. The fire died out of his eyes, his face. All trace of heat was gone, veiled behind a mask of ice.

Instead of green fire, flinty emerald chips.

"I can do without a woman," he said, with slow deliberation. A cold smile pulled at one side of his handsome mouth, and his eyebrows lifted in an expression of pure, undiluted arrogance. "Do you come to this country hoping to meet barbarians?"

"No, I did n—"

"Your search is not over so soon."

"Are *you* telling *me?*"

"When I want a woman I do not have to abduct a stranger at the airport."

"How comforting to know you have pulling power!"

"And even if I were such an animal, would such as you tempt me?"

Kate's lips parted on an indignant gasp.

"You were staring at me because you disapprove of my hairstyle, I suppose!"

His eyelids came down, as if to disguise his contempt. "No, Miss Drummond, I do not disapprove of your hairstyle, unwomanly as it is. And—"

Kate's eyes opened in horrified premonition.

"Who are you?" she croaked. "How do you know my name?"

"My name is Hadi al Hajar." An arrogant half smile lifted his eyebrows. "I am your guide, from the Tourism Ministry of the Barakat Emirates. Did they fail to notify you that I would meet you?"

Kate closed her eyes and breathed deeply to calm herself.

"No, they did not fail to notify me," she said, but couldn't stop herself adding, "I didn't expect to see you till after I'd been through Customs."

She could have wept with vexation. What a way to meet the man with whom she would be spending the next three weeks!

Why hadn't she reacted more calmly? It was so unlike her to have lost her temper so completely with a total stranger, that she could hardly recognize herself.

But the real fault lay with him. Why hadn't he waited till she got through Customs? Why hadn't he approached her and introduced himself instead of staring at her like a man with a grudge? *And* acting like someone trying to steal her case!

But these were questions she could not ask. If she was going to pull this out of the fire she absolutely had to stifle her resentment now.

Never had self-discipline required such effort.

Taking a deep breath, she put out a hand and tried her best to smile. "Well, anyway, I'm pleased to meet you, Mr. al Hajar. I'm sorry I didn't realize who you were."

He didn't unbend by an inch. He nodded once, abruptly, and turned his attention back to the carousel, ignoring her offered hand so pointedly that she longed to make another use of it.

But it would be foolish for her to vent her hostility—in action, word, or even by expression. *Save it,* she reminded herself firmly.

Her battered leather bag was only just coming into view again around the far end of the carousel. Time clicked back into focus, and she realized that it had taken only seconds to alienate the one official who, above all others, had the power to make or break her plans.

If he refused her access to sites or attractions on her list, what recourse would she have? None. Without his cooperation, Drummond and Venables could kiss their entire prospective tour goodbye.

Kate glanced up at the man as he stood, straight and unconsciously resolute, fists on hips, his legs a little astride, waiting for her bag to arrive.

No, she was just going to have to bite the bullet and be unfailingly polite and pleasant for three weeks to an arrogant macho idiot who probably was delighted to have wrong-footed her so early in the game.

It wouldn't be the first time. All over the world

there were men who resented the presence of a woman in business, though rarely had she encountered such spectacular fireworks.

Sometimes she could understand it. So often men in the cushy jobs in tourism were related to whoever was in power. They disliked work—half the time they had no idea how to go about it. And they didn't appreciate her telling them, either. No one, in her experience, got more mightily offended than an incompetent petty official expected to do his job—by a foreign woman.

As often as not, they were there for the bribes and payoffs, and could be quite shameless about asking what was in it for them. There were plenty of countries around the globe where Drummond and Venables Travel Adventures paid a ''head fee'' under the table to some tourism official for every single tourist they sent in. Not because he did anything to assist the agency's tours, oh no, nothing so straightforward as that. To ensure that he did nothing to hinder them. Like closing a site for ''essential repairs'' just as your group arrived after a three-hour bus drive. Like neglecting to notify you till after your brochures were printed that the site of a two-day trip in your program would be inaccessible this year.

And the connections of such people usually meant they were unassailable. You didn't report the president's cousin's son-in-law for corruption, not if you wanted to continue doing business with the administration.

Kate hated it, but it was the way her business had
to operate, and she had mostly gotten used to it. What
was an ever-present annoyance, though, was the in-
competence of such people, and the stubborn resistance to her legitimate demands.

She watched Hadi al Hajar speculatively. He didn't
look incompetent. In fact, that eagle gaze reminded
her of no other official she'd ever met. Kate had some
serious experience with officialdom, but she couldn't
place him. What were his weak points? What did he
want? She asked herself all the usual questions, but
drew a blank.

He looked as if he'd be more comfortable on a
craggy mountain pass waiting for the enemy to come
up the defile than guiding a hiking party along it.

Apart from their strange, no-holds-barred encounter, the man looked, if not cold, completely self-
contained. Kate wondered if that were all a front.
Would the offer of baksheesh soften him up? It did
almost everyone else.

"You are booked into the Hotel Sheikh Daud,"
Hadi al Hajar told her twenty minutes later.

She was beside him in the front seat of a battered,
dusty Land Rover, heading into the city. She wished
she dared to insist on sitting in the back, but he had
put her luggage there. She didn't like sitting next to
him. He had too high a body heat or something.

Until now they hadn't spoken. Kate had searched
for some innocuous way to break the stiff silence, but

all that came to her mind were stupid questions that would show him how hostile she felt. Like, *Why didn't you introduce yourself instead of sneaking up behind me to grab my bag?*

"That's right," she agreed curtly. She couldn't understand herself. She hardly ever had a problem being civilised with people she didn't like. Now she couldn't even smile. Kate took a breath and tried again.

"I understand there's a new casino there?"

Hadi al Hajar eased the car into a turn. In the distance was the sea. "Yes, the Shalimar Gardens opened this year. Do you wish to visit it?"

He sounded surprised and disapproving.

"Certainly," she said, struggling against the impulse to assure him that she herself never gambled for pleasure. Why should she care what he thought of her? "We'll be including it in our brochure."

"Are there no casinos in Vancouver?"

On the surface, an innocuous question, but she was sure he judged her with every word. Kate took a breath and deliberately looked out the window, willing the scenery to calm her quick, hot response. They were on a little height, heading down into the city. The sea sparkled brilliantly in the far distance. The sky was the richest blue she had ever seen, the sun a hot white hole in it.

"The presence of a casino won't convince anyone to take a trip they wouldn't otherwise take, not among our clientele, but some will enjoy an evening out during their visit," she said at last. And then, to show him that she didn't care about his opinion, she added, "I'll drop in tonight, if I'm not too tired."

An indefinable expression crossed his face. "You will not wish to go to such a place alone," he informed her with masculine condescension. "I will escort you. Tonight will not be possible, however."

A burst of sheer panic flooded Kate's blood at his words. *No thank you!* she almost cried. She couldn't tell whether this was merely another bid for masculine control or a sexual pass, but the first she was determined to resist, and the thought of the second made her hair stand on end—it would be like going to bed with a tiger!

So, although for obvious reasons it would be more pleasant to have an escort at the casino, she wasn't agreeing to anything that might leave room for misunderstandings.

Kate mimed a regretful smile. "Thank you, but I won't impose on your time like that. In any case, I'll only—"

"I am booked for three weeks. You have already paid for my time."

"I don't imagine you expect to be on call day and night."

"It is no trouble. We will go tomorrow night."

Kate breathed out irritably. "Does it make a difference when I go to the casino?"

She saw his eyelids droop. She wondered what expression he was hiding. He slowed the car and pulled over as an ambulance screamed up behind them.

"Tomorrow we have a very full day in Barakat al Barakat. You will not wish to tire yourself."

Everything had an edge. Like the sparks that fly off a cat's fur in winter, Kate thought.

She wondered what his background was. Maybe he was an only recently civilised mountain tribesman. She had heard they were a race apart, with their fierce mountain code of ethics—*parvanwali*.

It would be stupid to go head-to-head with someone whose cooperation would have so much impact on her plans, but even as Kate told herself so, her mouth was opening on argument.

"I'm used to looking after myself," she said coolly.

A muscle twitched in his cheek. "Are you? Why, then, did you request the services of a guide and interpreter from the Office of Tourism?"

That was ridiculous and stupid.

"Because I don't know the geography or the language of the country," she snapped. "Not because I need—"

"And do you know the culture?"

Their eyes met for a brief, hot exchange. Kate did not answer. To her fury, he took it as an admission of defeat.

"Then will you allow me to advise you? Do not go to the casino tonight. I will escort you—tomorrow night."

As if she were a child clamouring for a treat. She had to clench her teeth to bite back the retort that rose up. Never in all her travels, in all her meetings with strangers, had she met such smug arrogance!

Or was it just that she had never had such trouble controlling her reactions to it?

Breathing deeply to regain control of herself, she turned away to look out the window as the car made its way through the city down towards the sea. Silence fell between them, interrupted only by the loud beating of her heart in her ears.

When Hadi al Hajar stopped at a red light, Kate's eyes were drawn irresistibly to him, knowing what she would find.

He was watching her with that gaze of burning ice, and it seemed to enclose her, so that she could see nothing but his eyes.

Kate drew in a slow, nervous breath and wondered what demon his soul wrestled with to produce the darkness she saw.

Chapter 3

The Hotel Sheikh Daud looked like somewhere you only got to by rubbing a magic lamp. Kate had never seen a place so magically beautiful. Arched doorways, white plaster walls decorated with intricate patterns of mosaic tile, bathroom in green marble. Cabinets and doors in antique limed wood sculpted with breathtaking intricateness.

Outside, the terrace was tiled with terra cotta and shaded with plants. Beyond, she could see the sea and the famous sand beach with its intervals of twisted black rock. Rugged and enticing at the same time.

Not like the man behind her, who for some reason known only to himself had waved off the hotel porter and carried her bags all the way to her room. Kate fervently hoped he wasn't expecting to enjoy a little afternoon delight, because her polite facade would crumble into screaming fury if he moved a finger her way. Just the thought of it lifted her hackles.

She just wanted him out of here pronto, but he put down her bags, opened a door, and showed her out onto the terrace. There he stood with the bright sunlight glinting off his black hair, watching as Kate took her first real look at his country.

Her breath caught with delight as she looked around her. Ahead of them the sun-spangled water of the Gulf of Barakat lay spread in all its entrancing beauty, in shifting gemstone shades—turquoise, sapphire, emerald, lapis lazuli.

A miles-long stretch of pale sand curved in a wide arc between the sea on one side and a palm-forested escarpment on the other. In places black rock heaved up, the water lapping and slapping against it, enhancing the air of dangerous beauty.

She could smell the perfume of a thousand flowers mingling with marvellous spices, intoxicatingly mysterious.

"It's absolutely beautiful," she whispered, all her animosity dissipating in wonder and pleasure.

An overhead lattice of olivewood rested on two support walls at either side of the balcony. Carved into each support was an onion-shaped arched opening that framed the scene beyond like a window onto mystery.

The lattice was overgrown with climbing plants, providing a delicate, dappled shade for a third of the balcony. Beyond the shaded area was a small tumbling fountain to cool the air, and beside that, a teak table and chairs, with a teak-slatted beach umbrella. Palm trees grew high around the balcony, stirred gently by the breeze, casting their own cooling shadows.

It was half magic, all Eastern.

Below, at ground level, she saw a swimming pool, an open-air café, and just a glimpse of the renowned hotel gardens.

Pure heaven. In spite of the disturbing presence of the stranger, Kate sighed with a feeling of liberation so intense it was almost a homecoming.

Hadi al Hajar stood beside her, looking out over the scene himself, apparently lost in thought. The sun burned fiercely down outside the areas of shade, but a cooling breeze wafting from the fountain disturbed the skirt of her dress.

She had no idea how long they stood there admiring the scene together before she finally surfaced from her dreamless dream, but suddenly all the awkward tension of being in his presence returned.

"I suppose we should get down to work. There are a few details about the itinerary, I think."

Hadi al Hajar glanced at his watch and shook his head. "I am sorry. This is what was scheduled, I know, but your plane was a little delayed and I am expected elsewhere."

Kate smiled. She was quite happy to leave the discussion to another time. Just now she wanted to get away from him.

"It can wait, then. Thank you for coming to the airport for me. It's been good to meet you, and I'm looking forward to our trip," Kate lied brightly.

With his usual arrogance, he gave that only the briefest of acknowledgements. "I am sorry not to be able to offer you dinner tonight, but the hotel will take good care of you."

Neither of them mentioned the casino. He passed her the room key.

"Thank you, I'll be fine. I'm quite used to eating alone."

Kate stifled a sigh. The real romance was for her clients; her end was stage management.

He glanced at his watch. "I will be here to pick you up at nine tomorrow. A full day is planned, which I warn you we will not be able to complete if we do not begin on time."

She heard a reluctance in his voice as deep as any she felt, and was immediately, contrarily, annoyed. Why shouldn't he want to be her guide? *She* wasn't the one with the attitude problem!

"Now I must leave you. Tomorrow at nine."

"I am so sorry, Miss Drummond," said the distressed voice. "But it is simply not possible. Every other guide is already booked. Only Mr. al Hajar is available for the three weeks."

"All right," Kate said.

"Is there a problem? Was he not at the airport on time? Mr. al Hajar is a very—is one of our most experienced guides. What is the trouble?" Halimah sounded completely mystified, as if a woman would have to be insane not to want Hadi al Hajar's undivided attention for three weeks.

Kate was beginning to feel seriously stupid. Two minutes' thought would have told her that it would be impossible to change the arrangements now, and that it would only be stirring up trouble to try.

"It's quite all right. There's no problem. It's nothing personal against Mr. al Hajar," she lied fervently. "Please don't tell him that I made the request."

"No, of course not," said Halimah, and Kate knew it would be the next call she made.

Kate put down the phone, frustrated and deeply annoyed with herself. She had just made a bad situation worse.

But there was no point worrying about it now. Since she had a few hours of sunshine left in the day, like any Canadian, Kate was determined to make use of them. She slipped into her swimsuit and beach robe, and within ten minutes was down beside the magnificent pool.

As she had noted from her balcony, the pool was also shaped like an eastern archway—this time laid flat. Three straight sides formed a simple rectangular shape at one end, but the top end was carved like an onion.

It was enchanting. The body and immediate perimeter of the pool were tiled with beautiful antiqued blue, turquoise and green ceramic tiles, reminiscent of the sea. The water, stirred into life over them, created a dream-like ripple effect.

The arched shape was obviously a design motif for the hotel, and she could see why. It was the doorway to a magic land. Leap in, it promised, and swim through the depths to a mysterious, unknown world....

Which was pretty much just what she would be doing, Kate thought when, after half an hour in the cool seawater that filled the pool, she wrapped herself in her beach robe and settled down to work at a table under an umbrella.

She had a package containing her notes, her proposed itinerary, and the tourism ministry's information pack.

She had never before visited a country that so thrilled her with anticipation. There was so much magic here. Barakat was at a crossroads on the old Silk Road. Just about every culture of the ancient world had passed this way, leaving traces in the language, the land, the food, the customs and traditions, and even the blood of its people. It was a marvellous, mysterious mix, exotic and intriguing.

She already knew—but read again—that the country, until a few years ago called Barakat, which means *Blessing,* had been divided into three by Daud, the last king, for his three sons, Omar, Karim and Rafi.

Now it was called the Barakat Emirates, and each prince ruled his own area.

With the help of his personal cabinet. Following the tradition of the ancient ruling dynasty, each prince appointed twelve Cup Companions to act as his advisors. Although the title was an old one, the duties of the post were now very different from what they had been a thousand years ago.

Once upon a time the men had been literal "cup" companions—those with whom the monarch relaxed and unwound from the cares of rule. They did not discuss business or affairs of state, but only such matters as poetry, philosophy, wine and love.

Nowadays, however, the Cup Companions were influential in every area of the country's life—acting as the princes' advisors in fields as diverse as trade, the secret service, and public relations.

In certain areas—such as foreign policy—the Barakat Emirates operated as a single entity, and Queen Halimah Palace, here in Barakat al Barakat, the capital, was the seat of the joint government.

Kate couldn't help smiling as she looked at a photograph of the three handsome princes and their beautiful foreign wives in front of the most gorgeous government building she had ever seen in her life. She would be visiting the palace tomorrow.

"Would you like more juice?" asked the waiter, pausing beside her table. Kate looked up absently, then reached for the tall pitcher and tilted it to look inside.

The weather was very hot; she had polished off the entire jug of delicious mixed fruit juice without even noticing. And he was right, she was thirsty again. *"Shokran,"* she said, trying out her minimal language skills. "And could I have a bottle of water, too, please?"

With a graceful nod, he cleared the dishes and disappeared.

Kate glanced around her. The pool area was not very full, but the hotel's nearby open-air beach café was bustling. There were only a few people sprinkled along a beach of staggeringly picturesque beauty: within a few yards' walk you would feel completely alone.

Kate led a busy life. She could almost regret not being able to spend the whole three weeks lazing in the hotel, but when she turned back to her itinerary, inertia was lost in anticipation.

The emerald mines in the mountains of Noor. Spectacular caves in East Barakat. The archaeological site of Iskandiyar, founded by Alexander the Great himself, only recently rediscovered and now—though in a very limited way—open to the public. The site where the rebel Jalal's headquarters had been, and the amazing ancient tunnel under the River Sa'adat...

And most fascinating of all, the tantalizing, nebulous legend of the Valley. Al Darreh. The land, they said, that only the brave could visit. The land that only existed in the imagination—unless you were lucky enough to find it.

Kate could hardly wait.

* * *

But before morning came, she had the evening to get through, and after an exquisitely cooked but solitary meal on the terrace of the hotel's restaurant, to the accompaniment of a woman singing haunting love songs, it was still early and she was just too thrilled by her surroundings to go tamely back to her room and to bed.

Maybe a walk along the beach was what she needed....

There would be no reason for Hadi al Hajar to know that she had defied him, if she went to the casino. And nothing in the hotel information pack she'd read earlier said that women were not admitted unescorted.

Kate was wearing a simple dress in black, cut like her jade travel outfit—ankle length, short sleeves, wide neck. She never travelled without it, because it could be dressed up or down and was cool and wrinkle free. To dress it up tonight she was wearing a pretty necklace and earrings, with a fine spangly scarf draped over her elbows. She might not match up to the wealthy luxury that would be displayed by other patrons of the casino, but she was pretty sure her outfit wouldn't raise any eyebrows.

Just to make sure, as she was being bowed out of the restaurant, she said to the maître d', "Is it possible to go to the casino?"

"Of course, madame. Follow the path through the

bostan—the garden," he said, gesturing in the relevant direction. "Is members only, but you are hotel guest, you go also in."

Well, that was pretty definitive. Trying to subdue the faint feeling of defiance—she was, after all, only doing her job—Kate took the path that had been pointed out to her and strolled through a fabulous perfumed garden beside a tumbling water channel. Little flaming lamps at knee level lighted her along her way.

It was unbelievably romantic. Above her head the stars had never been more magical. Her clients would adore this spot. What a place to come with your lover!

That was not a lament. Kate was used to travelling alone. Even when they were considering themselves engaged, Michael had joined her on only about half her jaunts.

She had met Michael, a travel writer, on one of her working trips. They had both been spending a few days at the same resort—he to write about it, she to include it in a travel package. Against the sensual backdrop of an Indian island, perhaps it was no surprise that they had so quickly fallen for each other.

After that, whenever he could, Michael drummed up an assignment in whatever location Kate herself was investigating, and they had travelled together several times over the next two years.

Back home in Vancouver, though, they didn't move in together, for a lot of reasons. Michael loved his quiet, perfect apartment, but it was too small for two when he worked at home. And Kate was working very hard at her new business and wasn't ready to start devoting her time to creating a home. Still, they had talked about marriage as something that would happen one day.

In some part of her, Kate had been unsurprised by the discovery that Michael had cheated on her while she was away. Unsurprised, and curiously untouched. Maybe there had been unconscious clues, maybe he had wanted her to find out. And possibly they had just never been as close as they pretended to believe. The relationship had always been more comfortable and useful than passionate.

Michael had said he still wanted to marry her, but that was just stupid. Kate wasn't walking into that one. In fact, she was walking out.

The further she got away from the relationship now, the more grateful she was. They hadn't loved each other enough for marriage.

So it wasn't Michael she was regretting as she strolled through the divinely beautiful garden. She was yearning for something, or someone, but it was nothing she could put a name to.

Chapter 4

Hotel guests got into the casino simply by producing their keys, and Kate was welcomed without so much as a raised eyebrow. A hostess showed her in. She found a room exquisitely designed in shades like the sea—deep navy, turquoise, lapis and green—with none of the cheap gaudiness of casinos she had seen elsewhere.

She stood looking around her for a moment, caught by the glittering, crystal-encrusted Eastern lamps, the angled golden mirrors in the same delicate, onion-arched shape she had seen elsewhere, the richness of the fabrics that draped ceiling and walls.

The occupants of the room, a cosmopolitan mix of nationalities, looked like an advertisement for a mega-yacht. Kate had never seen so many precious stones in one gathering in all her life. The people glittered at least as brightly as the sparkling lamps, and though Kate rarely felt like a country mouse, she was well out of her element here. Her best outfit at home might have allowed her to hold her own, but not her smart little all-purpose black travel dress and pretty costume jewellery.

She'd be lucky if they didn't mistake her for a cloakroom attendant.

Hadi al Hajar was right. She'd have felt better with an escort, especially one as powerfully handsome as he was. For a moment she toyed with the idea of retreating and leaving this till another night.

But that was simple cowardice. She had carried off lots of difficult situations in her travels, Kate reminded herself, and each new success made the next easier. All she needed was a moment to orient herself. She'd be fine.

Opposite the doorway, a wall of windows framed the magical garden, with its dark shadows and rustling fountains. Kate was drawn across the room to look up again at a mysterious sky. The moon was richly golden, the stars glittered like frost on black snow.

The skin along her spine shivered with animal awareness. She would have noticed the familiar prickling earlier, if she hadn't been so overwhelmed. Now it registered, and with an inward command not to be an overimaginative idiot, Kate turned her head.

At the end of the room, trapping her in the net of his angry gaze, sat Hadi al Hajar.

Kate bit her lip.

He was at a blackjack table. With a slow deliberation that made her want to turn and run, he abandoned his cards, picked up his chips, and got to his feet. He slipped the chips into the pocket of his immaculate black tux and approached her, his gaze on her the whole time.

Kate stood motionless, hypnotized by the eyes that never left hers, her hands clasped tightly on her spangly stole as if it might protect her from his assault. If only the windows opened, she thought wildly, she might have fled into the garden.

"Madame?" With an abrupt effort, she tore her gaze away. A waiter was beside her.

"You like to order, madame?" He offered her a tiny menu.

"*Shokran,*" she murmured.

"*Al 'afou.* You are welcome, madame," the waiter replied.

She didn't need to turn her head to know that Hadi al Hajar was behind her now. Blindly she consulted the menu. It listed snacks and drinks, but her eyes, or her brain, couldn't find meaning in the squiggles.

"Do you have an English menu?" she asked stupidly.

An impatient sound came from behind her. In front the waiter's eyes widened in blank surprise. "Is not

English?'' he cried, bending his head to look. Kate felt totally stupid. Of course it was English.

Hadi al Hajar plucked the card from her hand and passed it back to the waiter. Whatever he said made the waiter disappear.

He took her arm in a strong, impossible-to-resist grip, and, sliding open one of the windows, forced her out into the garden.

So they did open. Oh, she was outclassed in every sense tonight.

She stumbled blindly down the little path beside him, into the dark, secret shadows of the garden, his hand burning its brand on her bare arm, accompanied by the dangerous silence of his anger and the sensual odour of tropical flowers, releasing their musk as the night made love to them.

Out of sight of the glowing windows, he stopped and forced her to face him. He glared down at her. ''Do you always flout the advice of your guide?'' he demanded harshly. ''It is an attitude that will not get you far in the Barakat Emirates.''

Maybe if he hadn't attacked she might have been more submissive.

''It depends on the guide, doesn't it? Opinions seem to differ. The maître d' of the hotel restaurant and the doorman here didn't agree with your reading. It was two to one.''

He ignored that. ''Go back to the hotel,'' he commanded in a low, impatient voice. ''It is that way.''

If he hadn't given her arm a little push, as if she

were some kind of bratty schoolgirl, she might have obeyed. Instead, Kate twisted away and stopped, facing him.

"You're my guide, not my father!" she exclaimed. "Don't tell me what to do!"

With his flashing eyes and neat, pointed beard, he looked like the devil himself.

"I do tell you what to do! Have you no respect?"

"I have a great deal of respect for self-determination. I'll leave the casino when I decide to leave, thanks!"

He loomed over her again, making her heave in a breath. But there seemed no oxygen, only perfume, in the air, and with a little intoxicating rush it went to her head. Kate suddenly felt drunk.

"You interfere with things you do not understand! You—"

His hands came up abruptly, and he grasped her in a tight, angry hold, the surface of his palms rough on her upper arms. The rasping touch was wildly sensual against her soft skin, and sweet burning spiralled into her back and breasts, down her arms till her fingertips sparked.

It's the perfume, Kate told herself wildly. *It's not him, it's just the flowers.*

She looked down, instinctively avoiding his eyes. She knew the long fingers, the prominent thumb, the oval, square-cut nails as surely as if they were her own—though how and why she had managed to memorize his hand's shape after so short a time was a mystery.

Then, fatally, as if under a spell that drew her irresistibly to her doom, she looked up into his face.

The electricity that had been building up in the air around them ever since the airport had suddenly found a connection, and now, as their eyes met, it was as though thousands of volts of loose electrical charge rushed to ground. Like children playing on a power grid, they were helplessly locked together, eyes and bodies, as sensual awareness flowed through them.

She wasn't sure whether time slowed, or the moment stretched out in real time. A muscle leapt in his jaw, and his emerald eyes were glittering black as he looked at her. Kate felt naked, stripped bare, body and soul.

He, too, was naked, and for one moment she both touched and saw the very heart of his being.

It was that touch, not the physical one, that shook him beyond his control. His hands trembling, he dragged her roughly against his body. Kate gasped, but his mouth gave no quarter as it clamped on hers and burned his angry, helpless kiss into her blood.

His lips were a brand, searing her so that she felt the mark of his kiss would be visible on her flesh ever after. His tongue scorched into her mouth, desperate for the moistness of her, hungry and punishing at the same time. Seeking, and helpless to resist taking what it found. She felt the hard plunging again and again, powerless in her turn to resist the heat that melted her.

When he lifted his mouth at last and stood back, Kate slapped him across his hard cheek with all her might.

It was a reaction so primitively animal she had no conscious connection to it. It was as if it had been done by someone else.

His eyes glittered like two cold, distant stars.

"Don't ever do that again," Kate panted.

Hadi's chest heaved as he struggled for control, and she waited for his reaction with eyes wide.

The night, the stars, the scent of flowers, and his own rushing blood were the summoners of a primitive passion that he knew she, too, felt. The ground was soft in the garden, there was total darkness beyond the little flares that lighted the path, and the bushes were thick.

His male brain knew that if he took her there she would not resist. She had slapped him out of passion, as any female animal fights—to test his strength. When he showed her his passion was stronger than her resistance, she would submit. It was the law of nature.

She waited, watching him. Waiting for him to prove himself a man.

His hands and his jaw clenched with the effort as he regained control. What insanity had consumed him?

"Go back to the hotel." His voice crunched like the gravel under their feet.

"*Don't* tell me what to do!" Kate cried, her blood pulsing with animal disappointment, which she read as anger.

Hadi al Hajar shook his head as if she were beyond reason, then his jaw tightened into an expression that frightened her.

"All right," he said, in a hard voice. "You're here, and you insist on staying. Let us make what use we can of it. Come."

Kate's heart was churning with conflicting feelings as she allowed him to lead her back inside. All she had wanted was to absorb the atmosphere a little so she could write a small blurb in the Drummond and Venables brochure! How had the situation managed to escalate to the point where she had been wanting him to drag her into the bushes and make love to her?

He led her to the roulette table. A number was called out as they approached, and she could hear the rattle as the losers' chips were raked down the chute. Under Hadi al Hajar's guidance she slipped into a chair which a disgusted heavyset German man had just vacated.

Kate opened her purse and firmly reminded herself why she was here. Her budget for the night would, if she bet carefully, keep her going for perhaps an hour.

Kate never pretended to herself that she was going to win. She would spend half her allotted budget here and half at the blackjack table, probably, and wander around to watch in between. Then she would feel she had adequately "done" the casino.

A lean, dark hand came down over hers, closing her bag, and then quickly lifted again, as if he did not dare to let that connection last.

He silently signalled a command to the croupier. A moment later the long rake moved out to position several stacks of chips in front of Kate.

The heat burned up in her cheeks. Kate suddenly felt exposed. But around the table only one or two incurious glances came their way. On the outside it had looked only as if a handsome man with his eye on a pretty girl had bought her some chips.

She stared down at the piles of chips in front of her—about five times more than she had been expecting to spend all evening—but she was afraid to challenge him now, not out of fear of his response, but from not knowing what emotions would arise from her own depths if she gave them an outlet.

"Place your bets, please, ladies and gentlemen," a voice urged. "Place your bets." But she sat stupidly, unable to muster a response.

"What number is your birthday?"

"The twelfth," she responded automatically, and watched as Hadi al Hajar pushed a stack of chips onto the green baize.

"I don't know how we'll get home," a loud, drunken masculine voice warned. Kate looked up. On the other side of the table a gorgeous but falling-down-drunk couple were arguing over a bet.

"On our winnings!" the woman said blithely. She was stunningly beautiful in emeralds and a gold dress so form-fitting she looked as though she'd been covered in gold leaf.

A certain stillness made Kate glance up at Hadi al Hajar. He was watching the woman with a look in his eyes that she couldn't decipher. She felt a tension in him, too, a watchfulness, and was sure suddenly that he knew the golden girl.

With a horrible, sinking feeling, she understood. Was this why he was at the casino tonight? And why he had not wanted Kate there?

Though she chided herself for an overworked imagination, Kate couldn't shake the idea that Hadi al Hajar had some agenda relating to the woman. Did he want the woman himself?

If she was right, it explained everything, including the wild passion of that kiss in the garden. It was the golden woman he was kissing, not Kate who, faced with such pampered beauty, was feeling particularly dowdy.

She supposed that he had changed tactics when she refused to leave. It was probably no coincidence that he had led her straight to the roulette table. Was he now hoping to use her, Kate, to make the other woman jealous?

Any other woman was welcome to him. But she couldn't stifle the outrage she felt at being used. She was glad she'd slapped him. She only wished she'd been holding a brick.

The croupier set the wheel spinning and released the little white ball.

"Kiss me for luck."

Kate almost leapt out of her skin. The voice, pitched low, had carried oddly, and for a crazy second she had thought she was hearing Hadi al Hajar's voice. But it was the man with the golden girl speaking.

A kind of frisson went through every person standing around the table at the tone in the man's voice. "Kiss me, Lisbet, and tell me you love me."

Kate, along with most of the others at the table, was now unashamedly watching. The couple kissed, and she felt a burst of deep pity for Hadi al Hajar, because there was no way he would get the golden girl as long as that other man was alive. Love itself seemed to enter the room to wrap them in an almost visible net of light as they kissed.

She glanced up to see how Hadi al Hajar was taking it, and her breath came in on a soundless gasp. Hadi was no longer in the here and now. He was somewhere else, in the place where ghosts resided, and it was his ghosts he saw as he gazed at the embracing couple.

She had never seen eyes so shadowed, a soul so lost.

The ball landed, and the couple broke apart.

"Noooo!" cried the woman, staring down at the wheel as the croupier announced, "Number twelve."

A loud, drunken scene ensued. The golden girl was urging her lover to bet on her lucky number again, but he steadily, if drunkenly, refused. "Cleaned out," he said. "Cleaned out, baby."

And Hadi al Hajar watched it all with a face like stone.

It began to seem slightly unreal to Kate. It was a little like watching a well-acted play. She wondered suddenly if the golden girl could be playing the scene for Hadi al Hajar's benefit, and her heart went out to him. God, what humiliation!

The scene ended at last, the golden girl storming out and her handsome lover following. Kate, along with many others, breathed a sigh of relief.

But to her grief, Hadi al Hajar grasped her wrist in a quick farewell and, with barely a word, followed the couple out.

"Place your bets, please, ladies and gentlemen. Place your bets."

Kate turned back to the table to discover that the pile of chips in front of her had multiplied in size. But all the interest had gone out of the game. She knew she should feel relieved at this discovery that what lay behind Hadi al Hajar's hostility was simply a freshly broken heart.

But she didn't. It wasn't relief she was feeling at all.

Chapter 5

In the morning Kate sat at the table on her own terrace with a pot of coffee and hot, delicious, freshly baked Barakat bread slathered with fresh butter and the hotel's own home-made mulberry jam.

Below her, she watched a horseman on a black horse gallop along the deserted beach, while behind him the sun climbed out of the dancing, sparkling sea. At this hour and from this angle the water was a brilliant mix of sapphire and emerald, with a hint of deepest amethyst in the depths, and diamonds appearing and disappearing over its surface.

She had awakened early, and had lots of time before Hadi al Hajar arrived at nine. Time to think over what had happened last night.

She couldn't make sense of any of it. Who was

Hadi al Hajar? That was the first question. He was working as a guide and interpreter, not the most prestigious job in any country. Yet last night he had had the air of a powerful, wealthy man—a man who had looked at the wealthy lover of the pampered golden girl as if he could challenge him on his own ground.

And he had certainly not treated Kate the way most people treated the person who paid their wages.

Kate spent a few minutes going over the correspondence with the Ministry of Tourism which she had brought with her, but she could find no solution to the mystery there. "Mr. al Hajar will meet you at the airport. He will act as your guide and interpreter, and is empowered to negotiate with you on the ministry's behalf."

Nothing hung together. At the airport he had had the air of a mountain tribesman. Last night he had seemed completely at home against a background of extreme wealth.

He had kissed her. That was what Kate had been trying to avoid thinking about, but it rushed on her now, demanding its quota of attention.

The kiss, at least, made sense from his point of view. He had been thinking of the golden girl, and he had been angry at Kate for coming on the scene, and one emotion had quickly shifted into another, with the wrong woman.

Her own responses were less easy to explain away. Kate didn't want to admit to herself that what she had experienced last night had been all new. The rush of passion she had felt, when an angry Hadi had pulled her so roughly into his arms and kissed her with such barely contained violence, was something that she had no previous experience of.

She had been shaken to the depths by his rough caress, utterly consumed. She had slapped him, and now she knew exactly what motivated a female cat in heat, biting and clawing the tom when she clearly wanted what was coming. Kate had never before felt on the edge of such a cauldron of primitive emotions. It had both thrilled and frightened her.

Her heart was pounding hard with the mere memory. When she closed her eyes she could feel his kiss all over again. Melting her into a river of sensation that began and ended—if it didn't exist endlessly— far beyond Kate's own body.

She forced her eyes open. She would have to be on her guard. It couldn't be allowed to happen again. Because last night she had been very close to losing control, and she did not want to lose control with him. He was too primitive, too incomprehensible…too dangerous.

Anyway, the woman he'd be making love to in his head was the golden girl.

But although that was final, Kate couldn't stop thinking about it. Couldn't help wondering who the golden girl was to Hadi al Hajar. Someone he had lost, or someone he hoped to win?

Shaking her head to try to clear it, Kate refilled her

coffee cup and turned to the English-language paper which had accompanied her breakfast.

But she didn't escape her thoughts for long. There it was—in a back page gossip column of the *International Herald Tribune*. A picture of the couple she had seen last night, the man on a white horse, the woman reaching up to kiss him. The caption read, *Sheikh Jafar al Hamzeh gets encouragement before the polo match from the English actress Lisbet Raine. Prince Karim is said to disapprove of the playboy Cup Companion's latest liaison.*

"Would they let me take a photograph?"

To avoid the heat later in the day, Hadi had brought her to the *Jamaa al Fannun*, Barakat's famous central market, first thing this morning.

The market was in a large, bustling square, with several ranks of stalls and shops around the perimeter, and it seemed to Kate's dazzled eyes as if everything anyone could ever want was on offer here, from handmade leather sandals and richly embroidered silk kaftans, haunting perfumed oils and black kohl, to roasted nuts and lamb *harissa*.

Over the whole scene wafted the rich odour of mingled oriental spices, sometimes carried on the smoke from the charcoal braziers, sometimes rising from the stalls where the spices themselves were sold.

The open centre of the square was lively with various artists and artisans. Snake charmers, dancers and musicians, kebab sellers, beggars and pickpockets all plied their trade.

Kate had watched as a potter's skilled hands transformed a thick rope of potting clay into a bowl, while at his feet a boy carefully rolled more clay into rope. Beside the potter his wife painted glaze decorations on his kiln-dried creations, in delicate Arabic calligraphy, her two daughters watching and helping.

"What does it say?" Kate wanted to know.

"The names of a couple who are to be married. It is the custom in Barakat to give such personalized pots or dishes as wedding gifts, since no couple can ever have too many. Wealthy people order expensive porcelain dinner sets in Paris and London, where some enterprising manufacturers have introduced a customized design. But ordinary people stick to the old materials. This clay comes from the banks of the River Sa'adat—the River of Happiness—which is thought to be sacred, and itself brings good luck. In addition it is very durable."

He was the best guide she could remember for a long time, and in the thrilling environment of the souk, the difficult atmosphere between the two of them was eased.

Now Kate watched, absorbed and fascinated by the sheer beauty of human expertise. The man's hands worked so perfectly together that as the rope of clay was laid on top of the last coil, it was already moulded into the rest, and the shape grew as if by magic.

Meanwhile, the woman's paintbrush moved in a graceful poem of swirls and dots over plates and bowls, cups and serving dishes.

"Why do you say no one can have too many?"

"Because by tradition when the last such dish is broken, the love goes out of a marriage and thereafter disharmony reigns. Since only dishes given at the time of the wedding count, people are naturally anxious to stockpile as many as possible. Especially among those tribes where the women are known to have hot tempers."

Kate looked at him, suspecting a trap. "Well?" she prompted.

"When a Barakati woman wants to warn her husband that the marriage is in trouble, she may deliberately smash one of their wedding dishes to make her point, thus bringing the whole enterprise that much closer to ruin. Combine that tradition with a quick-tempered wife and you will see that a wise man prefers to go into his marriage with plenty of leeway."

Kate laughed. What a wonderful people the Barakatis must be, she thought. Preparing at the outset for the inevitable problems of a marriage. Perhaps if her mother had had such an outlet her parents would still be together.

"Would she do a dish with my name for me?"

Hadi al Hajar turned to make the request.

The painter looked up at Kate with horrified dark

eyes, waving her hands. *"Laa, laa!"* she cried, making a rapid-fire comment.

Hadi explained. "She says it would be very bad luck for a woman to have her name alone painted on a dish. It would be sure to draw the evil eye, and you might never marry. I am afraid she would not understand if I tried to explain that you are a career woman and above worrying about such petty considerations as finding a husband."

Kate laughed. "All the same, I think I won't risk it. *Shokran,*" she added, smiling at the woman.

The woman's gaze moved from Kate's face to Hadi's and back again. Then she fixed Kate with a look and said something more, her glaze-stained, sundried finger punctuating her point.

"What does she say?" Kate pressed, when Hadi al Hajar hesitated. Behind him the woman insisted.

"She offers to paint the dish with our names together."

A little shiver of foreboding traced Kate's spine. "Why?" she asked, keeping her voice light. "We aren't going to be married."

Another exchange, at which the potter laughed loudly and threw in a comment of his own.

"Such a thing can bring good luck," Hadi translated. "It is a charm which young women often have recourse to, for with luck it may bind the man named to you."

Kate heard the words with a zing of primitive feeling. Hadi al Hajar—bound to her?

"No, thank you!" she cried instinctively.

He acknowledged that with an ironic bow. "Since the charm undoubtedly would not work until you had performed some noxious ritual with the dish, you have undoubtedly made the right decision."

"Like what?"

"This would be a secret kept from mere men, but perhaps it might involve drinking from the dish a mixture of which sheep's blood, urine, and perhaps a lock of my hair formed the main ingredients."

Kate gazed at him suspiciously, but he went on blandly, "Umm Aziz informs you that I am a good man and there are not a large number of good men in the world, and therefore advises you to—"

"How does she know you're a good man?"

"More country magic, no doubt. With a job like hers, she probably moonlights as a matchmaker."

"Will you ask her for specific details, please?"

"No," he said, and they laughed together.

And in that moment of mutual understanding and good humour, was it her evil genius that prompted her to say, "I'd love a picture! Would they let me take one to put in our brochure?"

She reached into her bag, drew out the digital camera she carried everywhere and held it up to the woman with a questioning smile.

The potter laughed toothily and called something to his wife. The girls smiled shyly and drew back against their mother.

That long, lean hand which she had come to recognize as a harbinger of interference covered the camera without touching her. Kate observed that careful avoidance with a distant outrage.

"You intend to take a photograph for use in your publicity?"

She looked at him in surprise. "Yes, why not? They seem perfectly happy to pose."

"Of course. But they don't know that you are not an ordinary tourist, do they? You intend to make money with your brochure. What will this family get out of it?"

Kate drew in a breath. "Well, I wasn't going to walk away without giving them something!"

"'Giving them something'?"

His coldness after that moment of warmth and friendliness shook her. "What's your point?"

"How much? A few barakatis?"

"No, of course not!"

"If you hired models to pose for your brochure in Vancouver, how much would you 'give' them?"

Kate glared. Why was he trying to make her out a monster? They had just been laughing together! "What, exactly, is your point?"

The potter was making soothing noises at him, clearly advising Hadi al Hajar to go easy with such a pretty lady.

"Kate, you're assuming that you can exploit these people for your own benefit. Why?"

Kate gasped.

"Exploit them? I'm not assuming I can exploit

anyone! Are you telling me they expect Actors' Equity rates? It's probably more than they see in a month!''

"I don't think these people are so far from the middle class as you imagine. But if they are, that should make you more willing, not less, to see that they get fair wages, shouldn't it?''

"I think you're crazy! Everybody would start demanding money from any tourist with a camera!''

Hadi al Hajar didn't smile. "And why shouldn't they? Do you think the rich have the right to take advantage of the poor all over the world? Why shouldn't the wealth be distributed in this way? The clothes and shoes you are wearing now, Kate—do you know where they were made? Were they made by hungry children at starvation wages?''

Kate was left floundering, so angry she couldn't think. "What are you talking about?''

"The rich nations enslave the world, Kate. But do not hope to perpetuate the injustice here in Barakat. We have very firm policies and laws to protect our citizens.''

"How *dare* you accuse me of—I—what is it you want? I *do* not exploit—!'' Kate babbled. She had never felt so challenged. She struggled to control herself.

"All I want is a picture! I'm not even sure we'll use it! But if we do, when our clients come here they'll recognize them and—''

"And give them a few dollars? This is a charitable deed on your part, in fact?"

Suddenly she got his drift. What an idiot she was! Of course he had to pay for that wonderful tux somehow.

Kate heaved a deep breath. Most people were much more careful and circumspect about it than he was, that was what had thrown her. But if he was going to be direct, so could she!

She looked Hadi al Hajar straight in the eye.

"How much?" she demanded rudely.

Chapter 6

His eyebrows went up above eyes as green as a cold northern sea.

"I take it you're acting as their agent," she said with biting sarcasm. "How much to let me take their picture?"

Hadi al Hajar looked at her, and she could see that, as insults went, she had paid him back in full.

"Is that how you respond to someone who challenges you, Kate? You accuse me of dishonesty so that you can escape the truth of what I say? Do you never examine your motives and assumptions? You must always be right?"

The questions hailed down around her, but Kate didn't flinch. Maybe he had reason to be annoyed, but she had never been so angry in her life. Everyone knew that you had to be careful as a tourist not to spread money around too lavishly for fear of disturbing a delicate balance. His attack was completely unjustified. Drummond and Venables did everything in their power to be fair to the local population, wherever they mounted tours.

"Suppose we stop with the guessing game and you tell me what I have to do?" she said waspishly.

He looked at her with narrowed eyes.

"We have a public agency in the Barakat Emirates. When newspapers, magazines and other agencies ask us for photographs, we have a fee schedule, depending on the intended use. If you still want to take this family's photograph, I will explain the circumstances to them. If they are willing, you will pay a sitting fee—*to them.* If you decide to use the photograph in your brochure, you will offer these people a contract and pay them a fee according to the ministry guidelines."

He spoke calmly, but Kate couldn't get over the sense of outrage she felt at having been accused so unfairly. That she was also deeply distressed because it had happened on the heels of a gently building intimacy between them, she did not allow herself to see.

Childishly she shoved the camera back in her bag. "I've lost the impulse now, anyway!"

It wasn't at all the money that made her change her mind, only that all the joy had gone out of the moment, but Hadi al Hajar nodded as if he had expected it, his eyes full of cynical lack of surprise.

He turned to the family, his hands spread, and said something that made the parents laugh, the children look puzzled. The potter called something to Kate, and they laughed again.

Hadi and the family exchanged polite farewells. Kate smiled and nodded regretfully, feeling at a terrible disadvantage. What had been said about her?

"Ma'assalaam!" the family cried, as they moved off.

"What did you tell them?" Kate asked. Suddenly, as the heat left her, she was feeling depressed.

"I said they had missed their chance at world stardom this time, but that *insh'Allah,* another opportunity would come their way."

She couldn't even smile. "And what did he answer?"

"That he hoped his chance would come before his teeth fell out."

They walked on in a pregnant silence. A man with a snake paused beside her, offering her the long golden body of his pet. She shook her head with a forced smile.

The magic had gone out of the day.

"Was it necessary to be so hostile about it?" Kate asked bitterly, when she could bear it no longer. "Could you just have told me the facts, without making me feel like a monster?"

He wasn't going to unbend by an inch. "I fell short of accusing you of criminal activity, at least!"

"I didn't accuse you of—" Kate began, but he interrupted harshly.

"You accused me of soliciting a bribe. Also of robbing the poor."

"Well, how was I to know you're so different from everyone else?" Kate demanded, distantly wondering why it was so hard to back down with him. "It's just the way of life out here, isn't it?"

He stopped dead in his tracks, grasping her arm so that she was forced to stop, too, and turned to look down at her, showing his teeth in an angry smile. The noise of the souk suddenly faded as she gazed up at him.

"Out where, exactly, is bribery and corruption a way of life?"

Kate closed her eyes and bit her lip. Now she really had put her foot in it. She faltered, but who was he trying to kid?

"I'm sorry, but you know it's the truth!"

"If you have had experience of corruption in the Barakat Emirates, I would like to hear the details," Hadi growled.

His expression was deeply intimidating. She didn't answer.

"You have been in the country less than twenty-four hours, am I right? What corruption have you seen? Something at the casino? The hotel?"

"I'm not talking about the Barakat Emirates in particular!"

The green eyes narrowed. "What *are* you talking about?"

The enormity of what she was suggesting to him suddenly struck her. It was one thing to bandy it around among colleagues, another thing entirely to say it to someone's face. She had been angry and hurt and had spoken without any thought.

Kate pressed her lips together and bowed her head to escape the expression in his eyes.

There was a long, horrible silence.

"Be warned, Kate," he said, his voice silky with disdain. "Take care before you advise your clients that officials in the Barakat Emirates are open to bribery. The Barakatis are a proud people—and very quick to protect their honour."

The incident coloured the rest of the visit. She wanted to have lunch in the little Parvan-type *chaikhaneh* at one side of the souk—a small covered area where the customers sat or lay on cushions and were served mint tea and delicious-looking local food on cloths spread on the floor. That was the sort of thing her clients would like, and Kate, too.

But when she suggested it, he brushed her request aside and took her to a more formal restaurant, where the customers were a mixture of nationalities. She suspected this was because the clientele at the little *chaikhaneh* were all locals. As if he had to protect them against her influence!

When they had ordered, Kate remembered something with a little pulse of satisfaction, and acted instantly on the thought. She unzipped her money belt, pulled out a wad of money, and passed it across the table.

Hadi al Hajar received it in his palm with narrowed eyes and a look that burned her.

"What is this?"

"Relax, it's not a bribe," Kate said flatly. "It's the money from the chips you bought last night, and your winnings. You left them on the table when you went out so quickly. I cashed them for you."

"It was my intention that you should spend them," he said stiffly.

Kate took secret pleasure in returning the same suspicious look. "Why? I paid a fee to the tourism agency for the hiring of a guide, but nothing was said about being financed to play at the casino."

"It was my private choice. I was your escort," he said, and she could see that he was angry again. Part of the *parvanwali* code was generosity to guests, she had read. Well, tough! Part of *her* code was financial independence. She rested her arms on the table and leaned across to get right in his face.

"First, you were not my escort," she pointed out. "Second, I wouldn't dream of wasting that amount of money on anything as pointless as a game of chance." She took a deep breath.

"Third, you kissed me last night. That doesn't entitle you to throw money at me. I'm a professional tourist agent, not a good-time girl. And believe me, I'm as proud as any Barakati you care to name!''

To her surprise, she saw the glimmer of a smile as Hadi al Hajar carelessly pocketed the money. "I will remember," he said.

In the afternoon they visited Queen Halimah Palace. Once the premier royal residence of the monarch, now it was the seat of the central government of the Barakat Emirates.

The pleasure gardens were open to the public on days when the *majlis,* or parliament, was not in session. One of the most admired examples of Islamic architecture in the world, the place was a must-see for any tourist and would be included in any itinerary Drummond and Venables offered.

But even though Kate knew this, even though she had seen photos of the gardens, still she was staggered by the reality.

Water appeared as the central feature in nearly every vista, offering wonderful relief from the dry, hot climate. Hadi led her past fountains and cascades, beside beautiful reflecting pools, along canals that descended through several levels via small waterfalls, and even behind one of the bigger falls, for a moment of peace and perfect coolness.

The gardens held several pavilions, some of which were open to visitors. There she saw masterpieces of art and carpets of unparalleled beauty. Paintings of generations of the royal family were on show, as well as objets d'art from various periods, including some from the fabulous Jalal Period by the greatest craftsmen of the age.

Kate had majored in art and art history at university, and she drooled at so much beauty being collected in one place. Like being let loose in a chocolate factory.

"Was all this really built by a woman?" she asked. "I've heard that it's just a myth."

"It is no myth. Queen Halimah is one of the great figures of Barakati history," Hadi replied. "She inherited the kingdom from her husband when their son, Jalal, was only an infant, and immediately embarked on a program of public works. She built not just palaces, mosques, and schools, but also roads, bridges, and wells.

"However, so much was undertaken in her reign that her name did, it is true, become a byword. Nearly any ancient structure is now attributed to her by ordinary people, and this has been the case for several hundred years. Some things attributed to her by the old writers we know cannot have been built in her reign. The great travel writer Ibn Katibi seems to have made several such mistakes.

"And of course, not all her grand projects were completed in her lifetime. Some of them are the result of decades of painstaking work. Halimah's son, Jalal, continued the building projects after his mother's death, and in his day the court teemed with artists, artisans and craftspeople, who flocked to Barakat."

GET 2

HOW TO GET YOUR
2 FREE BOOKS AND FREE GIFT!

1. Peel off the MIRA sticker on the front cover. Place it in the space provided at right. This automatically entitles you to receive two free books and an exciting surprise gift.

2. Send back this card and you'll get 2 "The Best of the Best™" novels. These books have a combined cover price of $11.98 or more in the U.S. and $13.98 or more in Canada, but they are yours to keep absolutely FREE!

3. There's no catch. You're under no obligation to buy anything. We charge nothing – ZERO – for your first shipment. And you don't have to make any minimum number of purchases – not even one!

4. We call this line "The Best of the Best" because each month you'll receive the best books by some of today's most popular authors. These authors show up time and time again on all the major bestseller lists and their books sell out as soon as they hit the stores. You'll like the convenience of getting them delivered to your home at our special discount prices . . . and you'll love your *Heart to Heart* subscriber newsletter featuring author news, horoscopes, recipes, book reviews and much more!

SPECIAL FREE GIFT!

We'll send you a fabulous surprise gift, absolutely FREE, simply for accepting our no-risk offer!

5. We hope that after receiving your free books you'll want to remain a subscriber. But the choice is yours – to continue or cancel, anytime at all! So why not take us up on our invitation, with no risk of any kind. You'll be glad you did!

6. And remember...we'll send you a surprise gift ABSOLUTELY FREE just for giving "The Best of the Best" a try.

Visit us online at
www.mirabooks.com

® and TM are trademarks of Harlequin Enterprises Limited.

BOOKS FREE!

Hurry!

Return this card promptly to GET 2 FREE BOOKS & A FREE GIFT!

The Best of the Best™

Affix
peel-off
MIRA
sticker here

YES! Please send me the 2 FREE "The Best of the Best" novels and FREE gift for which I qualify. I understand that I am under no obligation to purchase anything further, as explained on the back and on the opposite page.

385 MDL DNHR   185 MDL DNHS

FIRST NAME	LAST NAME

ADDRESS

APT.#	CITY

STATE/PROV.	ZIP/POSTAL CODE

Offer limited to one per household and not valid to current subscribers of "The Best of the Best." All orders subject to approval. Books received may vary.

(P-BB3-02) ©1998 MIRA BOOKS

The Best of the Best™ — Here's How it Works:

Accepting your 2 free books and gift places you under no obligation to buy anything. You may keep the books and gift and return the shipping statement marked "cancel." If you do not cancel, about a month later we will send you 4 additional novels and bill you just $4.49 each in the U.S., or $4.99 each in Canada, plus 25¢ shipping & handling per book and applicable taxes if any.* That's the complete price and — compared to cover prices of $5.99 or more each in the U.S. and $6.99 or more each in Canada — it's quite a bargain! You may cancel at any time, but if you choose to continue, every month we'll send you 4 more books, which you may either purchase at the discount price or return to us and cancel your subscription.

*Terms and prices subject to change without notice. Sales tax applicable in N.Y. Canadian residents will be charged applicable provincial taxes and GST.

"Nazim Gohari," Kate breathed reverentially. Nazim Gohari was the great artist of the Jalal Period, arguably the greatest in the country's history. "Is there any of his work here in the pavilion?"

"In the Red Pavilion there is a cup," he said, and Kate drew a breath.

"The Cup of Happiness?"

Hadi al Hajar shook his head. "The *Jahmeh Jahn* belongs to Prince Omar personally and is in his own treasury. Here in Queen Halimah Palace are kept only those treasures owned jointly by the three princes, which are on loan to the nation. Have you seen enough here?"

She could never see enough of such beauty, of course.

They wandered out into the gardens again. Deliciously shaded cloisters were defined by the columns in various colours of marble or stone that lined them—the Sandstone Cloister, the Alabaster Cloister and the Ebony Cloister. Each had some story about how the materials had been transported, the craftsmen who had sculpted them, or events that had taken place there.

Because she was not an ordinary tourist and had to cram her itinerary with as many different sites as possible, they quickly moved on to the Great Mosque and Queen Halimah's Tomb, the two other great architectural testaments to Barakat's golden age.

Kate had seen a lot of wonderful places in her travels, but nothing could compare to seeing three such buildings in a day. She began to feel that beauty like this was an actual substance, and that she was getting drunk on it. In the fabulous Hall of Mirrors—an arched, domed and pillared space that glowed with light from no visible source—she had the feeling that her brain structure was being modified.

"I won't be the same person when this is over," she murmured.

Hadi glanced down at her, a half smile playing on his lips. He, too, she thought, was like another person now. The mask he wore had slipped away, and again she had the sense of seeing his heart.

"What happened to it all?" she asked sadly. "Why does no one build like this anymore?"

The wonder was why, with so much talent and artistry in the world, there was so little in modern art that uplifted the human spirit in the way Islamic art and architecture did.

"The world has changed. Beauty can no longer survive here, and so it does not often trouble to appear."

The starkness of it shook her. Kate looked at him. His face was deeply shadowed now, and she realized that to see his heart was to see the deep scar that marked where pain had entered and lay within it. Her own heart twisted in acute sympathy.

At this moment they were alone in their part of the glowing, magical chamber. Impulsively, Kate put her hand on his arm. "You've known a special beauty that didn't survive, I think?"

The mask clanged down like prison gates over his eyes, and he was her enemy again.

"I am the guide, Kate, not a part of the scenic tour," Hadi said harshly, and turned to lead her out of that place of unbearable beauty.

Chapter 7

The next morning they left very early on a prolonged tour of the desert and the mountains. Like Hadi, Kate was wearing khaki pants and shirt and strong desert boots, with warmer clothes packed for when they got to the mountains.

In the morning they stopped briefly at an ancient, undated ruin of weathered, mudbrick arches, so time-worn they might almost have been a natural feature. It was a lonely, empty place, a powerful reminder that everything dies over time, including even collective human memory.

But lunch in a nearby village was much more cheerful, served to them by the women who ran a small "factory" where they wove their traditional tribal fabric for export. Kate was hoping to offer her clients a visit here in one of several optional day trips.

She was fascinated by the organization of the factory. Rather than working on a Western-style assembly line of the different processes—different women spinning the special yarn, dyeing it, weaving it, and then embroidering it with the traditional tribal design—each woman followed her own creation from beginning to end.

The women worked mostly in their own homes.

"We work together in small groups," Soraia Sahari explained. "When we have spun the yarn at Maryam's house, we go to the dye vats together and dye the yarn according to the amounts we need. Then we come here to our weaving frames, and work here until the weaving is done."

The women were at Soraia's house at the moment, each at her own weaving frame in the tree-shaded courtyard. The youngest, a beautiful, sparkling-eyed girl of about fifteen, was working on her first project. The oldest was a smiling, weather-beaten grandmother. Others had young children in cribs nearby, or helpfully fetching and carrying scissors and bits of yarn when needed. The older children, she was told, were in the village school.

"Then we go to Farida's house to do the embroidery. And when we have finished, we send our fabric to the agent, or to the clothing factory at Hamsa-Yemah. And other groups work the same way in their houses."

"What a pity you can't export your working methods along with your fabric!" Kate exclaimed.

"It would be difficult to build cars or computers in

Khanum Soraia's courtyard," Hadi observed dryly. He translated, and all the women laughed.

It was Kate's first foray out of the capital, and she was surprised by how prosperous the village was. The homes were beautiful examples of the traditional white stucco-covered brick, with domes and flat roofs built around pretty courtyards with fountains and palm trees.

"They are prosperous partly because the fabric is unique to this area, and they have secret techniques no one has been able to copy," Hadi explained. "The women of this tribe have made the cloth for centuries, and the secret is passed only from mother to daughter. There is a greater demand than supply, and we maintain centralized control over exports."

She knew that when the oil money began to flow in in the seventies, King Daud had put it into revitalizing the ancient craft guilds and other small local industries. It was a way of keeping the people in their communities, rather than letting unfettered economic forces drive the young ones to the cities. Here in this village, apparently, it worked extremely well.

"Is this a showcase village?" Kate asked, as they drove away.

"What do you mean?"

"Well, are there many villages that happy and prosperous, or is it a particularly successful one?"

He gave her a look that shamed her. "Are you such a cynic, Kate? Or is this another example of cultural arrogance? Do you really think no country can do anything better than it is done in the West?"

As before, his challenge caught her on the raw, making it impossible for her to back down or explain. And within moments they were arguing again.

Any time they seemed to be achieving a closeness, it seemed, she managed to say something that offended him.

"Will you take me to the valley called Al Darreh when we get to the mountains?"

Kate and Hadi sat around their own campfire, deep in the desert, alone with the stars.

Kate had never experienced such silence in her life. The desert stretched for miles around them. In the distance, here and there, villages and towns flickered with light like tiny points of consciousness in the void. To the north and east lay the mountain range called Noor. *Light,* he had said it meant, and she had seen why when the setting sun haloed the snowy peaks in shining white.

Hadi laughed. "If Al Darreh exists in reality, no one knows where it is. Some say that the mystics know. But then it is a metaphor for mystical knowledge, like turning lead into gold."

"But I've read a travel book where the writer visited it," Kate protested. "In the early 1880s. He said an old man took him there and the journey in was terrifying. And he wasn't allowed to say anything more about it."

Hadi shook his head. "That was convenient."

They had pitched camp in a ruin not far from the great River Sa'adat. It was a place that Kate knew would fascinate her clients as much as it did her, not least for its modern history: it was the site of the old rebel camp of Jalal, where Princess Zara had been held hostage and Prince Rafi and his brothers had struggled to free her.

Over the simple meal of *naan* and lamb stew that they had heated over their campfire, she and Hadi had discussed offering an expedition like this for her clients. In the morning she would negotiate with neighbouring villagers, to whom Prince Omar had given the right to act as tour guides and guards of the site, but tonight they were alone.

Now she set her empty plate aside and asked, "Will you tell me the story of the valley?"

"There are many legends surrounding Al Darreh. Some say that it has remained untouched by the outside world for thousands of years, that no invader has ever conquered it, and that the people there live still in the close and immediate connection to God that all humankind once enjoyed."

Sound travelled strangely at night in the desert. His deep voice seemed to be part of the silence. Somewhere an animal yipped its night song.

"The usual story, however, is that a thousand years ago it was a rich, fertile valley, where a wealthy sheikh ruled. He built a magnificent palace there, and his descendants enjoyed the blessings of the place unhindered for two hundred years—until it was threatened by the arrival of Genghis Khan.

"The sheikh's descendants, it is said, begged a Sufi saint who had taken up residence there to protect the valley and its people from the marauders. The saint used mystical skills to move a mountain and close the entrance to the valley—which until then had been readily accessible—so that Genghis Khan's troops passed by in complete ignorance.

"But there was a price for this escape from history. Thereafter anyone who left the valley could no longer find the way back, and no stranger could enter, unless by chance. So the people were completely cut off from the world."

Over the black mountain peaks in the distance a full moon was slowly making its way up the lush sky. The strange perfume of the desert at night teased her nostrils.

"Some were happy with this state of affairs, for the valley was rich in gardens and animals, water and sunshine, and so supplied all their wants, but many became anxious to visit the world outside. One by one these people took the risk.

"After only a little time in the outside world they knew what a mistake they had made and tried to go back. But although some had gone to great lengths to mark the way as they came out, none ever succeeded in returning to the paradise that was the valley.

"And those inside never knew why the adventurers did not return. Had they lost their way? Had they been killed? Or did they stay away because the outside world was such a paradise no one could bother to return?"

"Oh," Kate sighed.

"Each new explorer came out of the valley only to

meet those who had preceded him and were desperate for him to lead them back in. And gradually over the years the valley, which was paradise on earth, emptied, because men do not know when they are happy. Now it is said that only those whose own hearts allow it can find their way in.''

When he finished speaking they sat in silence for a long moment while the moon cast powerful shadows over the sculpted sand. A rocky outcrop in the distance moved and changed shape like a living creature.

''Oh, God, that's a really tragic story!'' Kate exclaimed softly.

''It is the story of the human condition.'' Hadi turned to stir the little saucepan that was heating their coffee over the fire.

''Is that all it is? Don't you think there must be some basis in truth for a story like that?''

''Perhaps some traveller stumbled upon a valley mysteriously deserted and started the tale,'' Hadi agreed. ''But now the story has been embellished, so that the valley wouldn't be recognizable even if we found it. That, too, is the human condition.''

''What about Iskandiyar, the lost city of Alexander?'' Kate argued. ''I read that no one believed it existed until that archaeologist looked for it in a different direction. And what about the tunnel here—that story was supposed to be just a legend, wasn't it? Until the bandit Jalal discovered it.''

Kate looked around her at the ruined building.

"And now he's a prince! You don't get more fairy tale than that, but it's true."

"He is a prince no longer," Hadi pointed out. "Jalal has renounced his titles, to live as an ordinary man. Perhaps he, too, had difficulty inhabiting paradise when he found it."

"Or maybe being a prince wasn't paradise for him," Kate argued. "It's a romantic thought—to give up everything for love."

She thought of Michael, who hadn't even been willing to give up his apartment to live with her, and laughed aloud.

"What amuses you?"

She shook her head. "Do you think that kind of love is possible for most people? Or does it only happen to the lucky few?"

Hadi leaned forward to stir the thick coffee brewing in a little saucepan balanced between two stones. When he spoke his voice was harsh, as if he would have preferred to remain silent.

"Whether they are few or many, those who experience such love are not the lucky ones. It is not something to wish for."

Kate breathed a long, slow breath and thought of the golden girl. "There speaks a man who has loved and lost."

"This is ready," said Hadi. "Give me your cup."

"Do you think true love always ends unhappily just because that was your experience?" Kate pressed, not sure what drove her, as she passed him one of the

cups from the cloth she had laid for their meal beside
the fire.

He poured coffee into one cup and then the other,
and she thought he wouldn't answer. But he set the
second cup down in front of himself and looked up.

"I think that love makes a man powerless," he said
evenly. "And it is better to avoid it."

A little shiver went over her. She struggled to speak
matter-of-factly.

"But they say when you love like that you don't
mind. That to be your beloved's slave is a delight.
Isn't that what it's all about?"

She thought of the comfortable warmth of her feelings for Michael and, with a sudden inner ferocity,
prayed to experience that true passionate love, the one
that fuelled poetry and deeds of honour....

"I did not mean powerless with the beloved." His
voice sounded raw. Kate closed her eyes for a moment, wondering how his voice would sound with a
woman against whom he found himself powerless. "I
mean powerless against the world. When there is
something in the world that you love and someone
threatens it...you are no longer master of yourself."

Kate gasped softly, his voice touching the place of
yearning in her. She wondered how the golden girl
had been able to resist the look in Hadi's emerald
eyes, that note in his voice.

She got to her feet and strode to a breach in the
perimeter wall to look out over the vastness that surrounded them. After a moment's silence she turned.

He was sitting where she had left him. Firelight

glinted in the unblinking green eyes, and just for a moment it was as if a wild animal crouched there, staring at her across the flames. Glossy and vibrant, and ready to spring away at the first sign of danger.

"So because someone might take what you love away from you, it's better not to love?" she said.

"I am not the first to say it, I think."

"People have said it in the past. People who lived in a more rigidly defined world than we do," she pointed out. "How many lovers nowadays really suffer that kind of interference in their lives?"

The question seemed to echo around the dark, empty courtyard. As if sudden tension in him had communicated itself to her, Kate found she was breathing through her mouth, listening intently to the silence.

"There are many ways to lose what you love," he said harshly. "Sometimes you yourself destroy it."

Kate shook her head. Could he really feel he had "destroyed" the golden girl she had seen at the casino?

"And you think unhappiness is the rule, rather than the exception?"

Looking into his coffee cup, he gave the little nod, his chin moving at an angle towards his shoulder, his eyes closing, that she had come to recognize as his last word on a subject. Then he drained the cup and set it to one side. He began to clear the remains of their meal. Clearly for him the conversation was over.

But Kate couldn't leave it there.

"So your message is, it's better never to dance, because sometimes people stumble?"

He made no answer.

"Suppose dancing is the only pleasure some people can hope to experience? Would your advice apply to them?"

Hadi threw her a look. "But that is not the case, is it?"

"Isn't it? Love is the source of all the good in the world, Hadi. And it's about the only thing left that's free. Even if you're naked and hungry, you can love, and feel better about the world because of it. How can you bear to be so pessimistic?"

Hadi set down a plate and got to his feet, and Kate suddenly began to doubt the wisdom of stirring these particular coals. He stopped in front of her, too close for comfort. He seemed to bring the heat of the fire with him, and it danced up between them in the desert night.

"Especially if you are naked and hungry, you can love," he said softly.

This time it was Kate's turn to answer with silence.

"If a man who has danced too close to the fire warns others away, Kate, is that pessimism?"

His voice had a resonance that made the night air shimmer. The two stood perfectly still, gazing at each other as his words grouped and regrouped in a soundlessly repeating echo.

Her heart pounded, her skin melted with excitement as the spiced honey of need he had created poured through her. Kate gazed up into his fire-shadowed eyes as the flickering light sculpted his face, painting temple, cheek and mouth with rich gold. The neat black beard added a devil's touch.

She looked even more like one of the *peri* now, he thought, with the firelight playing on her skin so that it seemed to glow with inner light, emphasizing the delicacy of her features, the haunting, dark-lashed eyes, the curving lips whose angry hauteur was softened now by the night and what was between them.

She watched him like a wild creature that both fears and wishes to be tamed.

"Is that what you did? Dance too close to the fire?" she said in a choked voice.

His hands rose and clasped her upper arms, and a jolt of heat burned down her body to her toes. Behind his head stars died and were reborn in their own timeless dance.

Her blood thrummed under his fingers and, as if that pulse were his lifeline, too, he sought her heart, enclosing her breast with hungry possessiveness.

"Yes, Kate," Hadi said harshly. "And I look at you and see another such fire, inviting me to my doom. But I will not go."

And then, in defiance of his words, he pulled her body hard against his, bent his head, set his mouth on hers.

Chapter 8

For a strange, waiting moment Kate went still under the passionate onslaught, as if listening for some distant sound. Then passion stormed through her, leaving her helpless to protest. It was passion that opened her mouth in feminine invitation under the tormented demands of his, passion that pressed her body against him, that thrilled to the hard hunger she felt in him.

She lifted her arms to wrap his head and draw him closer as he bent over her, arching her body up into his, her breasts pressed against the heat of his chest.

Sweetest hunger melted out through her body from every point of contact, spiralled along all her limbs. Her mouth burned with longing and fulfilment.

His hands pressed her with possessive strength, as if he were determined to increase the contact over every inch of their bodies. She felt the hard, moulding pressure down her back, against her waist, urgent over the curve of hip and thigh. He drew up her leg to make room for his hard flesh against her soft inner thigh, and pressed her more tightly against him. She grunted with the sudden kick of need.

As the sound vibrated against his lips, he lifted his mouth from hers, drew back, and she found herself trapped again in the net of his gaze.

"You are a beautiful and desirable woman, Kate," he said warningly. "I will dance with you, if you wish, but not close enough to be burned. Do not hope to make a mark on my soul. Nothing will come of what we feel."

Her heart thumped horribly, making her almost sick.

"Nothing?"

"The sexual pleasure that we see when we look at each other, my body wrapped in yours, yours in mine—this is inevitable. We knew it the moment we met. But do not submit to me, Kate, if you want more than this. I warn you. Tonight you look at the night and talk of love as a woman talks who dreams of finding it. Who yearns, not for the brief taste of passion that foreign women come here for, but for something more."

Kate licked her suddenly parched lips. "Do I?"

"Put such yearnings out of your heart, Kate, and enjoy what is to be enjoyed with me," he urged softly. "I know your body as if I had sculpted it my-

self from the sacred clay at the river bank. Pleasure
is certain between us, if we choose it.''

Then he sank onto his haunches and reached up to
draw her down beside him onto the hard-packed sand.

Kate resisted, and stood looking down at him. She
felt exposed and hurting, as if he had ripped off her
skin and then pushed her into the storm.

''Why did you do that?'' she demanded.

He gazed up at her, his eyes dark with challenge.

''Do you see what it is you're doing?'' Kate asked.

He laughed soundlessly. ''I invite you to my bed,
Kate. Is it not plain enough?''

She shook her head. ''You invite me, but at the
same time you push me away.''

He frowned up at her, his hand still clasped around
her wrist. ''I do nothing but tell you the truth.'' He
put his other hand under her palm and stroked it with
a touch that sent anticipation and yearning all through
her. ''Would it be better if I had not warned you?
Then you could have pretended to yourself that our
lovemaking was not empty, but full of possibility. Is
that what you want?''

She took her hand away. ''No. But I think you
knew before you spoke that what you said meant I
would refuse you. I think you said it so that I
would—''

With a sudden passion that defeated her, he pulled
her down against him, and lay back with her on his
chest. The breath caught in her throat as she gazed
down into his eyes.

His teeth flashed behind the dark beard. "I do not hope you will refuse me, Kate. I hope that you will make love with me. But not with stars in your eyes and dreams of Prince Jalal's fine love in your heart."

She said dryly, "If you don't want me to have stars in my eyes, Hadi, don't proposition me in the open air."

He frowned curiously. "What does that mean?"

With a wrenching regret, because she knew she belonged there, Kate lifted herself off his body and stood looking down at him.

"Think about it," she said.

Iskandiyar lay spread out below them as they topped a small rise in the rugged desert. A huddle of tents and huts sat on one side, away from the site, while long rows of roofs on stilts and a steel-and-canvas perimeter fence protected the remnants of the ancient city that had been founded by Alexander two thousand three hundred years ago.

At a little distance to one side, a modern building site was similarly protected from the harsh sun by a massive canopy, and on the other side a cluster of palm trees near an upthrust of rock promised water.

It had been an awkward, disturbed night, trying to sleep by Hadi's side, but the sun had finally made its appearance. After a morning of negotiation with the villagers in charge of the Jalal site, they had crossed the Sa'adat River into East Barakat and followed the newly built road to Iskandiyar.

Now Hadi pulled the Land Rover into the covered parking lot beside the building site, and Kate put on a broad-brimmed hat as they stepped out into the blazing sunshine to walk across to the dig. Power cables snaked everywhere across the sand from a large generator truck that hummed over the scene.

Two ancient stone lions, rubbed into soft focus by time and the winds, stood guard again at the gates, though beyond them, all that remained of the city they guarded were a few walls, some more or less square lines of brick and stone in the earth, and the white remains of pillars, some still tumbled, some restored. Kate entered the shade again with relief.

A small tour group being carefully shepherded around the site stood over the excavated floor of a house where two broken urns had been left in situ. A steel fence with a large red No Entry! notice, behind which the archaeologists were at work in the ground, divided the city in two.

As they skirted the fence, a dark-haired woman in desert khaki and a battered straw hat came out of a gate ahead of them and, turning to close it behind her, caught sight of the pair.

"Hadi!" she exclaimed with a smile, coming towards them with her hands out in greeting. "*Ahlan wa sahlan!* I didn't know you were coming today, did I?"

Hadi took her hands and bent and kissed her cheeks. "No, because I didn't realize you'd be here yourself today," he said. "Princess, may I present a compatriot of yours? Kate Drummond, Zara Blake."

Kate took a startled breath as the princess whose adventures she had been reliving only the night before put out a friendly hand. "Hello! You're Canadian? Where are you from?"

"Vancouver, Your Royal Highness," Kate stammered. "How wonderful to meet you!"

The princess smilingly shook her head. "I don't use my titles in my professional career. The protocol would just get in the way. Here on the site, thank God, I'm still Zara Blake—unless, of course, I'm having trouble getting something done!" She laughed. "Then the palace gravitas comes in very handy.

"Look, I'm just taking a break. I'm sure you both could use a cool drink. Will you join me?"

"Oh, *look!* Is that *her?* Isn't that the princess? Yoo-hoo! Princess Jana! Hello!"

Zara smiled and waved a breezy greeting, then, tucking her clipboard under her arm, she stepped between Hadi and Kate and put a hand under each of their elbows.

"Come on," she said in an undervoice, guiding them along a narrow pathway between two excavated buildings. A few minutes later they stepped inside a large, blissfully air conditioned caravan.

"Please take a seat," the princess said. "I'll just look in on the babe. How is he, Adilah?" she added, as a woman opened an inner door and came into the room.

"He has just fallen asleep," said Adilah softly.

The princess made a disappointed face. "Ohhh, already? Oh, well, I'll go and look at him. Adilah, would you be a dear and get Hadi and Kate some refreshment before you go for your break? I'll be right back!"

The room they were in was an office-cum-sitting room, with a large desk at one side. The walls were covered with aerial photographs of the site. When Princess Zara returned, Kate and Hadi were standing, drinks in hand, examining the various views.

"Now, what brings you to the Barakat Emirates, Kate?" Zara asked, moving to a dresser where she poured herself some cold juice. She flicked a glance from Kate's face to Hadi's. "Something special?"

She flung herself down on a kelim-covered sofa and gestured to them to sit, too.

Kate explained briefly. "And of course our clients will be thrilled at the chance to visit Iskandiyar," she finished.

"It's very gratifying to think we're on the tourist map already," Zara said. "We took a calculated risk, opening the site before the dig and the museum are completed. Will your clients mind that there's so little to see?"

"I don't think our clients would call an Alexander site 'little to see'! But anyway, there's always the cachet of being one of the first to visit." Kate grinned. "I intend to cash in on that myself."

Zara and Hadi laughed. "And accompanied by a

Cup Companion, too!'' Zara exclaimed. ''So how do you two know each other?''

There had just been too many clues that Hadi wasn't what he pretended to be for her not to have suspected something, but that he was a Cup Companion had never crossed Kate's mind.

''Cup Companion!'' she repeated in incredulous dismay.

Hadi laughed aloud, and Zara bit her lip and made a rueful face.

''Have I put my foot in it? Are you on your annual assignment, Hadi? Sorry!'' She looked from one to the other. ''And here I thought—''

Hadi simply shut down. His smile went, his eyes grew hooded. But he said, pleasantly enough, ''Yes, you've blown my cover, Princess. It's my fault. When I checked, you weren't scheduled to be here today.''

''I wasn't. But I'd invited Lisbet Raine to see the site and Jaf called to say he was bringing her today. They only left a few minutes ago. I'm sorry you've missed them.''

Kate flicked a glance at Hadi to see how he took that, but his face showed only ordinary interest. He was a master of self-control today, Kate thought.

''I've already met her. Jaf introduced us on the night of the Grand Reception,'' he said.

In an instinctive bid to run interference for him, Kate said, ''I saw them in the casino a few nights ago. She—''

Zara's eyes went dark with interest. "Really! *You* were there? How—"

Kate intercepted the look Hadi threw Zara, but she was miles from understanding it. The princess broke off abruptly, and Hadi said easily,

"Kate had to check out the casino for business purposes. As she was at pains to tell me, she herself doesn't gamble."

"I see," Zara said. She put her glass down and looked at Kate. "Now—you're dying to see the dig, I'm sure, and I think that group has probably gone by now. Will you let me show you around?"

"Which prince are you Cup Companion to?" Kate asked in the morning, as they hit the road again.

They had spent the night at a nearby village, in the home of a warm, hospitable couple with several dark-eyed serious children, who were excitedly undertaking to offer bed-and-breakfast accommodation for visitors. Between socializing and talking business, there had been no opportunity to talk privately with Hadi about the events of the day.

But there had been plenty of opportunity to think later, in bed. And plenty to think about. That Hadi was one of the influential Cup Companions was nearly unbelievable, but it was certain. Princess Zara certainly hadn't been joking.

"Prince Omar," Hadi answered now. They were heading up into the mountains, where they would spend a few days visiting caves and the emerald mines and several other sites.

And Kate still hadn't given up on her quest to find The Valley.

"Prince Omar of Central Barakat? He's married to Princess Jana?"

Hadi nodded.

"Does it matter that I know?"

"No. But you should refrain from telling anyone we meet, please."

"Is that for security reasons? What did Zara mean when she asked if you were on your annual assignment?"

"The Princes of Barakat subscribe to the view that an enterprise or an organization is best served if those in management and executive positions spend some part of their time actually working at ground level. In government, every official at management level or above, without exception, must spend one month of the twelve in such work every year. The idea is spreading to private industry here, as well."

Kate spent a moment absorbing the implications of that. "And do they all do it in disguise?"

"No. In many cases, that wouldn't even be possible. But the Cup Companions have in addition another task. The princes have revived the ancient practice of the Caliph Haroun al Rashid. Perhaps you know that the Caliph used to go out among his people in disguise, to make sure that his officials treated his subjects fairly. He would masquerade as a private citizen with a petition, to see whether his judges were asking for bribes, for example.''

''Oh, I think I've heard of this.''

''Yes, it is becoming public knowledge, because the princes themselves also do it. All Cup Companions are expected to go incognito at least once every year to see at first hand how public servants operate and are treated—sometimes within our own areas, sometimes in others. I am merely using this opportunity to combine both tasks.''

''Is Hadi al Hajar your real name?''

''I am Hadi Farraj ibn Wadil al Ahsheq Durrani. The foreign press call me Hadi Durrani.''

''And were you undercover at the casino, too? Princess Zara seemed to suggest—''

The Land Rover slowed as he turned to face her. His eyes were grave and level. ''Kate, I ask you not to speculate about what you saw at the casino.''

She was silent for a moment of surprise. She cleared her throat. ''Is this for—personal reasons?''

Hadi's eyebrows snapped up, and he took his eyes off the road again to throw her a look of surprise. ''Personal reasons? No. What could be personal about it? But I can say no more, Kate.''

''You can say this, I think. When you danced too close to the fire, Hadi—was it Lisbet Raine who burned you?''

Chapter 9

They were alone on a long stretch of road, and Hadi put his foot on the brake and pulled over onto the narrow shoulder.

He turned to look at her, his mouth as grim as the Reaper's. "What do you want, Kate?" he demanded harshly.

She was suddenly aware of the bleakness of the landscape. The road they were on was built up several feet from ground level, a narrow causeway of tarmac over miles of barren desert linking the sea to the rugged mountains.

They hadn't met another car for minutes past. The mountains loomed ahead, no more hospitable than the desert, no more friendly than Hadi Durrani's fierce, cold eyes.

What do you want? he had asked, and to her dismay her heart answered, *You.*

"You wanted to make love to me, Hadi," she pointed out. "Some women would demand to hear your entire sexual history for the past ten years before considering it. All I'm asking for is a little emotional background."

"My emotional background is not relevant to—"

"It is to me."

"Then your decision to refuse me was the right one," he said flatly. "If you wish to rethink that decision, I am very willing. But it is your attitude that must change. Mine will not."

"I don't think I've asked you to change your attitude. I asked you for the background. When we were at Jalal's camp, I thought you were in love with Lisbet Raine. Now that you've said—"

"In love?" His eyes narrowed. "What made you think it?"

"Just the way you looked at her that night. When they kissed, you looked as though—"

She broke off. As if he didn't want to know, but couldn't stop himself asking, he prompted, "I looked as though—?"

"As though your heart was being ripped out," Kate finished baldly.

His teeth glinted against the sun-browned skin, the black moustache and beard, as if to warn her of danger if she came closer.

"I have no heart, Kate. And its history is long dead."

She gasped, then said quietly, "That's a contradiction. If it has a history, it must exist."

Suddenly, as if he had reached the end of his tether, his hands clasped her shoulders and dragged her half across the space between, to face him. His eyes glowed with a banked heat that both terrified and thrilled her.

"My heart is not your business. My body is the only—" And then, driven beyond his endurance, he cursed, pulled her roughly into his arms, and smothered her mouth with a punishing kiss.

Sensation leapt through her system without rhyme or pattern, random bursts of pleasure that made her heart kick into a matching erratic rhythm, then steady into a fast, hard, urgent response.

The gearshift was digging into her waist, bringing her back to her senses. This was crazy. She couldn't give in to this. Kate put her hand down to hold the gearshift away and push herself up, only to find herself caressing his urgent erection.

Hadi lifted his mouth with a groan. "Not here, Kate! Not on the road. We must wait."

Kate snatched her hand away and sat upright, feeling that she had lost the high moral ground. "It's not—I wasn't—damn it, I thought that was the gearshift digging into me. I wasn't trying—"

He shook his head, trying to clear it, not hearing. "Never mind. We must get to the guest house."

For a moment he rested his head on his arms, on top of the wheel, breathing deep, slow breaths to calm his blood. Then, with a sideways glance at her that melted her into a heap of honey where she sat, he put the truck in gear and eased back onto the road.

Several hours later they arrived at a village guest house in the mountains. They had spoken little en route, mostly to discuss the scenery and where they were headed. They had stopped for a quick meal from the provisions packed in the Land Rover, but otherwise had driven without a break.

Kate was exhausted. Not by the journey, but by the emotional tension. She knew that Hadi believed she had changed her mind. She knew that he was expecting that here, tonight, they would make love. She knew she shouldn't—couldn't make love with him under the circumstances. She couldn't cold-bloodedly decide to make love to a man who deliberately kept his feelings out of the equation.

But she had found it impossible to say so in the confines of the car. So she was going to have to say it as soon as possible now that they'd arrived. She couldn't let him go on expecting all evening, all through dinner, that sex was on offer when they went to bed.

She had every right to say no. She hadn't thrown away any of her rights by mistakenly making him think she was interested.

But still she was intensely nervous. Not least because a part of her was willing her to let it happen. To go with the flow.

She had never felt the extreme physical reaction he aroused in her with any other man. His kiss, his eyes, his voice melted her more than Michael's passionate lovemaking. His rejection of emotional involvement hurt her more than her breakup with Michael.

That was stupid, of course. It couldn't be real. It was mountain sickness, or desert flu, or something. Rapture of the heights, wasn't that what they called it? Never mind that it had happened a few feet above sea level. It wasn't real.

But it sure felt real.

She was vaguely aware that he was speaking a different language now, with the guest-house proprietress. Parvani, she supposed, since they were in the mountain range that East and Central Barakat shared with neighbouring Parvan. Negotiations for their rooms were quick and uncomplicated, but the courtesies of the exchange, here in the mountains, took a little longer.

Meanwhile, two shy teenage girls, painfully pretty in the bright headscarves and long shirts over flowing trousers that were the mountain costume, ran in and out with sheets, bedding, and buckets of water, preparing their rooms.

Kate stood to one side, smiling benignly. At last the woman pointed them towards three tiny cabins with balconies on stilts that jutted precariously over the rocky slope. Kate followed Hadi up the steep incline with difficulty, as Hadi, carrying both their overnight cases, leapt up ahead of her as easily as the girls had done, sure-footed as a mountain goat.

He paused and waited for her, turning and laughing at her careful pace, and she saw him cast his eyes around the towering mountains with deep joy, and take a huge breath, like a man released from prison.

She realized that Hadi had come home. This was where his spirit rested.

She, too, of course, felt at home in the mountains, though the Noor Mountains were more rugged than those she had grown up with. Perhaps that made them kindred spirits.

The door of the room was unlocked and he went in ahead of her. By the time Kate got inside, he was out on the balcony, opening the wooden shutters that protected the narrow expanse of glass from the elements.

It was a very simple room—a hut, really. Thick rough planks of wood, aged and weather-beaten now, and sealed with white daub that gave a characteristic striped effect, formed walls, ceiling and floor.

The floor was scattered with aged kelims, the bed was a thick pad on the floor with another thick kelim for a blanket. Candles under glass globes would be her light, and the plumbing consisted of a handmade ceramic jug and basin, filled with hot water, from which a little steam was still rising.

It smelled wonderful. Fresh mountain air, and the faint tang of evergreen.

Kate moved to the window as Hadi locked back the shutters, and gazed out. It was a stunning view. Though the temperature had dropped as they climbed, she hadn't realized quite how far into the mountains they had travelled. Now she looked back over the long defile, and the desert was scarcely visible in an opening between two hills below.

In the distance, scrubby evergreens clung for their life to the steep slopes, but all around her deciduous trees were a mass of riotous colour, yellow, red and brown. Here in the mountains, it was fall. Off to the right one hill was neatly terraced on several levels, and a donkey was being led around the perimeter of one field.

Then Hadi stepped through the door in front of her, and without a word pushed her against the wall, wrapped his arms around her, and drowned her with the wildest, most passionately drunken kiss she'd ever experienced in her life.

Kate was breathless with surprise and excitement, too overwhelmed to prevent her own arms wrapping around his neck, her mouth opening hungrily under the wild onslaught of his. A murmur of satisfaction sounded in his throat and the next thing she knew, she was lifted so that her feet left the ground, and was carried to the bed.

Exerting every ounce of self-control she had, Kate tore her mouth away from his. "No, Hadi, no!" she gasped. "I told you no!"

His arms still around her, he lay down on the bed,

dragging her with him. His devil mouth laughed up
at her. "You told me no?" he repeated. "Kate, we
had to stop because we were on the road in plain
sight! You held me here—" He took her hand and
pushed it down to his abdomen, wrapping her fingers
around his aroused flesh. "Remember?"

The touch shook her. That he could be so fiercely
aroused by her, and that his arousal was so fierce her
fingers could not meet around it, made the blood
pound into her thighs, leaving her light-headed.

His hand wrapped her head and drew her face
down for his kiss. Kate's eyes closed against the
swoop of passionate hunger that rode through her, but
she pushed her head back to resist.

"I thought it was the gearshift!" she cried. "It was
digging into me and…" It sounded stupider than she
could have imagined. "I was going to tell you as soon
as—I didn't expect you to jump on me like this!"

His hands stilled in her hair, his eyes narrowed as
he frowned up into her face. "You thought I was the
gearshift?" he repeated, as if it was the most unbelievable idea in the world. Well, it came close. "Are
you serious?"

She nodded. "I'm serious."

"Then you were deliberately fooling yourself."
With an abruptness that took her breath away, he
lifted her hand again, wrapped it around his flesh and
held it there. "You couldn't have made such a mistake without wanting to."

She couldn't deny that, though willful naivete

wasn't usually her strong suit. The promise she felt under her hand made her swallow hard, and she resisted again and lifted her hand away.

"Maybe, but the fact remains—"

"No, don't speak." His hand stirred against the back of her neck and head, massaging her with firm possessiveness. "I understand you. Don't say yes, Kate, you don't have to. You don't have to do anything...."

Loud voices were clamouring for her to shut up and let him have his way, but something else was stronger. Her heart, maybe, that wanted to be part of this, too. And couldn't be if she gave in to his empty passion.

She struggled up to a sitting position on the mattress. It was hard and ungiving, like him, she thought.

"I'm sorry, Hadi, but I can't. I'm really sorry, I had no idea this would happen."

"No idea?" he repeated in soft disbelief.

"I would have made it clear if you'd given me a little time."

His teeth glinted in an angry smile. "We have been driving for hours, Kate."

"I know we have, and I tried to tell you, but it seemed—I'm sorry. Please can we leave it at that? Could you just go to your own room, please? I'd like to—"

"This is my room," he said, with flat emphasis on every word.

"What? Well, then, where's—"

"This is our room, Kate. I only asked for one."

She closed her eyes. "Oh, God. Well, I know it'll be embarrassing, but we'll have to get another one, please."

Hadi pushed himself to sit up and drew his legs to an easy cross-legged posture that looked as natural to him as breathing. He looked like a miniature Parvani painting, she thought irrelevantly.

"No, we will not get another room. It would be more than embarrassing, it would be insulting to our hostess."

"Why?" she demanded harshly. "What will she care?"

"This is not Vancouver. This is not even Barakat al Barakat. This is the heart of the country, Kate, and the people here are as strict and old-fashioned as they are hospitable. I told the woman we were married."

Kate gasped, "Told her we were married!" she almost shrieked. "What did you do that for?"

"Because I want to make love to you. And I thought you wanted the same. But the people here would be very shocked if a man and a woman who were not married asked to share one room. Bad enough that we travel alone together."

She wasn't sure she believed him. "So what would you have told her if you hadn't thought that I was willing?" she demanded cynically.

"I would have said that I was from the Ministry of Tourism and was here to show a foreign businesswoman the caves. And I would have asked for you to have a room beside her own if possible.''

"That's Victorian!''

"The fact that such attitudes are no longer current in the West does not invalidate them, Kate. Right and wrong in such matters are not absolute.''

"Can't you just tell her your wife is feeling sick or something?''

"A man whose wife is sick stays by her side. If I now ask her for a separate room, she will know that I have lied. It would hurt her feelings very much. I will not do it.''

Kate felt panic threatening in her stomach. "Well, then, I will!''

She made as if to get to her feet, but his hand on her arm stopped her. "No.''

It was an empty threat anyway. She couldn't speak a word of the language. How would she ever make such a request understood?

"Then please can we go to another hotel?''

He laughed, but it was not with mirth. "Where do you think we are? We have come to the end of the road, Kate. Tomorrow we take donkeys to the mines. There is no other guest house within ten miles of here, if that. It will be dark soon and the mountains are cold at night.''

"You did this deliberately!'' she cried, feeling goaded. She did not want to spend the night in this sparsely furnished room with no one but Hadi Durrani for company! No television, no books—what would they do?

He laughed again, this time with more mirth. "Of course I did it deliberately! But I would not have done it if I had thought you were so changeable."

"I didn't change my mind. I thought—"

"You thought you were massaging the gearshift. I know," he said ironically. As if the conversation bored him out of his skull, in one easy uncurling he got to his feet. "Our hostess will have dinner ready for us in an hour or so. You will want to freshen up before that. I, too. Use the hot water sparingly."

He went out.

Chapter 10

They ate by lamplight on the main balcony of the hotel, looking out over the mountains. Far in the distance Mount Shir presided majestically over the scene, and a breath of air from its chill white peak seemed to move down over them as night deepened.

It was a welcome relief after the hot nights in the desert, but it wasn't doing anything to lessen the heat between Hadi and Kate. That fire had been lighted and nothing, it seemed, was going to extinguish it. Not even Hadi's impatient irritation with what he saw as her female weakness and indecision.

"You must make up your mind to come to me, Kate," he told her. "I will not argue with you, and I will not try to convince you. I want you. You know it. And you want me, this I know. But you must choose what you do about it."

That was what he said, but his actions belied him. Consciously or unconsciously, in his rough, impatient way, Hadi set out to seduce her.

His voice was pitched low, increasing the intimacy of their little corner of the otherwise empty balcony. They leaned against cushions, with the exotically spiced meal spread in front of them in the traditional way, on a cloth on the floor.

He did not touch her, but their elbows leaned on adjoining cushions, and his body heat brushing her was more potent than most men's caresses. He showed her how to eat the fresh mountain herbs and goat's cheese. He offered her delicacies from his own fork.

Of course she was too weak to resist.

Once he leaned over her to reach for a cushion. His breath did no more than blow gently across her throat, but electricity flooded her unexpectedly so that she made a little noise of reaction. He turned a look on her of such smouldering, unconscious intensity that she gasped again, and for a moment they were locked there, gazing into each other's eyes, the cloud of desire boiling up around them.

Then, with superhuman effort, he turned away.

It didn't help that the food was succulent and delicious. It didn't help that any murmur of appreciation she made seemed to strike him as halfway to invitation, or an expression of the desire she was trying to deny.

He said nothing. But she saw it in the way he

paused, like a man shot and waiting to sense how fatal the wound might be. In the way he closed his eyes and struggled for breath.

Every movement that either of them made seemed to take the voltage up another notch. Kate had never before felt such a sense of power, and it was heady. But it was matched by his power over her, so that she felt both strong and weak at the same time.

At last she complained, "You don't play fair."

Hadi threw her a look that was almost outrage. "*I* don't play fair?" he demanded. As if involuntarily, he grasped her arm, pushing her back into the cushions, bending close over her so that her blood sang with his nearness.

"It is you who lick your lips and moan as if to invite me to push you back on the cushions and bury myself in you! It is you who toss your head like a woman wanting to entice her lover! Yet you say you will not have me! Why do you do this, if not to tempt me to—"

His mouth came down, but she turned her head. His kiss slipped down her cheek, her ear, and into her hair, while her skin ignited everywhere.

"It's you who almost touch me every two minutes, you who make sure I feel your body heat with every movement!" Kate cried, struggling to sit up as he reined in his passion with terrible effort.

Her own frustrated desire powered her words, and she shot them at him, one by one.

"I told you I don't want sex for sex's sake and I

meant it! That doesn't mean I'm not tempted! You said you wouldn't try to seduce me, Hadi, but you haven't stopped since we sat down! You want to get me to the stage where my body overrules my head, and—''

She broke off when his breath caught with a helpless grunt and his face went white. She knew she had hit him deep and hard.

''What—what is it?'' she breathed.

''I do not seduce you!'' he rasped.

Kate gave a helpless little laugh. ''Hadi, what do you call it?''

''Call what?''

''Do you really not see what you're doing?''

She could sense a dreadful tension in him. A muscle in his jaw leapt, and leapt again.

''What is it?'' she breathed. ''What have I said?''

''Am I such a monster?'' he rasped. He rolled to his feet and went and stood at the railing, looking out over the mountain, his back to her. She saw that he was struggling with some powerful emotion. Her throat was dry with surprise and fellow feeling.

For a few moments there was silence, broken only by the sound of someone calling to an animal further down the valley, the shrill cry of a bird or wild animal among the trees.

Then he turned and came back to her. She thought that this was how a man's face looked when he had fought a battle and only barely survived.

It was this that undid the last of her resistance. The

understanding that he acted not out of a cold heart, but out of suffering.

They returned to the sparse little cabin only late, after a long, congenial visit with their hosts—the proprietress, Safra, her husband, Arsalan, who was a baker, their older children, and one or two neighbours—that was born of Hadi's clear reluctance to be alone with her.

They had discussed business, a little, but that had not been allowed to be the focal point of the evening. Poetry and government and philosophy and farming had all been thoroughly aired, as far as Kate could understand, for at intervals Hadi broke off to give her a quick précis of the topic of the moment.

It was a side of Hadi that she hadn't seen before— laughing and light-hearted and easy. He was at home here, a mountain man, and a shell seemed to have fallen away. Here amongst his own people he seemed more reachable than he had in the desert.

Once someone spoke to her directly and he reluctantly translated, "They say I will have to teach my wife Parvani."

Kate was blank for a moment, and then remembered, and blushed.

His eyes burned with an unreadable emotion as he looked at her, and she knew he regretted the deception. Kate smiled pleasantly.

"It wasn't my idea," she reminded him sweetly.

"Tell them that of course I mean to learn the language."

As at every such meeting, Kate asked him to question their hosts about the Valley.

"Safra says it is far from here," he translated, for it was their hostess who answered. Kate sat up with a little jolt. This was the first time anyone had spoken of it in such concrete terms.

"Two days' ride, they have heard. And you must have a guide who knows the way."

"Ask her if there's someone who will take us!" Kate cried excitedly.

The woman laughed, and Hadi translated, "No one around here knows the way, except perhaps the hermit in the cave higher up. And she warns you that the path is said to be very dangerous. Some have died in the attempt."

"Ma az darreh yahft shodeem, nah oo az ma."

"What did she say?" Kate asked. The woman had spoken to her with particular emphasis and glowing eyes.

"'We are found by the Valley, the Valley is not found by us,'" Hadi translated. "It is an old saying. People do not find the Valley by searching for it. Usually they stumble upon it after being lost in the mountains."

But the evening could not be prolonged forever, and shortly after this exchange, they said good-night. The trees cast sharp, black, moving shadows as Hadi led her back up the stony slope to the little cabin under bright moonlight. The air was tangy with ever-green and rich with the smell of the earth.

They entered to find that the daughters of the house had come in to make the room welcoming. Lighted candles cast a warm, intimate glow over the simple room. The bed had been drawn back, and fresh flow-ers had been strewn across the rough linen sheet and pillows.

Kate bit her lip. ''Do they think we're on our hon-eymoon?''

Hadi didn't answer. ''Take the bed, Kate,'' he said, bending to roll up one of the kelims from the floor. ''I will sleep outside.''

But she was sure of herself now. She moved close to him and shook her head.

''No need for that,'' she assured him softly. ''Share the bed with me.''

A short bark of laughter escaped him. His eyes burned all the insulation off her nerves, leaving her raw and leaping with electricity.

''Impossible.''

She came closer, and he stiffened.

''I am not strong enough for that,'' he said roughly.

Kate slipped her arms around his waist. ''I think you're strong enough,'' she whispered, lifting her face for his kiss.

The passion that blazed up in him, body and spirit, as he understood her intent, made her tremble and faint.

"Oh," she breathed, but her breath was stopped by his rough embrace, his wild, demanding, smothering kiss.

Afterwards she lay in his arms, her cheek against his shoulder. He held her with a possessive cherishing that she thought was half unconscious.

One candle still burned, throwing its soft light against the darkness.

"Will you tell me about the time you danced too close to the fire and were burned?" she asked quietly.

"It was a long time ago. I haven't thought about it for years, Kate. It is not important. It does not affect me now."

But she knew that it was, and it did. "I'd like to hear it, anyway."

There was a long silence. When he spoke at last, his voice was low and hesitant.

"I grew up in the Noor Mountains. In an area not so far from here, across the river. It is now part of Central Barakat, while here we are in East Barakat.

"My father is a sheikh, Kate, with a certain area under his command. I will inherit that command, and be our clan chief, when he dies. A tributary of the Sa'adat River divides our valley, and the other side of the river is governed by another clan, who historically are our enemies. Hend was the daughter of that clan chief.

"I met Hend's brother, Arif, at university seven years ago, in Barakat al Barakat. We were drawn together at first because we missed the mountains, but we became close friends, and we vowed that when we each inherited our father's position we would declare our clan enmity finished.

"When we returned home during the summer break, we used to meet, without our fathers' knowledge. And one day, Arif introduced me to his sister."

He paused, his eyes looking within. "Hend and I fell in love. It was sudden and complete. We met secretly, with Arif's assistance, all that summer, for my friend was happy to promote a bond that would unite our clans more certainly.

"The three of us rode together almost every day, and the whole valley understood what was happening, even our mothers. But it had not yet come to our fathers' ears. I told Hend I would speak to her father before I went back to university, but I put it off again and again because her father was a deeply old-fashioned man, and whether he approved or disapproved of our engagement, everything would change from the moment I spoke. Our happiness that summer was…" He shook his head, unable to find the words. "I knew—we all knew—that such moments in life are rare and short-lived. But I did not guess then how little happiness is granted to us.

"And then I went and spoke to him. He said no. He was very angry, especially with Arif. He would not hear of it. Hend was his only daughter and he could not bear that her children should be the grandchildren also of his enemy."

Kate made a noise of sympathy and stroked his naked chest beside where her cheek lay.

"You must understand how things are in the mountains. We are not—not like western city people, Kate. I was a virgin, and Hend, too. I would not have thought to touch her before she was my wife. That is our way.

"But we have another way, in the mountains. If a man abducts a woman, she is afterwards forced to marry him. It is old-fashioned, and most families nowadays would not hear of marrying their daughter to such a man. But Hend's father was old-fashioned. I told Hend that if she agreed I would abduct her....

"I can no longer remember how long she objected before she gave in to my persuasion. For a long time afterwards I told myself that she had been unwilling throughout, and only gave in because I never gave up trying to persuade her. But perhaps it was not as bad as that. Perhaps she did truly agree."

"And you abducted her?"

"I kept her with me for two days, and then took her home and demanded to marry her. Her father was extremely angry, but he finally agreed, and I went home, jubilant, to prepare for the wedding."

His voice grew tight. "Her father betrayed me, but his betrayal of Hend was a thousand times worse. Within a week, she was married—but not to me. Her father found a man who did not care that she was 'spoiled.' Arif told me she did not know it until the ceremony, and her cry of grief and dismay when she saw her bridegroom silenced all who were there.''

''Oh, God!'' Kate whispered, aghast. ''It's a wonder she didn't go mad!''

He closed his eyes. ''She did go mad. Her father forced the ceremony to a conclusion in spite of the distress of the guests, in spite of the fact that Hend was weeping and fainting. And she was sent off to the house of her husband—'' He swallowed convulsively. ''They said she never smiled again. Five months after the wedding, Hend drowned in the river.''

They sat in silence, listening to a night bird.

''What a dreadful story,'' Kate breathed at last. ''I am so sorry. You must have blamed yourself for a long time, and that would make it so much harder to bear!''

''I still blame myself. The fault was mine. If I had not done what I did, her father would not have been able to trick her in that way. But that is not the worst of my guilt.''

She was silent, listening as his voice struggled for calm.

''While we were together, I made love to her. Again, she protested that it wasn't right, and I overruled her. I said that the plan would not work unless... I told her we were married in our hearts and would be soon in reality. We were so in love that it was not difficult to convince her.

''I know that Hend admitted to her father that she

was no longer a virgin when she returned. Perhaps he
would not have sought to marry her so quickly without that. But if a child resulted…

"Do you understand me now, Kate? Do you understand why I say that love is dangerous and not to
be trusted? Why I offer you only the pleasure that we
give each other with our bodies, and nothing more?"

And as he spoke his body grew hard again with
hunger, and his hands became urgent on her flesh, and
his mouth sought the solace of her willing lips.

Chapter 11

In the morning they rose early. Hadi dressed in the mountain costume of loose white trousers and shirt with a dark vest, and now his transformation was complete. He was a mountain chieftain, completely at home in his surroundings.

Kate dressed more warmly, too, because they would be climbing, and the caves would be cold.

They ate breakfast in Safra's kitchen, good coffee and warm bread. Hadi had arranged for two donkeys the night before, and when they heard the tinkling of the bridles, they thanked and paid Safra and went out again into the deliciously fresh morning air.

A salt-and-pepper-bearded old man sat on a third donkey. He wore a long brown robe, sandals on bare feet, and a faded purple keffiyeh on his head, banded

with a rope of polished metal discs. One of them
caught a beam of early sun, so that it was hard to
look straight at him.

"*Assalaamu aleikum! Sobheh shoma bekhair!*"

"*Waleikum assalaam! Sobheh shoma annoor!*"

Kate was pleased to be able to use the greeting the
family had taught her last night. The man looked at
her with eagle gaze, piercing but benevolent, and
spoke to Hadi in Parvani.

"Your wife speaks our tongue!"

Hadi felt acutely uncomfortable, certain from the
old man's tone that he had guessed they were not
married.

"A few words," he said.

"There is no shame, my son," the old man said,
lifting a hand. "You have told no lie, though you
think you have." And while Hadi was still blinking,
he said, "You wish to visit the Valley."

Kate, who had been paying close attention, caught
the words *al Darreh,* gasped, and demanded, "What
is he saying? Is he talking about the Valley?"

After a brief colloquy, Hadi said, "He will act as
our guide to the Valley if you wish it. But he warns
us that the way is dangerous and that we must trust
him completely. If we obey him, he says, we will be
safe."

Kate stood silent, absently stroking a donkey's soft,
nuzzling nose, gazing between the two men. The old
man returned her gaze with amused understanding,
but said nothing.

"Do you trust him?" she asked at last.

Hadi said, "He is probably the hermit Safra mentioned last night. What we call in the mountains a *Pir,* or Wise One. He will not hurt us. But that doesn't mean he can save us if one of us falls from a pass."

Kate had never felt such a yearning as now entered her heart. It was a deep, powerful conviction that in the Valley she would meet her true fate. That without her knowing it, the Valley was her whole reason for coming to this country. And that if she did not find that fate, she would wander forever seeking.

It wasn't rational. She was probably half crazy with the thin air, or the after-effects of a loving that had made her drunk.

"I want to go."

"It will not be easy, Kate," Hadi warned quietly. "We will be two days walking or in the saddle each way. It is not an outing at a leisure centre. The mountains are dangerous."

"Are you willing to go?"

"I? Yes. But I was raised to it."

"I want to go," she repeated.

It was clear that the old man understood the exchange, for he barked something at Hadi now, who translated, "We must give our word never to tell anyone any part of the way or try to take them there."

A moment later, mounted on the donkey, she set off up the trail after the old man.

At noon on the second day—it felt like a year to Kate—they stopped for lunch on a bleak plateau.

The sun was high and hot. Kate was so stiff and sore, after a day and a half in the saddle and a night trying to sleep on the hardest ground man had ever called bed, that she thought her butt was going to fall off. She walked a little, trying to bring life back into her bruised thighs, and gazed out over the harsh, inhospitable landscape.

They were on a plateau between two mountains. Ahead of her she had her first really unobstructed view of Mount Shir, whose white top glowed in the sunshine. All around, lesser peaks fell away down to the desert plain somewhere in the distance.

At her feet, the ground sloped sharply into a rugged valley. Pine and scrub clung precariously to the slopes, and opposite she could see a herd of goats, hear the distant, faint tinkle of a bell. Kate breathed deep of the freshest air she had ever tasted.

She felt she had been through fire. She would be forever changed by this trip. She had travelled to plenty of exotic locales, but she had never been anywhere so remote. Never walked paths so terrifyingly dangerous. Never stared down to certain death as she inched her way along a narrow ledge between a rock wall and a crevasse with a donkey nuzzling her from behind.

And never had she felt such nervous anticipation as now. The *Pir* had told them they were close. They would reach the Valley in about an hour after lunch.

When she returned to their little camp, Hadi and the old man between them were setting out provisions from the saddlebags. *Naan* from Arsalan's ovens, some goat's cheese, a pot of soup that was still a little warm from last night's campfire, and some sweet halvah formed their meal again.

But it tasted like food for the gods here in the mountains. And Kate was putting away a staggering amount of it at every meal.

She bent painfully to sit on a rock, grunting as her muscles screamed a protest. Hadi smiled at her as he handed her a cup of soup.

She glowed back at him, her heart in her eyes. Going through hardship together was a powerfully bonding experience, it seemed. She thought she would be perfectly happy to go through time locked in this one, blissful moment.

She had learned that she loved him. Last night, lying beside him wrapped in a single blanket that scarcely kept the cold out, she had found it difficult to sleep on the hard ground. Hadi drew her head onto his shoulder and told her a story of the mountains. It was while she was drifting off under the tender voice, soothed as a child is soothed, that Kate had realized the state of her own heart.

He was Cup Companion to a prince, scion of a noble family, who would one day be clan chief. They were a world apart. And worse than that, he had put a guard on his heart and sworn never to love again.

Nothing could come of it. But still, Kate was happier than she could remember ever being.

It wasn't the custom among the mountain folk, she

had discovered, to talk while eating, and here on a mountainside it seemed to make sense.

But when they had finished eating and were packing up the remains of the meal, they chatted together in the way that had developed between them, Hadi interpreting where necessary, but Kate and the *Pir* often understanding each other without his intervention.

When they were ready to mount again, the old man reached into his saddlebag and pulled out two strips of cloth. He gestured, saying something to Hadi, who reacted with sudden anger.

"Na!" he said brusquely, with a chopping gesture of one slim hand.

Kate shivered with surprise.

"What is it? What did he say?"

A dialogue ensued, the old man calm and imperturbable, Hadi increasingly irritated, Kate watching with growing alarm. Hadi was seriously disturbed, but she could tell that the old man had won when Hadi slapped his hand against the saddle, shaking his head.

"What is it?" she whispered.

"We must go back."

Disappointment stabbed her. "Back?" she cried. "Why? What's wrong? Did we take the wrong path?"

"No. But he says that from here we can only go blindfolded."

"Blindfolded!" Kate repeated incredulously. She remembered some of the hair-raising, narrow paths they had taken, where one misstep would have meant death. "But that's impossible!"

"Exactly what I said. But the *Pir* is adamant. He will take us no further without blindfolds."

It might live forever as the most terrifying hour of her life, Kate thought. Perhaps birth had been comparable, though nothing less—and this blind journey wasn't unlike birth. The brutal passage from a familiar world to an unknown one, guided by a stranger, fraught with danger.

They went on foot—the *Pir,* followed by Kate, followed by Hadi. The donkeys, tied together in series, came last, the rein of the lead animal in Hadi's hand.

Kate was startled by the primitiveness of her own animal responses. She had never felt such fear.

When a cool wind blew on them, she sensed a vast emptiness on her left, and her mind conjured up a picture of a drop of hundreds of feet only inches from where she stood. The old man reinforced this image by pressing her shoulder against the rock face on her right, a clear message that she was to keep close against it.

He called the instruction verbally to Hadi, who interpreted for her, but Kate was already plastered against the rock like a slow-moving limpet as she crept along.

Her heart thrummed in her ears, her breathing rasped behind the blindfold.

She didn't know what was worse—the fear of fall-

ing, or later, when the wall on her left closed in and
they went for ten minutes with the defile getting narrower and narrower until the donkeys could scarcely
pass.

It was the longest hour of her life. Sometimes para-
noia swept her, and she was convinced that this was
some kind of conspiracy between the other two, that
they had disappeared, leaving her alone in the middle
of nowhere. Then she would call wildly, and reach
for Hadi. The moments before his hand found hers
were sheer hell.

Sometimes she suspected that she alone was blind-
folded, that Hadi's whispered curses were only stage
dressing. That it was all a game to humiliate her—or
worse.

Sometimes she feared herself. That when the old
man told her to do something she would madly disobey and plunge into the abyss as the price.

She went through every form of mistrust there was,
and somehow overcame them. She sweated buckets,
and when at last the old man stopped and allowed
them to take off the blindfolds, she could see that
Hadi's forehead, too, was drenched.

As a fiercely independent mountain man and Parvani, used to relying on his own wits, she reflected,
it might have been an even worse experience for him
than it had been for her.

For long seconds they gazed at each other, two
comrades who have been through an ordeal together.

Then Hadi laughed and, dropping the reins, wrapped her wordlessly in his arms.

Together they took their bearings. Behind them was the narrow, dark tunnel they had just passed through. It was no more than a tall cleft between two masses of rock. The slightest shift of the living rock, it seemed, might close it.

"I suppose that's where your saint moved the rock. You can see how Genghis Khan would have missed it," Kate observed dryly.

They had been steadily descending through the tunnel. Now they had debouched onto another sloping rocky ledge that curved around the rock face to the right. On the left, beyond the ledge, the ground sloped steeply down to a treed ravine.

A few yards away a waterfall fell from another cleft in the rock to the valley floor. A cluster of trees, their leaves gold and yellow with the approach of autumn, ran down the slope. If this was the Valley, they must be at the very tip of it.

The old man beckoned them on, and they followed him around the concavely curving rock face, and suddenly the vista opened up, and they looked out over the Valley.

It was long and narrow, running generally east and west, Hadi noted, which would give it maximum sun. It looked fertile, with the waterfall forming into a tumbling little river that wound all along its length.

Down below, on a flat plain by the river, was a large, spreading stucco mansion, white and domed, in

the typical Parvani pattern, with a huge walled garden
where trees grew and flowers still bloomed.

Here and there along the river were the ruins of
other, much more modest houses, against which the
largest one might easily have been considered a palace, and a tumbled minaret showed that even here the
devout had not been out of sound of the call to prayer.

They followed the ledge, which became a path and
led them down to the valley floor. On their way a
curious deer watched them and other animals fled into
the brush.

"It must have been abandoned for many years,"
Hadi said. "Look at the wildlife."

There was a peace, a stillness, across the Valley,
and Kate could imagine how this place would live in
the hearts of those who had to leave it.

"Why would they ever have left?" Kate marvelled,
as they made their way down to the little palace.

"It's possible they didn't leave, but died out.
Maybe the population was just too small to be via-
ble."

They arrived at the place at last, and pushed past
a rotting door into the garden. It was thoroughly overgrown, but still the remnants of ancient water channels and a fountain were visible.

They tethered the donkeys and their guide settled
under a tree as Hadi and Kate turned towards the
house.

Chapter 12

It had been a beautiful house once, of perfect proportions. Built around an inner courtyard surrounded by a roofed terrace onto which every room opened. The walls were thick, with arched doorways from room to room, some still with beautiful Barakati lanterns suspended from the pointed arch.

Most rooms had patterned marble floors, with decaying rugs still scattered on top. Intricate mosaic tiling climbed the walls to shoulder height, every room with a different pattern and colouring. Even now, under the twin plagues of time and neglect, the colours and patterns captivated, and the memory of what the house had been was strong.

Arched niches still held the bronze ewers or musical instruments that the owners had placed there.

Heavy tapestry curtains shrouded doorways, caught
back by rotting silk ropes. Low couches lined the
walls, with tables in hand-carved hardwood still in
front, strong with the memory of trays of mint tea.

Two things became evident as they moved from
room to room around the inner courtyard: that the
house and furnishings had been left intact, as if those
who left had intended to return, and that it had suf-
fered no vandalism during the centuries of its abandonment.

In the inner courtyard a square pool about four feet
deep, with a fountain in the centre, stood empty except for a few gallons of stagnant water in the bottom.

Kate asked, "How did they get the water here? Did
they have to carry it in buckets? Or was this built to
catch rain?"

"See those channels?" Hadi pointed to a small ceramic conduit that ran between the pool and the wall
of the courtyard on two sides. "They are functional.
The architect tapped the river or some underground
spring. It's silted up now, that's all."

He moved over to where the channel met the wall,
knelt down, and cleared away dead leaves and earth
to reveal a metal sieve. After a few moments' struggle, he was able to lift it off. Behind it, the channel
was choked with earth, stones, dead leaves, the body
of a small animal.

"A filter further up must have broken, to allow all
this down."

Kate knelt to help him clear it, and tacitly they set to work to restore the water channel together.

It wasn't easy. But the longer they worked, the more determined they became. After the first few minutes, Kate found the labour actually soothing to her aching muscles. It was curiously pleasant, working in the dappled shade of the courtyard, or outside the house, in the perfect silence of the scene, where the old man nodded his understanding of their mission and continued to sit gazing out over the Valley.

They had to make their tools from tree branches, whether the broom to sweep or the rake to clear the long channels, but after a while the water itself lent its help, pushing against the blockage, and a small trickle gave them promise that their goal was within reach.

Kate took a towel and shampoo from her saddlebag and, using a big ceramic bowl from the kitchen, cleaned and scrubbed the walls of the channel and the pool, as well as the fountain that sat in the centre, and then the tiled floor that surrounded it, while Hadi went on working to clear the channel and repair the broken ceramic that lined it.

They lost count of time as they worked, but at last the muck that blocked the channel shifted, and the trickle became a stream, and then suddenly a gush of water came through, swirling with leaves, twigs and earth for a few minutes, then running clear and fresh and delightful.

They stood with their arms around each other, smiling in very human satisfaction as the pool filled with water, and when even the fountain burbled and bubbled in faint memory of its old use, they laughed in delight.

They were filthy from their endeavours, of course, their clothes soaked and stained, their hair caught with twigs, dead leaves and dust.

"Shall we?" Hadi murmured, with a smile straight from childhood, the invitation to adventure. It took them only a moment to strip naked and step into the sun-dappled pool, where, splashing and gasping with the icy coldness of the water, they cleaned themselves.

And then, their skin alive with sensation, their hearts bursting with the simple joy of shared labour and natural beauty, they stood upright in the sparkling pool and looked at each other.

And for the first time, their eyes were fearless.

Wordlessly taking her hand, Hadi pushed their discarded clothes into a little heap in the sunshine, spread their towels over to form a rough mattress, and lay down, drawing Kate down to lie on top of him.

Her skin shivered with the burning touch of his. She lifted herself on her arms and smiled down into his face half-questioningly as his arms gently wrapped her. His hands stroked her back.

"Kate," he said. "I love you."

A tiny shaft of pain pierced her heart, but only so that sweetness could escape; sweetness that flooded through her, rivers of plenty where none had been before. She closed her eyes on a smile, opened them again to look her fill of the warmth in the emerald depths of his gaze.

''I love you,'' she said.

His body leapt against her, strong and demanding, and he slipped his hands into her damp, spiky hair and drew her head down for a sweet, tasting, testing kiss that was in all ways like a first kiss.

As his mouth touched and tasted, his tongue teased, his hands still enclosed her head, lifting and guiding its movement, to bring first her mouth, then her cheek, then her ear, temple and eyes, within reach of his hungry lips.

Her body melted into need as his mouth caressed her, gently, questioningly, as if it was something he had never done before, and he savoured the newness of it.

His hands began to stroke her, with the same questing wonder, as if her body were all new to him. And his touch was also new to her. It was the touch of love, and her heart clenched so tightly in response, and opened so completely, that she thought a human body was not capable of containing so much feeling.

When their bodies joined at last, and moved into the urgent rhythm that was necessity to them both, they looked into each other's eyes and saw tears. Then the anguish of love consumed them, and they cried out their submission to what swept them.

They heard each other's cries, and for each of them

the pleasure and the pain spiralled up and up until it fountained up into the Light, and for one precious moment conquered gravity, to dance in the air in a sparkling, original pattern that was theirs alone.

"Why did you bring us here?" Kate asked the old man later, as they sat around their campfire eating. Darkness had fallen swiftly over the Valley, and now they could hear more clearly the bubbling river, the scurrying of animals.

The *Pir* only smiled.

"And why can't we come back? Why is the whereabouts of the Valley kept secret?"

"'Because the Valley is more than a valley. It is a legend, and must remain one,'" Hadi translated.

"Why?"

"'You have many questions. I can give you an answer, but you may struggle to understand.'"

She nodded.

"'Humankind thrives best when it understands that it has fallen from perfection and strives to return there. On that level, it is not the Valley, but the myth of the Valley, that is significant. There are other such stories in the world, because each generation, and each people, needs one.'"

Kate blinked, trying to take that in. "Camelot," she breathed. "Atlantis. Do you mean they are all the same?"

"'Some individuals will be stirred into remembrance by such stories. Then they will bear in mind at all times that they have one origin and one destination—we come from God and we are going to God. And for such people to strive and work among us is the health of all humanity.'''

"But it's such a waste!" Kate cried.

The old man smiled at her and spoke softly. "'Do you call it a waste that there is a place of beauty in the world?''' Hadi translated, and Kate had no answer.

Next morning, as the sun rose behind the mountains and light crept over the Valley, they walked by the little river, past the ruins of smaller, older houses that told the story of human habitation lasting over centuries.

"I wonder why they left, after so many generations of habitation?" Kate murmured. They were standing over the remains of a very old structure whose buried walls were now no more than raised elevations in the soil. Long ago, no doubt someone had used the stones to build the house nearby, now itself fallen into ruin.

Hadi only shook his head. The stories were too encrusted with myth for the truth of the Valley's abandonment ever to emerge.

They planned their future together as they walked. She could open an office of Drummond and Venables in the Barakat Emirates and supervise all their Eastern business from there. Or Hadi could ask Prince Omar for different responsibilities, which would allow him to live abroad for part of the year.

He talked about Hend, a little. "I was young and full of confidence, and took a terrible risk. When destruction followed, I saw myself as the culprit. I felt that love had led me astray, and I learned to distrust love.

"Until you, Kate, I avoided anyone, anything, who touched my emotions beyond a certain depth. I saw you at the airport and I knew you were a woman who was dangerous to me."

Kate gasped. "Dangerous!"

"To my way of life. I knew that to be involved with you would be to dance too close to the fire."

"How did you know?"

"I cannot say how." Hadi shook his head. "Something stirred in me as you looked at me, something that had not been disturbed for a long time. And when I touched you—I was touched by fire. Even at the very beginning I had to be sure to avoid all physical contact, because when I held you…" His green eyes darkened with feeling. "After I left you at the hotel I knew I should keep away. But my work meant I could not keep away."

Kate laughed. "I almost played into your hands, then, because I phoned Halimah and tried to get another guide."

"How easily we might have run from our destiny," Hadi observed. He kissed her. "I know you did. I should have been relieved when Halimah told me, but instead I was angry. Already I felt possessive about you, though then I didn't see things that way."

"And when did you know that you—"

"That I love you? Yesterday, as we came blind-folded to this place. I had trusted the *Pir* with my life because you wished it, but it did not come easy to me. I did not like being out of control."

"Oh, wasn't it awful! Didn't you want to just rip off the blindfold?"

"Of course. But I had given him my word, and one must always keep one's word with a holy man."

He paused, lost in thought for a moment, and she prompted, "And so?"

Hadi smiled. "The terror I experienced was so fierce it seemed to…to burn up all the false ideas I had surrounded myself with. And in the darkness of the blindfold, I saw the truth of myself. The truth was that Hend's death had turned me into a coward. That to run from you and my feelings for you was not strength, as I believed, but weakness."

Hadi stopped and turned, drawing Kate to face him. Behind them in the distance, he saw the *Pir* waiting with the donkeys to take them back to the world.

"I saw that true strength is not to run from the fire, Kate, but to go through it, and win our heart's desire. And I saw that you were my heart's desire. I have been through the fire, Kate. Have I won you?"

She smiled, and melted against him, and whispered her answer against his hungry lips.

Epilogue

"Hadi, look at this!"

At the urgent breathless tone in her voice, her handsome sheikh put down his own paper and looked up.

"What is it, Kate? What have you seen?"

"Lisbet Raine and Jafar al Hamzeh have been awarded some kind of—of knighthood, or something, by the princes!"

He smiled. "Yes, the King's Heart. It is a very distinguished award."

"This writer is speculating that she did some undercover work of some kind for them…. Hadi! Was *that* what was going on that night?"

"Beloved, I did explain to you that there will be some things about my work for the princes I can never talk to you about, did I not?"

"Yes, but—oh, can't you just give me a hint? I had a feeling it was all an act that night. Was it?"

The smile was never very far from his green eyes nowadays, when he looked at her. "It was an act," he admitted.

"And were you—were you—"

"I was—one of the stage managers."

Kate sighed. "Oh, I'd love to know the whole story. She was so beautiful that night, and I thought—I really believed that you loved her."

He got up and came lazily over to where she sat, in dappled shade beside a rippling fountain. He drew her to her feet and slipped his arms around her, holding her lightly but with the possessiveness that always melted her.

Overhead the sun burned hot, but just here, they were cool enough.

"Yes, Lisbet has a golden beauty quite unlike yours, but my taste is not Jaf's taste. My heart was already given that night, though I didn't know it, to my *peri*-woman," said Sheikh Hadi Farraj ibn Wadil al Ahsheq Durrani. "And I will never get it back."

KISMET
Fiona Brand

To Wi-hiloh,
my friend always.

Dear Reader,

I've always been fascinated by the concept that we have lived not one life, but many, and that through those lives we have been in a relationship with one special person who is so closely tied to us that they can be called a soul mate or a twin soul. This fantasy lies at the very heart of the romance genre, and in the hearts of many people.

The opportunity to write a sheik hero just cried out for a plot that resonated through time, and of course, I couldn't resist. Have you ever read about people who have retained memories of past lives? Or have you ever met someone's gaze for the first time and felt a deep sense of recognition, a shifting sense of déjà vu? This is the theme of my story "Kismet."

I hope you enjoy it!

Happy reading!

Fiona Brand

Chapter 1

The year 1192
The Holy Land

Prince Kalil Husam al Din, General to Saladin and named Al Saqr—The Falcon—by his men, sat his horse, still and solitary, as the sun reached its meridian and burned down with a white-hot intensity that stung his eyes and burned metal into skin.

Heat waves shimmered off stone and sand, distorting the crazed puzzle of hills and gullies even further, sinking and pooling into the maddening illusion of water, so that his nostrils flared and his mouth ached with the need to drink.

A faint breeze stirred the tangled mane of hair that hung, coal-black and loose, about his shoulders as his

narrowed gaze swept the arid terrain. His war stallion
blew softly and dipped his head in the vain hope of
finding a tuft of grass growing from the sandy soil.
The sudden movement broke Kalil's stasis; abruptly
he shifted in the saddle, his normal immunity to the
discomforts of heat and battle, thirst and fatigue gone.
He had already removed his helm; now, with muscles
weary and stiffened from too many hours in the saddle, he drew off his gauntlets and pulled the heavy,
overheated mail hauberk from his shoulders.

A hot gust of wind sent tangled strands of hair
whipping about his face as he secured the garments
on his saddle. Kalil frowned at the added complica-
tion of the rising wind as once again his dark, cold
gaze skimmed the deceptive dips and hollows of the
barren hill country, and touched on the distant
smudge marring the white-blue arc of the sky.

His bare fist tightened on the reins.

The oily curl of smoke was all that remained of his
home. The tiny village had been razed to the ground,
the cool, quiet refuge of palace and gardens looted
and burned by the retreating remnants of the Coeur
de Lion's armies as they cut a bloody swath from the
Holy Land to their last coastal bastion at Acre.

His throat closed against a raw throb of grief and
rage, but with a practiced flick of a mind hardened
by too many battles, too many years spent campaign-
ing at Saladin's side, Kalil dismissed what he couldn't
change with his own strength and intellect, and forced
his attention to the demands of the present.

With a last brooding sweep of the stony puzzle of hills and gullies for the marauding band of soldiers that had pursued them through the night, he wheeled and returned to the ragged column of refugees that were all that remained of his men and his household. Some were mounted on an assortment of horses and camels; most were on foot, carrying children, possessions, and leading livestock, their faces slack with exhaustion and lined with strain. Loaded carts, from which food and drink were being dispensed, were clumped together in the inky well of shade cast by an outcropping of wind-carved basalt. Hooded, jessed falcons flexed their wings desultorily beneath the wearing heat, and his leashed hunting dogs lay sprawled beneath the carts, lean flanks heaving, tongues lolling a startling pink against the burnished browns of their coats and the bleached mosaic of the desert floor.

Kalil's gaze skimmed the rough gathering, his mind automatically inventorying his people even as he hungrily sought out the blaze of colour that was his own dark blue mantle, with his crest, the falcon, emblazoned in gold on the rich cloth.

Despite the grimness of the past hours, a smile tugged at Kalil's mouth when he saw that the mantle, which he'd secured around his wife's shoulders as they'd retreated from the ferocity of the attack, had been discarded against the heat of the day, and his lady's veil had slipped—again. His dark mood dissolved into something close to delight as he surveyed

the guard around Laure: Gan, the whipcord-lean
Frenchman, and his wife, Ila—both of whom were
bonded to his lady, and now to him—and his two
most trusted lieutenants. Sulaimon and Yusef were
both studiously looking anywhere but at Laure, their
backs stiff with offence at the outrageous sight of her
moonlight-pale skin and pretty lips, the ever-errant
tendrils of her dark hair fluttering in the breeze.

Laure's dark green gaze fastened on his, and Kalil's
heart swelled in his chest, threatening to burst with
the strange intensity that gripped him still, despite the
cold demands of the trade agreements that existed between their two houses, the exchange of jewels and
silks for ships and gold, and the practicalities of marrying to secure his lands and his ancient bloodline.

They had met and bedded on the day they were
wed, but from the first he'd been filled with longings
and needs he'd thought long buried by darkness and
blood. He was twenty and eight, already a widower
twice over, and yet he'd been overwhelmed with the
need to converse in a voice not choked by battle and
too often forced to stony silence; to laugh and play
and speak as a simple man and not a blooded warrior
of The Faith. His discomfort had endured through the
entire day of their marriage, the formal completion of
the contracts, the interminable feasting. The few compliments he'd finally managed to choke out had fallen
on deaf ears—his lady hadn't understood a word.

Lady Laure de Vallois sat her horse, exhausted yet
spellbound, as the strange, fierce husband she'd trav-

eled half a world to wed returned from his lonely vigil on the hill. He was garbed for battle still, although he'd shed the heavier metal accoutrements against the burning heat of the day, securing them behind his saddle along with his battle shield and mace. Freed of the constriction of his helm, his hair hung long and tangled and barbaric about his broad shoulders, so that she longed to run her fingers through the dark strands, comb out the knots and bring a smile to the hard, sculpted planes of his face. A fine linen surcoat clung damply to his chest, and a leather belt fastened his dagger and sword at either hip, the hilts glinting with the rich gold of his crest as he rode amongst his people with the muscular, catlike grace of a man who spent much of his life in the saddle. He looked grim and formidable, but despite the long hours of battle and flight, purpose and energy burned from him, igniting a ripple of hope everywhere he passed. She could see why his men loved him, why small children risked the ire of the big bronze stallion he rode to dash up and touch his leg and chatter shyly at him. His people adored him. He was their hope, their falcon—and now hers—as bright and wild as the desert itself.

Her stomach tightened as he approached. His stallion sidled close enough that their legs brushed, and she caught the musky, sweat-sharp scent of his skin, the spicy scent of his hair. Despite the heat and her exhaustion, a fierce wave of longing swamped her.

Lips twitching, he reached over and tugged her veil into place so that she felt smothered all over again.

''For Yusef and Sulaimon,'' he said in careful Arabic, so she could catch each word. A rare smile entered his dark eyes. ''And for me.''

His fingers brushed her cheek through the filmy veil, and on an impulse—one of the many unladylike impulses that had made her difficult to school to the high standards demanded by her powerful family—she caught at his hand and clung, driven by the numbing fear of the past few hours and a sudden desperate need to break through the frustrating, invisible barriers that closed her out of much of her husband's life. She had been used as crudely as a piece of gold by her family to buy influence and trade concessions in these foreign lands—a hedge against the treacherous ebb and flow of politics and the greed of Philip II and the Church—but that cold fact didn't change who she was inside, or the girlish dreams she harboured still. She needed her husband to have at least a modicum of affection for her, and from Kalil she needed…more.

His startled gaze clashed with hers. An awkward silence swelled between them; then his hand turned, gripping hers. His palm was hot, calloused, his grip close to painful as he carried her hand to his chest and pressed it there so she could feel the damp heat of his skin beneath the linen, feel the heavy pounding of his heart. The gesture, in full view of his people, his men, was intimate, unconscionable, and it made her heart race.

"You make me weak as a child," he muttered in Arabic, almost too fast for her to comprehend. *"Kalila."*

A shudder swept her at the low, rough register of his voice, the raw intensity of his expression. She'd studied the language, ever absorbed by learning and the few books that were available to her, determined to become fluent in Arabic. She knew *kalila*. It was a word—and a name—close to her lord's own, meaning dearly loved.

He pressed her palm more deeply into his chest, his pitch-black gaze boring into her. A rough sigh left his lips. *"Tu es mon coeur,"* he said hoarsely, using her language.

You are my heart.

The breath stopped in her lungs. Her eyes closed against a dizzying rush of emotion, and the faintness that had assailed her of late chose that moment to sweep all the strength from her limbs, making her feel as ill as she'd felt on the sea voyage from Nice, so that she clung to her lord as fiercely as she'd clung to the ship's railing.

She heard his sharp demand that Ila attend her, then a flood of Arabic, low and concerned, as he urged his stallion closer still to her mare.

His arm came around her thickening waist, warm and muscled, and she leaned more heavily against him, soaking in the heady, tingling heat of his presence.

"The little falcon is strong within you," he whispered. His breath sifted across her cheek. "Do not be concerned, this will pass."

Her stomach heaved. She swallowed and tore the veil from her mouth, bumping his jaw in the process. His head jerked back, he muttered something low beneath his breath—no doubt a soldier's curse of some kind—but she couldn't allow that to concern her. She was afraid that at any moment she would lose the few sips of water she'd managed to swallow. "You know this by experience?"

Her blunt question was met by a gasp from Ila, who was busily soothing Laure's mare. Laure looked up in time to catch the tail end of a masculine grin, quickly hidden; heard Yusef's outraged chuckle behind her.

"I have not borne a child myself," Kalil admitted, the register of his voice low and tinged with what could only be amusement, "but I am fortunate to have the acquaintance of women who have. This is a situation often discussed within the ranks of married men."

There was another stifled snort from Yusef.

At that moment Kalil's stallion nickered and sidled, nostrils flaring. Kalil's head came up sharply. In the short time they'd been conversing, the breeze had lifted further still, scouring the desolate hills on a low whistling moan, providing cooling relief, but bringing with it a stinging whirl of dust and sand, and masking sounds that might otherwise have been heard.

He issued a series of low commands and sent her a searing glance as warriors spread out in a ring around the women and children. Yusef, Sulaimon and Gan took up defensive positions close by. Servants hurriedly secured livestock, and the falconer worked feverishly to unhood the falcons against the possibility that they would have to be released. Bows were made ready, arrows nocked. The cold slide of metal against metal hissed through the air as swords were unsheathed.

A grunting cry signaled the attack. Hooves thudded, pebbles rattled and the attackers burst into view, coming from two directions, catching them in a pincer action.

Kalil roared a command. The hounds were loosed and streaked, baying, toward the approaching enemy. The falcons shrieked and attempted to launch themselves in a flurry of wings and raking claws, beating at the air in fury as their jesses held them captive.

The clash of metal and the whinnying of horses filled the air as the exhausted men rallied, meeting the attack with a discipline lacking in the thin, desperate remnants of the Lionheart's starving, impoverished army.

Soldiers poured around the tight knot of women and children like hungry dogs wild for the kill, and horses reared in a confusion of dust and noise as men and animals locked in combat. A piercing scream rent

the air. Laure's head snapped around in time to see a
soldier on horseback dragging one of the palace
women along the ground as if she was a bundle of
rags—a pretty girl she recognized as Yusef's daughter. Yusef cried out in agony and spurred forward in
a desperate lunge to reach his child.

A bloodied hand caught at her mount. The mare
reared, whinnying in terror. Hard fingers curled
around Laure's ankle and jerked. She tumbled sideways, awkwardly scrabbling for the reins, the chaos
of battle sliding away as the stony ground rose up to
meet her, pounding all the breath from her lungs. Her
headdress and veil were torn away. Bony fingers sank
into her hair, and white-hot pain flared in her skull as
she was hauled to her knees. She felt the cold burn
of a blade at her throat and rough fingers at her breast
tugging at her amethyst brooch—a birth gift from her
parents and one of the few precious reminders of
home she'd brought with her to this new land. A
strangled cry erupted from deep in her chest. Abruptly
she hit out, knocking her attacker's hands away. A
face leered at her, one-eyed and scarred, a filthy beard
trailing from cheeks burned raw and peeling from the
sun. The blade at her throat was withdrawn and lifted
in a swift arc. For an interminable moment the bright
flash of the sword held her paralyzed, blocking out
the grunts and screams of battle, the snarling fury of
the hounds engaging, the sickening stench of death.

A blood-chilling roar cut through the odd stasis that
held her. A shadow fell over her attacker, silver

scythed the air, and he tumbled, as lifeless as a broken doll, body in one direction, head in the other.

Iron-hard hooves lashed at the ground, dust spewed into the air and the sweating bronze flanks of Kalil's stallion swept close enough that her heart should have leapt with fear, but she remained kneeling, frozen, her mind still locked on the gleam of the blade that had been about to behead her, the shock of watching the soldier's own head severed from his body, the sensation of his fingers dragging through her hair as he fell.

A lean hand gripped her upper arm, hauling her to her feet. Kalil's fierce gaze fastened on hers. His voice was rough and urgent—incomprehensible—his hold strong as he leaned lower still, intending, she realized, to sweep her up onto the horse. His arm curled around her waist, when abruptly the fighting surged around them. A staff caught him in the back, and he pitched forward, crashing to the ground beside her as his warhorse screamed and reared, striking out with his hooves. Kalil's sword landed a scant distance from her, glittering silver striated with the dark gleam of blood.

Kalil gained his feet almost immediately, as lithe and muscular as a lion, but he was rapidly surrounded by three of the attackers, with only a mace in his hand and his shield warding off blows in the other. The mace was deadly enough, but lacked the reach of a sword. Through the haze of numbness that still held

Laure, a part of her registered that he *needed* his sword.

Her fingers closed on the warm metal of the hilt, slick with blood and coated in gritty dust, and bile rose in her throat. For a split second everything in her rejected the incomprehensible whirl of battle, the violence and the savagery.

One of the soldiers went down beneath the mace, but as he fell, Kalil took another blow to the back and stumbled, correcting almost immediately to knock the crude club from the hand of his opponent. The soldier howled and clutched at his hand, and Laure felt the brief impact of Kalil's gaze as he spun to engage the hissing swing of a sword. As he parried the blow, the soldier with the injured hand darted, snake-quick, beneath Kalil's reach, snatched the dagger that hung from her lord's hip and, as Kalil pivoted on the balls of his feet to meet this new threat, plunged it deep into his chest.

For an endless moment time seemed to stand still, the clamour muffled and distant, then an eerie keening pierced the roar of battle, and Laure realized the sound had burst from her own throat. The sword dropped, no longer important, as she stumbled over bodies and weapons, heedless of the skirmishing as Sulaimon and Yusef cut the remaining soldiers around Kalil down as if they were clumps of grass. She dropped beside Kalil, dry sobs tearing from her chest, her hair a wild tangle as she framed his face with her hands. His dark eyes flickered, locked with hers, still bright and fierce. She thought he whispered, *"Kalila."* Then the light slid from his eyes, and his face went blank.

For long seconds Laure couldn't move, frozen beneath the lash of this new shock.

"Non," she said hoarsely, shaking her head. *"Non!"*

This was *not* possible. She wouldn't allow it to be possible. She tried to remember the Arabic that would make him open his eyes, get up, *move,* but now, when she needed the words the most, her mind was incapable of remembering anything but her native tongue.

She shook his shoulders, barely able to move his heavy form as she exhorted him to get up, her throat closing thickly over the words so that they came out as little more than a hoarse whisper.

A hand closed over her shoulder, the grip like iron. She flinched, jerked away from the alien touch, then recognized Yusef.

"Non," she muttered again, clinging to Kalil's shoulders, but Yusef's grip was relentless as he pulled her away.

With a fierceness and strength she hadn't known she possessed—had never had to possess in the comfort and wealth of her life—Laure lunged free and sprawled on her hands and knees beside her lord. Her hands wound in his garments as she clung to him and pressed against the familiar warmth of his big body. Her fingers wrapped in the thick black mane of his hair, brushed the hot satiny skin of his neck. Her

hands closed around the dagger. She tried to pull it
from his chest; it wouldn't move. Swallowing, gritting
her teeth, she knelt and wrapped both hands around
the slippery hilt and wrenched with all her strength
until it came free.

Grief exploded inside her. *Too late.*

If she'd had the courage to take up his sword and
throw it to him, or if she'd somehow distracted just
one of those soldiers, he would be alive now. She
knew it, and the knowledge seared her. Kalil was a
warrior seasoned by years of war, one of Saladin's
fiercest, most successful generals. In single combat
she knew him to be unbeaten. He had saved her life
just minutes ago. He had stayed with her, protecting
her, *distracted* by her, when he should have been
fighting with the support of his men. All she'd had to
do was find enough courage to help him.

Anguish swept her, an icy wave that rippled the
length of her spine. When he had needed her most,
she had failed him.

This time, when Yusef hauled her up and away
from Kalil, his bruising hold brooked no argument.
The dagger half slipped from her grasp, and in a wild
panic to retain some physical link with her husband,
she clutched at the weapon that had killed him, the
knife he had always carried with him and used to slice
his meat…and hers.

Another shuddering wave of grief and guilt washed
through her, so that she shivered, chilled, despite the
heavy heat of the noonday sun. She felt the burn of

the blade biting into her palm, a trickle of wetness as her blood mingled with Kalil's as she was dragged unceremoniously toward the milling, frightened horses; then she was lifted and dumped onto the back of Yusef's sweating stallion.

Her fingers clutched at the coarse hair of the horse's mane as she fought to keep both her balance and her grip on the dagger. The slice in her palm throbbed and stung, but she ignored it. It was only a cut; she would live.

Gan stumbled forward to take control of the horse, one arm bandaged tightly across his chest. Ila hurried toward her, dark hair wild, clothing ripped and smeared with blood, pale blue eyes blank with shock. Laure submitted to Ila's perfunctory examination, but when the other woman tried to take the dagger, she resisted, keeping it close.

Ila tore a strip of cloth from her own hem and bandaged the seeping cut, all the while talking, her voice low and jerky, her gaze darting frequently toward her husband, as if reassuring herself that he was still alive.

When Ila was finished, Laure wrapped one arm around her belly in a gesture as old as time, protecting the child within. A tiny flutter shimmered deep inside her as the baby kicked, and grief slammed into her like a black wave. She tipped her head back and stared, half-blinded by tears, at the falcons wheeling above. Someone must have loosed them, and she realized on a beat of cold that Sulaimon would have done so. He had cared for the fierce birds with love and steady devotion, but the falcons had belonged to Kalil.

The fingers of one hand automatically found her brooch, which still dangled from a torn strip of her bodice. Her thumb rubbed across the large, faceted amethyst in an absent, soothing gesture carried over from childhood. The wind tugged at her hair, blew coldly across her wet cheeks, and this time when the faintness and nausea came, she didn't fight. As her legs lost their tenuous grip on the horse's flanks and the harsh hills and burning sky whirled into darkness, she remembered that she had never told Kalil she loved him.

Pain lanced coldly in her chest. Somehow, of all the things she had failed to do, that seemed the worst.

Chapter 2

Present day
Ransome, New Zealand

Laine Elizabeth Abernathy sat bolt upright in bed, a stark wave of grief and longing anchoring the dream in her mind with such clarity that for long seconds she floundered, caught somewhere in a precarious no-man's-land, grasping at reality.

The alien echo of a word—no, a *name*—still vibrated in the air.

Kalil.

She blinked, and the familiarity of her room registered, pushing back the shock of blood and death, the hot scents of dust and sweating horses.

A morepork hooted from somewhere within the

deep, shadowy reaches of the gnarled pohutukawa tree that shaded her back lawn, the noise striking an unnerving note after the strangeness of the dream.

Shoving covers back, she stumbled from the tangle of her bed, ignoring the indignant yowl of the neighbour's cat, a weighty ginger fur ball called Hector.

Hector had moved in with her over a year ago and had flatly refused to leave, despite a number of one-sided conversations she'd had with him, all involving the word *scat*. Much as she liked cats, now that she was divorced and living on her own, owning one seemed the final insult.

She was already a librarian *and* an Abernathy, having resurrected her honourable but staid maiden name. In the small town of Ransome, with its history of flamboyant, risk-taking, ill-fated Ransomes—of which family she was now the sole survivor—that added up to two strikes against her. Being labeled a cat-obsessed spinster was not going to happen.

She fumbled for the lamp switch, wincing as the cut on her palm throbbed. With a mild curse that, if either of her parents had been alive to hear it, would have earned her an instant scolding despite the fact that she was thirty-two years of age, Laine sat down on the side of the rumpled bed, squinted at the clock and sighed. Five-thirty. Too early to get up, too late to go back to sleep. If she was a serial killer, right about now she'd be considering going out on a rampage. The small town of Ransome might never recover.

Smothering a yawn, she peered at the cut, which she'd sustained the previous day while cleaning out her deceased great-aunt Hannah Ransome's attic. The slice from a dagger, which had tumbled out of a secret compartment in an old leather-bound volume, wasn't that deep, but it seemed to be getting infected.

Gingerly she flexed her fingers, resolving to get antibiotics if the cut got worse, then lifted the dagger from the bedside table where she'd placed it the previous evening, along with the book itself and the exquisite amethyst brooch that had also been contained in the secret compartment. The book was old enough to be intriguing, and the brooch was even more so, with its pretty jewel and the mystery of a crest and initials scored into the gold, but it was the dagger that commanded her attention. The chill of the metal burned into her palm, and she felt again the unnerving, shifting sensation, the tightening at the base of her spine that she'd felt when she'd first opened the book and found the secret compartment.

The fact that she felt any kind of emotional response to any of the objects in Hannah's attic was odd in itself. Every second of sorting through her aunt's stored booty had been loaded with the foreign and the exotic, much as Hannah's life had been. If there was any country on the planet that Hannah hadn't trekked or climbed or flown over, and then proceeded to buy a souvenir from, Laine would personally eat every book in Ransome's library.

After having cleaned out thirty boxes of dusty junk

and carting everything to a secondhand dealer, and with half that much again still to deal with by the end of the weekend, Laine was heartily sick of "treasure," but the mystery of the dagger and the brooch, hidden together in the musty old book, had pulled at her.

At first she'd thought the dagger was just another cheap, rusted ornament, but the metal was so heavy she'd been curious enough to wash it. The crumbly brown substance, which she had decided must be blood, had dissolved, leaving the blade smooth and glittering in the morning light. It was constructed of solid silver, with a falcon worked into the hilt in gold—not an ornamental piece so much as the weapon of some long-ago desert warrior, worn at the grip, the inlaid falcon rubbed smooth, as if it had been used on a daily basis.

Picking up the brooch, she studied the initials, LdV, and the crest, both of which were still clear enough to make out. A ripple of excitement burst through her that she might actually be able to trace the origins and the age of the brooch. The sensible thing would be to assume the brooch and the dagger had been produced in recent times, but Laine didn't think so. The brooch was a beautifully worked piece, heavy and strong, designed to fasten a cloak or a wrap. Aside from the fact that there were no jeweler's marks evident, something about the stark design suggested a more primitive time. She was no expert on ancient jewelry, but she was willing to bet that the brooch was at least several hundred years old.

The implications of her find, the huge span of years that had passed since the people who had owned and treasured the dagger and the brooch had lived, made her heart thump. She adored books and history, but these objects reached beyond the impersonal chronicling of events. There was an intimacy inherent in both items, their everyday use so obvious that she could almost see a sun-browned hand sheath the dagger, then lift the brooch to his lady's cloak to secure the heavy folds of silk....

The clarity of the vision made her blink. Abruptly she set the items back down on her bedside table, startled to see that a good fifteen minutes had passed while she'd sat holding the brooch, daydreaming. The tantalizing mystery of the people the antiquities had originally belonged to intrigued her, maybe too much. But the way the two objects had been kept, nestled together down through the centuries, one a blatant symbol of male power, the other gentler, softer, definitely feminine, suggested that the people they had belonged to had been intimately linked.

Not that she would ever know. The items would probably remain a mystery, as mysterious as the sheik who had shocked the small community of Ransome by buying Aunt Hannah's island and taking up residence there.

No one had seen much of the exotic and wealthy Sheik of Jahir, and speculation was rife, although in

Laine's book he was a definite letdown in the fantasy department. He was small, neat and fifty-plus, with a pencil moustache, and the only heart that was pumping any faster over him was Mavis Appleby's. And that only happened to be so because Mavis had just struggled free of the entanglement of her fourth marriage and was now on the lookout for husband number five.

Now, the sheik's groom...

She'd glimpsed him around town a few times, once while he was checking his horse float, wearing nothing more than jeans and short riding boots, his nicely muscled chest bare—giving all the women heart attacks and sending the men hanging around the local Town and Country store into deep depression.

Laine sighed, allowing herself to dream a little, but only a little. She was in her thirties, with a politely uneventful and unsuccessful marriage behind her, a master's degree in English and history, and a doctorate in dreaming. Lately she'd even done a little dreaming about the sheik's hired hand—intensely erotic, moody dreams that had confused her and stuck with her through the day because she wasn't in the habit of dreaming about men, no matter how good-looking. She'd had enough years of disappointment in her marriage to be pragmatic. She was no stunner and never would be, and if the sheik's hired hand even looked her way, she would fall over herself with surprise. He was exciting, and exciting was the last thing she was. Dreaming and fantasies aside, she was…cautious.

Hector brushed past her and landed on the floor with a thud. He picked his way disdainfully to the door, planted his furry butt and eyed her with an expression of great patience. He began to purr, the rumble sounding like a small lawn mower starting up.

Reluctantly Laine got to her feet and reached for her dressing gown. "Sucking up now?" she muttered. "Breakfast, that's what you want. All I am is a convenient cat hotel."

Which reminded her that, aside from going to work today, her prime purpose in life was to buy Hector cat food.

Hector trotted after her as she headed for the bathroom.

"No," she said sternly, eyeballing Hector as he made a dive for the bathroom door. "You are definitely not coming into the bathroom. I have to have some privacy in my life."

Exasperated, she eased the door closed, careful not to catch Hector's whiskers.

She had to stop talking to the cat; it was only encouraging him.

Ransome's sidewalk baked quietly in the summer noonday heat as Laine stepped into the hushed shadows of the local Town and Country store and stood for a moment, breathing in the wholesome scents of leather and feed and linseed oil, and adjusting to the

dimness after the blast-furnace heat and glare outside.
As she made her solitary purchase, she chatted ami-
ably with Liz Baker, who still looked the same sixty-
ish age she'd looked when Laine had been a teenager,
and who, according to local legend, had served behind
the counter forever.

Liz made a comment about the weather heading
their way and how much they needed the rain. Laine
made a polite rejoinder as she lifted the box of cat
biscuits, turned briskly away and collided with the
solid barrier of a broad, very male chest. Her purse
flew in one direction, the cat biscuits in the other. She
had a confused impression of bronzed skin, startled
dark eyes, the gleam of coal-black hair and the musky
scent of hot male skin; then hard fingers closed
around her upper arms as he steadied her.

"Are you okay?"

The low demand sent a small shock through her,
not least because she'd expected a foreign accent. The
man she'd walked into was the sheik's groom. His
voice *was* foreign, but not in the way she'd expected.
He had an American accent, albeit with a tantalizing
European intonation that denoted someone who had
traveled a great deal.

She muttered an automatic reply as she stepped
back, her heart pounding too fast as she searched
around for her purse, then bent to snag the leather
strap. When she straightened, he had her cat biscuits
in his hand.

"You might need these."

She caught the edge of a male grin. *Hector's cat biscuits*. She could feel herself blushing as she muttered a thank-you.

Oh, yeah, what would she do without a week's supply of Kitty Kat Chews?

As she walked toward the door, Laine pulled in a deep breath and let it out slowly. Her pulse was still hammering, and she was having trouble steadying her breathing. All she wanted to do was get back to the library and sit in a cool, quiet corner for a few minutes while she got her composure back.

The fact that her composure was so badly dented after such a minor incident was alarming. It wasn't as if she was in imminent danger of being asked out on a date, and he wasn't exactly a wild animal on the prowl. There was also the very obvious fact that she wasn't the kind of woman who attracted a lustful male response, which had always suited her. In her opinion, sex was badly overrated. If she never had sex for the rest of her life—she refused to call it "making love," because that was the lie of the century—she wasn't going to cry about it.

Unfortunately, as much as she wanted to avoid the whole issue of sex and sexual attraction, the uncomfortable problem was that the sheik's hired hand turned her on.

She had dreamed about him a number of times— too many times to dismiss—intense, disturbing dreams that had left her wrung out, her pillow damp with tears. She was almost certain he had starred in the dream that had catapulted her out of sleep this morning. After years of a marriage that had been more comfortable than exciting, then the limbo of separation and divorce, the sharp, hot stab of arousal was intrusive and scary. After eight years with Robert, she didn't know if she wanted to venture into the murky waters of relationships ever again.

She was still a dreamer—she couldn't see that ever changing—but when it came to romance, she had a cynical edge now. And this sneak attack of her hormones was *definitely* no romantic dream.

Sheik Xavier Kalil al Jahir watched Ransome's prim librarian walk through the dim shadows of the store and out into the hot glare of the dusty street, his gaze intent.

Hannah's niece.

Awareness clenched his belly muscles, and his groin warmed and tightened.

That was new, he thought dispassionately.

He'd been celibate for more years than he cared to count, ever since his wife had become seriously ill. Karen had died over eighteen months ago, but since her death, he hadn't felt the need for even the most basic of relationships.

He didn't want a relationship now. After five years of sharing Karen's battle with leukemia, he'd needed to get away from his business, his home and his family—all the ties that still held him to Karen and her death. All he'd wanted was the company of his horses, the confirmation of sun and sweat and hard physical work, and isolation, lots of isolation.

Apart from his need for solitude, common sense told him to leave the local women alone, because he didn't plan on living here permanently. This island was a retreat from all the pressures of his life, and one of those was the pressure to resume a healthy sex life, to marry again to ensure that his ancient bloodline continued.

Not that Jahir's bloodline was about to disappear from the face of the earth any time soon, he thought wryly as he took his wallet from his pocket to pay for the feed and fertilizer he'd ordered. He had three sisters with children, plus a raft of uncles and aunts and cousins. The island of Jahir was overrun with an embarrassingly long list of successors to the sheikdom, aged from six months to eighty years. If he failed to produce an heir, only the purists would lament that fact.

The voice of the woman behind the counter registered. He forced his attention back to the list of items he needed, but for the first time in the past month his mind wasn't on horses or farming.

The woman behind the counter chatted and smiled as she took care of his purchases. Kalil kept his answers brief, careful not to allow the conversation to traverse into any kind of intimacy. He valued his privacy. At the moment, he needed it—the hollow emptiness of everything that had gone wrong in his life was still too vivid and raw for him to want the pres-

sures of new friendships and a social life. He was
aware that the locals had decided that his uncle, who
spoke little English, was the sheik, which suited him.
They would find out who he was soon enough.

As he walked out into the sunshine and began loading sacks of feed onto the trailer that was coupled to
the rear of the Range Rover, he was aware that the
shady wooden building that housed the library and
council offices was directly across the street. He knew
he wouldn't be celibate forever; before Karen's illness
he'd had a normal, healthy sex drive. But of all the
women he'd met since his wife's death, he hadn't
expected Laine Abernathy to be the one to knock him
off balance.

When Laine walked back into the dim confines of
the library, her assistant, Ellen, was stationed at the
window. Ellen was nineteen going on thirty, with
short, spiky blond hair, three rings stuck above one
eyebrow, a tiny bead glinting to one side of her nose
and a barbell stuck through her navel. Today she was
wearing a long, filmy orange skirt that rode low on
her hips, and a lime-green crop top that left her brown
midriff bare. A radical fashion statement for the small
town of Ransome.

"Did you see him?"

Laine stowed her purse and cat biscuits in the bottom drawer of her desk, only too aware of whom
Ellen was referring to. "Who?"

Ellen rolled her eyes. "You know. *Him.* The guy

who works for the sheik.'' She folded her arms across her chest and leaned on the sash window, eyes sleepily narrowed as she continued to watch the Town and Country store. ''Oh boy, he can put his shoes under my bed any time.''

''He's probably married, with eight kids.''

Ellen grinned, her gaze still locked on the action across the street. ''He doesn't wear a ring. I checked.''

Laine joined her at the window. ''A lot of men don't wear wedding rings.'' Her husband hadn't.

The groom was loading supplies. Muscles bunched and rippled beneath the bronzed skin of his back, and sweat gleamed in the deep groove of his spine as he hefted sacks of feed from the pallet that sat in the inky shade of the store's overhang and tossed them onto a trailer. When he was finished, he dusted his hands off on his jeans, then went down on his haunches to check the trailer coupling. Faded denim stretched across his tight, muscular butt.

Ellen grinned and fanned herself. ''I've seen married, and *that* definitely doesn't look married.'' She leaned forward, squinting. ''Mmmm…he's a little older, but that's cool. Has he got an earring? I forgot to look. I was too busy checking out his chest.'' She sighed. ''*Please* tell me he's got an earring.''

Laine could feel herself growing warm all over again. She'd gotten a good look at his face *and* his chest. ''I didn't notice an earring.''

"That's okay. I can get turned on without body piercing."

An image of Ellen's current boyfriend popped into Laine's head. Harvey was clean-cut; he usually wore a shirt and tie, and pressed slacks. He drove an aging Fiat and worked in the local bank. "Just as well, since Harvey doesn't have any piercings."

Ellen gave her a sideways look. "Oh, yes, he does."

Laine closed her eyes briefly. It figured. Never trust a guy driving a foreign car—even if it was a four-door and on its last legs. "Don't tell me where."

Ellen shrugged. "It's no big deal. Ever since he slept with Molly Jones, the whole town's known where Harvey's pierced."

The Range Rover pulled away from the kerb, revealing the skinny, potbellied form of Silas Baker—the owner of the Town and Country, and a member of the district council. Now that there was nothing to obstruct his view, he peered across the road, eyeballing Ellen, the light of battle in his eyes.

Ellen gave Silas the finger.

Laine lifted a brow. "Keep doing that and your job's going straight down the toilet. Silas co-signs your paycheck."

"Beady-eyed old turkey." Ellen gave Silas the finger again, just in case he'd missed it the first time. "Every time I go over there, he stares at me like I just landed from Mars. This town should get a life." She marched over to the returns desk, picked up an armload of books and thumped them down beside the tray of cards. "Come to think of it," she said quietly, "*you* should get a life." Her gaze flicked over Laine's skirt and blouse. "Seriously, you've got a great figure and fabulous hair. I'll lend you some clothes. You could get laid like *that.*" She snapped her fingers. "What you need is an affair, a hot one-night stand."

Laine barely registered Ellen's offer of sexy clothes, or the concept of a one-night stand, which was so utterly alien to her that she had never considered it, even in joking. Her whole being was focused on the concept of getting a life.

She considered that she had a very good life now.

She was independent, successful in her career and she owned her own home. Her parents' and Hannah's legacies had left her comfortably well-off, so much so that she didn't have to work if she didn't want to. She didn't date, but apart from occasional loneliness, she hadn't seen that as a problem. Now she could feel the lack in herself of the vital spark that Ellen had in abundance—that her aunt had had until the day she'd died.

She wasn't old, but she didn't feel young, either. Laine couldn't remember ever feeling young, or carefree. She'd always studied hard, and had found it difficult to play as a child, preferring books to dolls. She'd only ever dated and made love with the man she'd ended up marrying. She'd met Robert Howell at the university where he now lectured, and had stayed married to him until she'd found out that one of the reasons their marriage was so uneventful was that Robert hadn't needed sexual adventure at home because he'd satisfied that particular appetite by having a string of affairs with faculty members and his students. Her lack of outrage when she'd found out had prompted her to take a long-overdue look at their relationship. They hadn't so much been married as flatted together.

She was thirty-two, and even though she'd been married and divorced, in some ways her marriage had left her untouched. She had never had an orgasm. She knew that some women just didn't, but to Laine, that seemed symptomatic of her life—as hard as she'd tried, she'd just never managed to hit the highs.

She sat down at her desk and studied the pile of returned books, for the first time in her life weary of books and the cool, cloistered stillness of the library that had always been her sanctuary. She wanted more.

She felt unsettled—subtly dissatisfied with every aspect of the life she'd so carefully constructed—but she didn't have the first clue about what it was exactly that she wanted, or how to go about getting it.

"I got myself a life once," she said, picking up a book and forcing herself to search for the card. She found the card and slipped it into the pocket before slapping the book closed with more force than was required. "It sucked."

Chapter 3

Laine carted another box of junk down the dilapidated front stairs of Hannah's house and loaded it into the rear of her station wagon, wincing as the bandaged cut on her hand throbbed.

A brisk wind gusted in off the sea, tugging strands of hair loose from her knot as she closed the rear door of the wagon on an almost full load. She'd already made two trips across the causeway into town to take boxes of junk to the secondhand dealer—this would be her last load of the day. Dusting her hands off on her jeans, she strode back into the house, which had a melancholy air now that most of the furniture had gone.

It was an old colonial farmhouse that was slated for demolition...if it didn't fall down first. It had been built by the founder of the town of Ransome, Charles Ransome, a colourful early settler who was rumoured to have made his fortune gambling. He'd fathered a brood of Ransomes, had drunk and womanized himself half to death, then finished the job by riding one of his half-wild stallions, which had then proceeded to throw him over a cliff into the sea below.

She climbed the narrow stairs to the attic, ducked down to squeeze through the tiny door and sighed at the jumble she still had to sort through by the end of the weekend. When Aunt Hannah had sold the island to the sheik, she'd done so with the provision that she would live out her life in the house, which she'd done. Hannah had died six months ago, and in that time, Laine had sorted out the tangle of Hannah's affairs and cleared most of the furniture from the house. However, after the last storm, the sheik had notified her through his solicitors that the house had been condemned and had to come down. She'd had a month to finish clearing it out, and the deadline was Monday.

Sun shafted intermittently through the attic windows as she packed a stack of dusty notebooks that turned out to be Hannah's travel journals into a box. Half an hour later, Laine checked her watch, saw that it was past three and pushed herself up from her kneeling position on the floor.

Her head spun as she straightened. Her hand shot out, reaching for the support of the wall, and pain jolted the length of her arm. She stood for long seconds, cradling her hand and holding her breath, until the throbbing in her palm and the faint dizziness subsided.

She'd felt tired and a little off-colour when she'd gotten up this morning, but she'd put that down to ovulation. She'd always been sensitive to the cycles of her body, and they were as regular as clockwork—actually, as regular as the lunar cycle. When the moon was full, werewolves might howl and witches might ride their broomsticks. She ovulated. But now she felt worse than just a little bit off-colour, as if she was coming down with a dose of the flu.

Picking her way around trunks and tea chests to the open sash window, she examined her bandaged hand and flexed her fingers. She frowned at their stiffness, which she hadn't paid much attention to before, because she'd thought it was simply the bandage restraining movement, but now she noted a pinkish tinge around the base of her fingers. Despite all her care, she had an infection. When she got home, she would have to make an after-hours appointment with Janice to get some antibiotics.

Movement outside the window drew her eye. The day was gloomy now, sun and sky almost completely blotted out by heavy cloud. Sunlight penetrated the murky layer in places, shafting into the sea and giving the expanse of ocean a leaden cast. There was a man on horseback down on the beach, the horse an unusual dusty bronze that gleamed richly in the dull light. Her breath caught in her throat when she saw who was riding the horse. An electric sense of recognition lifted all the hairs at her nape, the sensation so sharp and immediate that for a dizzying moment she was rocked by the certainty that she had seen the sheik's groom on horseback before, even though she knew she never had. She had seen him in town a number of times, and once on the island she'd driven past him on the short section of road that stretched from the island causeway to the fork of Hannah's drive. She knew he was responsible for the expensive and beautiful Arabian horses she occasionally glimpsed from the attic window, but she had never actually *seen* him with the horses.

At that moment his head came up. His gaze fastened on hers across the width of the windswept beach and she froze, her heart thumping hard in her chest. On horseback, wearing a sleeveless T-shirt and jeans, he looked more primitive than civilized. His hair was loose and whipped into a rough tangle by the wind, and even from this distance, the strong planes of his face, his wide mouth and tough jaw, were clearly visible. Her stomach clenched. The sense of recognition, the wild conviction that she had seen him this way before, hit again, confusing her even further.

He lifted his hand, acknowledging that he'd seen her, and spurred the horse onto the bank bordering the front lawn, as if he was about to dismount and walk into the house. She gripped the window ledge, ignoring the hot flash of pain in her hand. This wasn't the first time she'd seen him, or he her, but other than the incident in town yesterday, this was the first time either of them had voluntarily acknowledged the contact.

Instead of dismounting, he reined in and turned to look at the sea. Moments later he urged his horse down the bank and back along the beach. As she watched him ride away, an odd sense of melancholy gripped Laine.

Releasing her hold on the window frame, she let out a breath. Okay, reality check. She wasn't the heroine of some romantic Valentino-type movie; she was a small-town librarian who was attracted to a man who was way out of her reach.

Unfortunately, baldly acknowledging her problem didn't make it go away. The blood was still pounding through her veins, and she was suddenly very aware of all the most female parts of her body.

For the first time in her life, against all the odds, she *wanted* a man.

Years ago she'd thought she wanted Robert, but she'd never felt like this, as if some inner part of her was unraveling. It was crazy. Maybe the way she was feeling was all wrapped up with the fact that she was ovulating and her hormones had gone haywire? Maybe the odd, intense dreams she'd been having had affected her at some subliminal level? Or maybe she'd landed slap in the middle of an early midlife crisis?

Scary as the reasons were, she was beginning not to care about why this one particular man could upset her with barely a glance. Despite the fact that the man on horseback was a stranger—a fantasy—she wanted to know what it felt like to be close to him. She already knew what he smelled like, that his skin was hot and satiny, that the muscles beneath were hard packed. Now she wanted more. She wanted his tongue in her mouth, his hands on her breasts, then gripping her bottom. And just once, she wanted to sleep with him, to stretch and rub herself against the rougher male textures of his skin, and soak in his wonderful hot, musky scent; to wallow in the sheer animal comfort of being so close to him.

With a sharp intake of breath she turned from the window and caught sight of her reflection in an antique mirror that was leaning against the wall. On impulse, she walked to the mirror, unbuttoned her shirt and let it drop from her shoulders.

The checked cotton fell away to reveal the lacy white bra beneath. Despite the dust coating the mottled glass, she could see the hard points of her nipples and the dusky shadows of her areolas through the filmy material. Somehow, in her state of arousal, that part of her, which she'd always ignored or been embarrassed by, now seemed unbearably erotic. In the half-light of Hannah's attic, the feminine shape of her body, the pearly sheen of her skin, seemed mysterious and exotic instead of ordinary.

Awkwardly, because of the pain in her hand, she drew the pins from her hair and let them scatter on the floor. The heavy coil unwound and fell down her back, so long that it reached past her hips. With her shirt off and her hair loose, the woman in the mirror looked...younger, and nothing like Ransome's staid, boring librarian. She hugged her arms around her breasts in an instinctive, protective gesture and shuddered at the acute sensitivity of her skin.

The wind rose on a grumbling rumble of thunder, sending a flurry of humid air through the attic and a scattering of rain against the windowpanes. Another shiver coursed through her, this one leaving her feeling distinctly feverish.

What was she doing? Expelling a disgusted breath, Laine snagged her shirt and fastened it. Her hand ached and throbbed with every small movement, but she got the job done. Attempting to wind her hair back into its coil was a different matter. After the fifth attempt, she gave up on the hairpins and simply wound her hair into a rope and knotted it at her nape, hoping it would hold.

She was going to drive straight to the doctor's house when she got off the island. She felt awful, her head swimmy, her skin ultrasensitive. She hadn't done nearly as much packing as she'd wanted, but she was leaving now—deadline or no deadline. If the sheik wanted to knock the house down before she was finished, then that was just too bad.

Kal reined in as he rounded the curve of the bay and turned the big stallion back in the direction of the old Ransome house. The horse jibbed at the abrupt change, intent on regaining the sanctuary of his stable before the rain set in.

Kal ran a soothing hand over the horse's muscular neck as he brooded on the distant view of Hannah's old wreck of a house.

He should have gone in and introduced himself to Laine Abernathy. He'd ridden here for the express purpose of seeing whether or not she was working in the house today; then he'd lost his nerve.

A scattering of rain hit his face. He lifted his head, savouring the bite of the wind, the chill edge of the storm to come. His gaze locked on the dark outline of the attic window. He didn't know what to do about his attraction to Laine or the strange, intense emotions that had gripped him so powerfully he'd slept only in snatches last night.

A gust of wind tugged at his hair, so that it whipped around his shoulders. His gaze narrowed against small, stinging pellets of rain, but he ignored the discomfort. In a sense, he'd known Laine for years, because Hannah had spoken about her niece and shown him snapshots. He knew that she had been married and was now divorced, and since he'd moved to the island he'd learned that the faded snapshots hadn't done her any kind of justice. The photos had shown a mildly attractive woman who wasn't inclined to do anything as frivolous as smile for the camera, but in person her colouring was striking—her skin moon-light-pale and so fine it looked like alabaster, her eyes an unusual clear, deep green. The clothes she wore were plain, bordering on masculine, but the dark, businesslike colours and straight lines didn't hide the fact that her slim figure was curvy in all the right places, and her hair... It was long and midnight-dark, rich and satiny. He'd never seen it down, not even in photos. He wondered if anyone ever had. Apparently she slept with it coiled in that tight knot.

She barely spoke. Maybe that was what riveted him about her. The rest of the women in the small town of Ransome were chatty and personable and so openly curious about him that he kept his visits to town to a minimum. In contrast, Laine Abernathy was a virtual hermit.

A wry smile tugged at the grim line of his mouth as he gave in to the horse's impatient snort and let him amble back in the direction of the stable. He ought to know a hermit when he saw one; he was practically one himself.

A hermit, but definitely not a monk.

Chapter 4

The wind buffeted Laine as she loaded Hannah's
journals into the car, whipping at her hair so that
strands worked loose from her makeshift knot and
tangled across her face. The sea was grey and turgid
with whitecaps, the air filled with a thick misty drizzle
that blotted out the view and made her stomach sink.
A storm had been predicted, but this was looking suspiciously like cyclone weather.

The winding, rutted drive to the causeway took no
more than a few minutes to negotiate. When the narrow stretch of water separating Ransome Island from
the village of Ransome came into view, she braked
and stared in dismay through the sweep of the wind-
screen wipers. The causeway was almost under water.
The tide wasn't full yet, but the sea was running high,

the wind whipping at the waves so that they broke across the slick concrete. She checked her watch, then sat back in her seat and let out a disgusted breath. She'd timed it so she would make it before high tide, but she'd forgotten about the full moon. The bigger than usual tides combined with the bad weather had completely obliterated her safety margin for completing the crossing.

Putting the car in gear, she backed up and turned. Five minutes later she parked outside the house, collected an old eiderdown from the pile of linen she'd stored in the back of the car, extracted her bag and made a dash through the rain for the front door. On impulse she went back to the car, took out the pile of journals and carried them into the sitting room, where she'd dumped the eiderdown beside an old armchair. It wasn't much of a bedroom, but it had a fireplace and good lighting, even if the huge iron monstrosity hanging from the ceiling was possibly the ugliest chandelier in recorded history. As a child she'd always kept a wary eye on it, frightened that it would come crashing down. Even now, years later, she still had a habit of skirting the chandelier whenever she walked into the room.

After dusting the chair off, she turned to the fireplace. The house had power, and the temperature wasn't cold, but even so, she felt chilled. If she had a fever, and she thought she most probably did, then she was going to need a fire.

Wind and rain hit her as she stepped out of the

back door, so she had to cling to the rickety banister for support as she negotiated the steps, nursing her throbbing hand and shivering as rain plastered her shirt to her skin.

The small shed that Hannah had used to store firewood creaked with every heavy gust of the wind. She pulled the door wide, wedged it back with a piece of wood she found lying on the ground and stepped into the murky interior. There was a scuttling sound, and a cobweb caught in her hair. She brushed the sticky strands aside, too tired and too wet to worry about mice or the spider. Gingerly she collected logs and carefully stacked them in the crook of her arm so she didn't have to use her sore hand. As she stepped outside, a violent gust of wind shoved the door at her, catching her shoulder. The wood tumbled from her grip. Automatically she clutched at it with both hands. A log caught her bandaged palm, and nausea swept through her in a wave.

When her stomach stopped rolling, she pushed the door back into its previous position with her shoulder and anchored it against the shed wall with a heavier piece of wood. Taking a deep breath, she crouched down and gathered two of the logs she'd dropped, maneuvered them into the crook of her arm and carried them inside. Her progress was slow, and she was getting soaked to the skin, but after the third trip she decided she'd had enough for the night. The next problem was that there was no axe to cut kindling with, and even if there was, she didn't think she could manage that, so she needed to find sticks and twigs. Minutes later, after she'd managed to fill a plastic grocery bag with the unexpected treasure of a pile of wood chips and bark on the sheltered side of the woodshed, she tramped inside to light the fire.

There was no problem finding newspaper, but by the time she was ready to light the fire, even the simple act of striking a match was excruciating, because she had to use her hurt hand, and she'd begun to shake uncontrollably—so cold her teeth were clacking together.

She dropped the first match, then scattered more as she tried to extract another from the box. On the third strike, the match flared and she held it to the newspaper. When the first flames licked over the kindling, a shudder went through her, and she shuffled closer to the building warmth until the heat penetrated her wet jeans and shirt. After she'd added the first log, she peeled out of her soaked clothing and laid it on the hearth to dry before wrapping herself in the eiderdown and settling in the sagging comfort of the armchair. As she stared at the flames, the storm steadily increased in ferocity. Wind and rain battered at the old house, wailing around the roof and pounding the uneven old glass in the windows like lead pellets from a shotgun.

She fed the fire when it dropped, stacking it high, then checked her watch, incredulous to note that it was only nine o'clock. Normally at this time of year it stayed light until later than this, but the storm had brought night early, plunging the island into premature darkness.

She considered examining the mysterious brooch and dagger, which she'd brought with her on the off chance that she would find some clue as to where they'd come from or who they'd belonged to, but decided she was shaking too much to handle the antiquities. The last thing she needed now was another cut.

When her clothes were dry she pulled them on, shivering as the warm fabric came into contact with her skin; then she cuddled back into the quilt. For a while she flipped through one of Hannah's journals, trying to read the fine script that had faded through the years, tears pricking at her eyes as she heard Hannah's voice in the abrupt, cursory notes describing everything from the wonders of the pyramids to the steamy depths of the Amazon basin. Finally she put the journal down and reached for her bag. She didn't feel like eating, but she should have something. There was still a peanut butter sandwich left from the lunch she'd packed, a muesli bar and half a bottle of water. Her stomach turned at the thought of the peanut butter sandwich, so she forced herself to slowly munch her way through the muesli bar, then sipped the water until it was gone. When she'd finished her makeshift dinner, she switched off the light and sat watching the flames, listening to the storm until her eyelids drooped.

* * *

A rending screech shocked her out of sleep, followed by an explosive detonation of sound. Shards of plaster rained down on her head; a split second later glass shattered, and wind and rain hammered into the room. For disorienting moments Laine couldn't think, couldn't move, her mind a frozen blank, the glow of the fire her only reference point. Then the icy chill of rain soaking her shirt registered, and she stumbled to her feet, cradling her hurt hand as she pushed the already sodden quilt aside. Out of pure instinct she bent and groped for her bag, her fingers tightening convulsively around the strap of her holdall as she clumsily slipped her arm through the loop and hooked it over her head so that the bag hung beneath her arm. As she straightened, the eerie, long-drawn-out moan of metal tearing froze the blood in her veins.

The house was collapsing around her.

She was halfway across the room when a massive gust of wind hit the old building with all the power of a gigantic fist. The floor beneath her feet shuddered, tilted, as if the house was caught in the rolling grip of an earthquake. Something heavy flexed and shifted above her head. A shower of sparks lit the room with a cold blue radiance as electrical wires cross-connected and fused; then Laine flung herself to the floor...and into darkness.

Light woke her, so bright she winced, her mind groping in blind confusion until she realized that the light glaring into her face came from a torch. Recollection flooded back. The storm. Hannah's house. A cold shock of adrenaline cut through her. She needed to think, move, but she felt odd, floaty…and cold, so cold….

"Out. *Now.*"

The voice was rough, curt. A hand curled around her arm, the heat of it fiery against her chilled skin as she was hauled to her feet. The strap of her bag pulled uncomfortably between her breasts, and the bag itself banged against her hip, so that she swayed off balance. She heard a muttered curse; then an arm clamped around her waist, pinning her against the furnace heat of a large male body. Her head swam, her stomach rolled, and for the second time that night she passed out.

Kalil swung Laine up into his arms and carried her outside into the storm. Wind hit him with all the force of a locomotive, but the tension in his gut eased the second he cleared the rickety steps of the house.

He paused in the scant shelter of the Range Rover and set her feet down so he could pull the door open, bracing it with his shoulder as he eased Laine onto the passenger seat.

Rain swirled into the lighted cab, instantly wetting the interior, but he ignored the rain as he leaned over Laine and checked her pulse and breathing, then began methodically checking for injuries. They were both soaked; a little more water wouldn't matter.

He didn't find any injuries other than small cuts—

and an older wound on her hand, which she'd already bandaged—although he couldn't be certain until he'd conducted a more thorough examination back at his house.

His jaw tightened as he put the vehicle in gear and eased carefully through the quagmire that used to be Hannah's drive. He hadn't found any discernible head injury, yet she was unconscious. She could have internal injuries, in which case they were in serious trouble. He didn't know how long the cyclone would take to blow itself out, but he was betting on another twenty-four hours, minimum. He was good with first aid. After years of nursing Karen and learning how to administer drugs and injections, he'd turned into a damn good nurse, but he was no doctor.

Minutes later the headlights of the Range Rover picked out the wrought-iron gates that guarded the entrance to his house. He stabbed the remote, barely clearing the gates as they swung wide, then jerked to a stop beside the front door.

The unearthly howl of the storm rose over the dull roar of surf on the cliffs below, striking an eerie note as he lifted Laine out of the front seat. She was still unconscious, and shivering so hard her teeth were chattering. Grimly Kal entered the house, shouldered his front door closed and strode toward his suite, not bothering with the niceties of removing his sodden boots as he took the stairs two at a time. He headed straight for the shower, pausing only to unloop the bag she'd hooked around her neck and drop it on the floor before he pulled the lever, waited the few seconds it took for the water to heat, then stepped beneath the warm stream.

Laine's eyes flickered open when the delicious stream of warmth abruptly stopped. Dazedly she registered that she was leaning against a solid male frame, and that she was having trouble standing. The man holding her was tall and dark and instantly recognizable. He was fully dressed, as she was, his hair long and coal-black and streaming with water as he propped her up in an elegant, marbled walk-in shower. A shiver went through her as she remembered the rending screech that had pulled her from sleep. "The house?"

"It was still standing when I drove away. Tomorrow might be another story. The roof was gone, and it looked like the house itself had been pushed off its foundations. It won't take much more for the whole lot to collapse."

She closed her eyes, aware that she should pull away from him, but she felt limp and exhausted. "Sorry about this. I'm sick. Flu, I think. Or maybe it's my hand. Hurts."

He helped her out of the shower. She groped for the wall, then sat down on the edge of the tiled bath, shivering as her skin cooled.

He handed her a towel, his gaze sharp. "Do you need help?"

Laine gazed at him blankly for a second before his meaning filtered through. A violent shiver jerked through her; she locked her jaw against it. "I'll be fine. I just need dry...." For a moment he didn't move, his dark gaze cool and appraising, and she revised her estimate of his age. She'd thought he was twenty-five, but maybe he was older...thirty, but no more.

"I'll get you one of my shirts to wear and see if I can find anything else that might fit. You're stuck here until morning, at least. If the weather doesn't let up, maybe another day. I'll leave the shirt hanging on the door handle."

The door closed behind him. Laine let out a breath, toed her soaked sneakers off, then began peeling off clothes, nausea rolling through her every time she had to exert any pressure on her sore hand. The shirt was difficult, because the buttons were small and her fingers were shaking uncontrollably, but removing her wet jeans was the worst because they clung stubbornly to her hips and she had to drag them down in increments.

The dry shirt was big, the sleeves hanging way below her hands, the hem at her knees, but Laine scarcely cared. The cotton was thick and soft, and it covered her. She rolled up the one sleeve that she could and left the other dangling.

Her hair was a bundled mess at her nape, with strands hanging loose. She shouldn't leave it to dry like that, because it would matt and then she would never get it untangled, but she didn't have the energy to deal with it now.

She deposited her wet clothes in the bath, then used the bath mat to blot up the puddle of water she'd made on the floor, but even that simple act left her breathless and exhausted.

A rap on the door told her she'd been too long. Careful not to move too suddenly or jolt her hand, she picked up her bag and walked out of the bathroom into a large, masculine bedroom.

She saw that he'd changed into dry jeans and a white T-shirt. His hair hung damply around his shoulders, unusually long for a man and black as a raven's wing.

He gestured toward the bed, which had the covers pulled back. "This is where you're sleeping. Lie down, and I'll check you out. And don't argue," he added, when her head came up. "You're moving okay, which means you haven't broken any bones, and you probably don't have any internal injuries, but you did pass out. Something's wrong with you, and I'm the closest thing to a doctor you've got."

Gingerly she eased into the bed, shivering at that first contact with the cool sheets, her skin so ultra-sensitive that even the fine cotton weave felt abrasive. Exhaustion and cold aside, she was also aware that this must be *his* room, his bed, but after a house practically collapsing on her, that fact seemed a mere detail. It was a bed, and she didn't know how much longer she could keep her eyes open. "How close?"

He shook out a thermometer and inserted it beneath

her tongue. His gaze touched on hers. "Close enough. My wife died of leukemia. It was a learning curve."

His wife. She lay quietly with the thermometer in her mouth while he took her pulse, silently digesting the information that he had not only been married, but that he was now a widower. Somehow she had never imagined him married at all. With the hard masculine beauty of his face, that silky mane of hair, he didn't look in the least domesticated. Ellen had been mooning over him in the library, but as confident and experienced as she was with men, Laine didn't think even Ellen could handle this guy. Civilized or not, he looked as wild and aloof as that big stallion he rode. She couldn't imagine him helping out with grocery shopping or doing the laundry, let alone putting his feet up and watching TV. Dimly she recognized that a part of her didn't like it that he'd been married— the same incomprehensible, stubbornly female part of her that had been vulnerable enough to fixate on a virtual stranger. Her eyes flickered, slid closed as she pondered the tension in her chest. She knew what it was, but she couldn't fathom why it should be there, or just *why* she should feel hurt.

Chapter 5

Kalil put Laine's wrist down and took the thermometer out of her mouth. Her pulse was a little fast, which wasn't surprising, given the trauma of the past half hour, and it was no big surprise to see she was running a temperature. When he'd checked her over in the Range Rover, her skin had been icy, her teeth chattering. Even now, despite the insulation of the feather quilt, chills jerked spasmodically through her.

Hypothermia was a consideration, but he'd discounted that. Despite the storm, the weather wasn't cold; it was the middle of summer. The cyclone had dropped temperatures, but not by much. She'd said she thought she had the flu. That was a possibility, but he'd also seen the way she favoured her hand.

Kalil sat on the edge of the bed and pulled the quilt

back far enough to extract her bandaged hand. When he unwound the wet bandage and saw the puffiness of infection, he let out a breath. He didn't need to be a doctor to know that what Laine Abernathy needed was a stiff course of antibiotics. Relief eased some of his tension. When he'd driven over to check on her and seen the state of the house, he'd braced himself for a situation he couldn't handle, but he could do antibiotics.

After rousing her enough to take a pill and drink some water, he cleaned and bandaged the cut, loaded another quilt on top of the one she'd bundled tightly around herself, then walked downstairs to lock up the Rover and the house.

As he climbed the stairs a short time later, a massive gust hit the house. The lights flickered, then resumed, which meant the mainland power had just been knocked out and his emergency generator had cut in. Retracing his steps, he went to check on the fuel supply for the generator, then checked the rooms on the seaward side of the house for damage. Everything was intact, as he'd expected. When the house had been designed, he'd specified tempered glass for all the windows. The architect had looked to cut corners, but Kalil hadn't seen any point in constructing a house with quarried stone if the windows were fragile. Money was no option, and he knew what he wanted. Some instincts, he thought, never die. There was nothing subtle about the design; in his family it was time-honoured—he'd built a fortress.

When he checked on Laine, he saw that she'd kicked off most of the bedclothes, and that her skin was dewed with perspiration. After getting some more water into her, he collected a bowl and flannel and sponged her face and arms and legs. He made her pillows more comfortable, tucked the sheet back around her and paused to broodingly consider the woman lying in his bed, before he dealt with all the wet clothes.

He'd spent the previous night tossing and turning and wondering what it would be like to have Laine Abernathy in his bed. After five years of celibacy, this wasn't what he'd envisaged.

After loading wet clothes into the washing machine and putting her sneakers in the hot-water cupboard to dry, he examined her bag. It was made of raffia and was soaked. It should dry out easily enough, but the contents would also be wet.

He began tipping items onto a towel: an empty water bottle, a sandwich wrapped in plastic, a leather purse and a battered leather book, a piece of what felt like jewelry wrapped in silk...a hairbrush. Something heavy caught in the lining, then slid forward. Silver and gold flashed under the muted lights as a dagger tumbled onto the thick toweling.

Kalil's gaze fastened on the familiar shape of the crest inlaid into the hilt, and without warning his head swam and his chest felt tight, heat burning in the centre like a hot coal. His fingers brushed cold metal, and emotion swept him, as fierce as the cry of a hunting falcon, as dazzling as hot sun glancing off steel.

His. The dagger was his.

All his life he'd experienced moments of what he could only describe as déjà vu. Sometimes those moments had slipped over into something even more powerful—a vivid picture, an inner certainty, knowledge he couldn't possibly have. On rare occasions, a recognition of objects and places.

When he was a small child, he'd sometimes spoken in different languages, fragments of archaic forms of Arabic, Latin, Greek and French. He couldn't remember doing it, and he couldn't speak those languages now. His parents had taken him to specialists, concerned that he might have some mental disorder. Physical tests hadn't shown any abnormalities, and the psychiatrists had been stumped. His first memory of the strangeness that haunted him was when he was seven and his father had given him a tour of the ancient armoury in the palace. Kalil had stopped by the collection of swords, pointed at a battered blade with a gold falcon worked into the hilt and announced that it was his. His father had gone pale and looked at him for a long moment, then nodded and allowed him to take the sword to his room and prop it in the corner by his bed, even though he was too young to have a blade and almost too small to carry the heavy weapon.

After that, the visits to the psychiatrist had stopped. His father, brought up with Eastern mysticism, had understood that his young son's perceptions were, on occasion, overlaid by those of an earlier time. His New Zealand-born mother had found the episodes more difficult to accept, but she'd married into an Eastern family, an Eastern culture. Acceptable or not, she'd had to cope with what was happening to her child. She had watched Kalil with worried eyes, and for her own peace of mind had researched everything she could find on the whole area of psychic phenomena and reincarnation, but as the years had passed and the moments of oddness had lessened, she'd relaxed. Her son might possess something extra in his makeup that her other children didn't have, but all in all, he was no different from the rest of her brood.

Kalil straightened, the ancient blade in his hand, his gaze shuttered and cold. The dagger was his, the crest recognizably his family's. To his knowledge, the crest hadn't changed in over a thousand years. Some ancestors had embellished around the falcon a little more, some had added words, but the falcon in full hunting cry had never altered. The dagger belonged to his family. It belonged to *him*. He'd never seen it before, and Laine Abernathy was carrying it around in her bag along with her peanut butter sandwich.

It posed a question, a lot of questions. Where had she gotten the dagger? The easiest answer was Hannah, which didn't sit right with Kalil. Hannah had been many things—an intrepid explorer, a souvenir hunter—but she had never been a thief. Somebody had been, though. The dagger was a priceless artifact dating back to the time of the Crusades. It had been hand forged by artisans for Al Saqr, one of Saladin's most successful generals.

The knowledge burned in his mind, as vivid as the glitter of light off the blade. The dagger had been made by Tantalus, a wily Greek rogue with hands mottled and deformed with burns, a tongue as sharp as the wrong end of a whip, and a skill with metals that would have made him rich, if he hadn't drunk his profits.

Kalil couldn't "remember" what went before that basic recall, or what came after, but he could see Tantalus's dark, lined face, the avaricious gleam in his beady eyes, as clearly as if he'd spoken to the Greek just minutes ago. It was always the same; every now and then something jumped out of the murk that was his mind and bit him on the ass.

But all weirdness aside, the one thing he was clear on was that the dagger was his. He had been there when it was made.

He didn't know why he remembered anything, or what purpose there was in remembering, but questions and confusion aside, Kalil had decided early on that for him the situation was black and white. He knew who he was in this life, and he had known since he was seven years old that in the twelfth century, amid the blood and the despair of the Crusades, he had been someone else. He had been Al Saqr.

* * *

At two in the morning he fed Laine another antibiotic. She was still feverish and barely conscious as she swallowed the pill and sipped water.

Kalil sat back in the chair he'd pulled up beside the bed, sprawled his legs out and tried to get comfortable as he listened to the storm battering the stone walls of the house. He'd slept in snatches, if at all, but he was too aware of the woman in his bed, and too unsettled by the episode with the dagger, to relax fully. Folding his arms across his chest, he settled deeper into the armchair. With any luck, Laine's fever and the storm would both break by morning.

A sharp sound pulled him from sleep. For a brief moment he was disoriented; then memory flooded back.

Laine. She'd kicked the bedclothes off. The sheet was tangled around her legs, and her skin was sheened with perspiration. Automatically Kalil reached for the bowl of water and the cloth on the bedside table, and began sponging her down. Her hand gripped his wrist, knocking the bowl of water from his hand so that it cascaded onto the floor.

"Kalil," she whispered, and tears squeezed from beneath her lids.

Shock ran through him. She had said his name with the ease of someone who knew him intimately, but they had never been introduced. It wasn't beyond the bounds of possibility that at some time in the past she had found out from Hannah what his second name was, but there was no logical reason for her to use it.

He was almost certain she didn't know he was the Sheik of Jahir.

She released her grip and lifted her hand as if she was reaching for something. He caught it, rubbing her palm soothingly, and then her voice came again, low and stumbling, as if she was explaining something, the words blurred, an almost incomprehensible mixture of French and...*Arabic.*

Her eyes flickered, opened, and a chill skimmed his spine. They were fever bright and eerily fixed. She stared at him blankly, cupped a hand around his nape and pulled his mouth to hers. He tensed, bracing himself on the bed as she clung to him, arching so that her breasts rubbed against his chest. Her fingers wound in his hair, anchoring him more firmly against her, and he shuddered as her mouth moved against his. The kiss was urgent, desperate, as if she feared losing him, and he felt her nipples turn hard, pressing into his hot skin through the layers of clothing.

A groan rose from deep in his belly. He should pull back, ease free, but for the first time in years he felt sharply, achingly alive, the blood pounding through his veins. For the first time in years he was free of death and despair, and he *wanted* Laine Abernathy. He wanted to unbutton the shirt she was wearing and see her naked. He wanted to push his jeans down, get on top and slide into her. But as savage as he felt, he couldn't do any of those things. He didn't know who Laine was kissing, but he was sure of one thing: it wasn't him.

Her hand slid down his chest, brushed the tight point of his nipple beneath the soft cotton of his T-shirt. Every muscle in his body locked. The touching was intimate and deliberate—familiar, as if they'd already made love many times. His stomach clenched as her hand smoothed down his torso, slid between the waistband of his pants and his tautly held lower belly, and closed around him. Kalil went rigid in her grasp. Her fingers tightened, and he came on a harsh groan, the abrupt shock of climax jerking through him in hot, shuddering waves as he caught her hand hard against him. The last convulsive twitch played out, and he pulled free, still sweating and shaking and semi-aroused as he stumbled from the bed, raking hair back from his face.

As he grabbed more clothes from his drawers and peeled off his jeans, his gaze fixed on the woman in his bed. After years of abstinence, he'd just been had by Ransome's librarian, and she didn't even know what had happened. She'd already fallen back into a deeper level of sleep, her lashes velvety dark against her pale skin, mouth lush, nipples tight, dark points beneath his shirt.

"Who are you?" he murmured.

There was something about Laine that drew him, but the feeling wasn't defined like the moment of certain knowledge he'd experienced with the dagger. From the first, sensory impressions had swamped him, and they still did. Every thought he had about Laine was tangled up with his libido.

One thing was for sure, the quiet reserve she wore like armour was only a disguise. Laine Abernathy was a wildcat in bed.

As he stepped into the shower, excitement stirred through him, tightened low in his belly. Her touch had unlocked something raw and barbaric in him, and now he wanted a lot more than the hurried fumble they'd just shared. He wanted her beneath him, and when he penetrated her, he wanted her eyes open, on *him*. Most of all, he decided grimly, next time he wanted her awake.

He didn't know who she imagined she'd just had in bed with her. There weren't many eligible men in town: the tall, skinny guy from the bank, or maybe Silas Baker's son. There were bound to be more. Ransome serviced a relatively large rural area, but he had been here less than a month, and in that time he hadn't exactly been interested in checking out the single male population.

His jaw tightened as he flicked off the shower and reached for a fresh towel. He didn't care who the opposition was, he would deal with it, and soon. The next time he got Laine in bed there would be no confusion at all about who it was she was making love to.

At four in the morning Laine started shaking again, the chills so violent that Kalil finally slid into bed with her, piled the quilts over them both and wrapped his arms around her. As her shudders gradually subsided and he drifted toward sleep, he remembered that earlier in the evening, just before Laine's mouth had fastened on his, she had spoken in Arabic. The words had been husky and slurred, but some of them he had understood well enough. She had called him her beloved.

Chapter 6

Laine woke to the insistent howl of the wind and rain drumming on windows still shrouded with heavy drapes. She had no idea what the time was, because the storm had blanketed everything in a preternatural gloom, although she sensed that it was late in the day rather than early.

She flexed the fingers of her sore hand. It throbbed a little, but not painfully. She felt altogether healthier than she had in days, her mind clear, the flu-like symptoms gone, although she still felt tired, her body curiously disconnected.

Remnants of the previous night surfaced as she swung her legs over the edge of the bed and padded to the bathroom. She remembered being rescued, waking up to find herself being held upright in the shower, then climbing into bed and having her temperature taken. She washed her face and hand, and studied herself in the mirror. She looked pale, and her hair was a mess. It had stayed bundled in its knot, but strands had escaped to trail down her back. As she secured the loose strands, another memory swam up out of the dim confusion of the night, although she wasn't sure whether it was a memory or a dream. She remembered being kissed.

Her stomach clenched as she stripped off the shirt and stepped into the shower. Awkwardly she began soaping herself, trying to keep her hair and her bandaged hand dry at the same time, but she was having difficulty concentrating. She was a librarian and a scholar; she had no problem separating reality from dreams. She *had* dreamed last night, and *he* had been in her dream, but that kiss had happened—it had been real. She could remember the hard pressure of his mouth. She could remember how he tasted.

Abruptly she turned the water off, stepped out onto the bath mat and toweled herself dry.

She felt strange, unsettled—alive and female in a way she never had been before. It was as if she'd been asleep for years and was only now waking up, and her acute sensitivity scared her.

She spread the towel on the heated rail and reached for her clothes—which had been laundered, neatly folded and left on the vanity counter—relief flooding her as she dressed. The clothes represented control, and after the past twenty-four hours, she was desperately in need of some of that.

After brushing her teeth with the new toothbrush and toothpaste that had also been left out on the counter, she unwound her hair and, using the comb she found, began untangling the knots. When she was finished, her hand was beginning to throb again, so instead of attempting to put her hair up, she compromised by twisting it and letting it fall in a rope down her spine.

She paused, her hand on the handle of the bathroom door, suddenly reluctant to leave the privacy of the small room.

He had kissed her.

Heat shafted through her. Her skin was flushed and oversensitive, her nipples tight and aching. Closing her eyes, she leaned her forehead against the cool, smooth surface of the door, wondering if she was going mad.

After years of being happily single, happily celibate, she didn't know why her body should do this to her now. For Laine, the sex act had always been firmly tied to emotion, which made the way she was feeling now even more bewildering. She barely knew the man she was fixating on.

Pulling in a breath, she opened the bathroom door and walked out into the bedroom.

While she'd been showering, the curtains had been pulled back, and the two sets of bifold doors that had been hidden behind the drapes had been opened, revealing a paved terrace overlooking gardens and lawns. Drawn by the view, she stepped outside and looked around. The wind had dropped, and the rain had subsided into a drifting drizzle. The temperature had risen, and steam wisped off the formal paved area below, wreathing a marble fountain and lending a primordial quality to the tropical plantings. Despite the calm, big purplish clouds still obscured the sun, making the light yellowish, and signaling the onset of more wild weather.

As she glanced around, the size and scope of the sheik's house became immediately obvious. It was built of massive blocks of quarried stone, the lines stark and simple. It wasn't so much a house as a walled fortress, the whole, including lush gardens, enclosed by heavy walls. The room she presently occupied was part of the central tower, which was also winged by two smaller towers. Off to the right she could make out another line of buildings, which must be the stables, but other than that utilitarian roofline, everything her eye encompassed was distinctly mediaeval. Mod cons aside, the whole place could have been transported straight from the time of the Crusades.

She heard a step and turned as the sheik's groom walked through the door with a tray. He looked as if he'd been out in the rain; his T-shirt was damp and clinging to his shoulders, and his hair, which was now pulled back into a ponytail, was sleek with rain.

He set the tray down on the bedside table and

joined her on the patio. "You look a lot better than you did last night."

"I feel a lot better. Thanks a lot for pulling me out of Hannah's house. I think you probably saved my life."

He shrugged. "I knew you were stuck in the house, because I could see the lights. I also knew the old place wouldn't stand a cyclone. I should have gotten there sooner."

She stuck out her hand, then grimaced and retracted it when she realized it was her bandaged one. "I'm Laine Abernathy."

He nodded. "Hannah Ransome's niece. I bumped into you the other day."

She waited, but he didn't supply her with his name. She met his gaze steadily. "I don't know your name."

His face was curiously still; in the gloom, the planes and angles of his face shadowed. For a moment she thought he wasn't going to answer; then the odd tension dissipated. "My given name's Xavier, but most people call me Kalil."

Kalil. A wisp of memory surfaced, then slipped away just as fast. She frowned. The name was familiar, but she couldn't put her finger on when, or where, she'd heard it.

He strolled back inside. She followed, watching as he selected a bottle of pills from the tray, which also held a plate of cut sandwiches, a bowl of fruit and a pitcher of water.

He shook a pill out of the bottle. "How are you feeling?"

"Better. Well enough to go home."

"You won't be going anywhere for a while yet. You've slept most of the day. It's after four, and the tide's almost full in. And this calm won't last. We're in the eye of the cyclone now; the tail end of the storm will be on us before long. I'm afraid you'll have to spend another night."

A raw spasm went through her at the prospect of spending another night with Kalil. The previous night she'd been so ill she'd hardly been aware of him, but that was all changed now.

He poured a glass of water and handed it to her, along with the pill.

"Antibiotic," he said briefly. "You haven't had the flu. That cut on your hand got infected. Poisoned your whole system."

"The cut." She let out a disgusted breath. "I was planning on making a doctor's appointment when I got home. I didn't bother before because it was so shallow it just didn't seem to warrant that much trouble."

"It was bad enough to knock you over."

She took the pill and drank the glass of water. As soon as she'd drained the glass, she poured another, abruptly thirsty. As she sipped her way through the second glass, he reached for her bandaged hand.

She sat down on the edge of the bed, while he

pulled up a chair, and allowed him to unwind the bandage.

"Is your tetanus shot up-to-date?"

She nodded, then winced when she saw the cut. It looked clean, but the flesh was still puffy and pink around the shallow slice, and fluid oozed from the centre of it.

He examined the cut, frowning. "What did you cut yourself with? It's not deep, you don't need stitches, but it's sure caused you a lot of trouble."

"A dagger," she said flatly. "It was dirty—I think it had dried blood on the blade. God only knows how old the blood was or who it belonged to. I'm just hoping it was *very* old…if you get my drift."

A wisp of amusement curled his mouth, but his gaze was cool, remote. "A dagger. That's an unusual thing to cut yourself with."

"There weren't many *usual* things in my aunt's attic. I could have sold tickets when I started cleaning it out. Do you know she actually had a sarcophagus?"

"You're kidding."

His amusement turned into a full-fledged grin, and her heart started thumping harder.

"Nope, and it was full. No mummy, though. Hannah drew the line at ghoulishness. She filled it with books. Said the sarcophagus kept the silverfish out better than anything."

His shoulders began to shake. "Silverfish. That was Hannah."

"You knew my aunt?"

"I met her when she came out to Jahir researching the old trade routes."

Laine couldn't repress her own grin. "She sold you that line? You realize she was really looking for sunken treasure."

His grin deepened, and she felt herself go all warm and melty inside, which was not a good sign. She'd never felt like this. She didn't want to feel like it now…all fizzy and happy, like a teenager on her first date. "We showed her a couple of wrecks and she was happy. She drew the line at putting on scuba gear."

He began smearing ointment on the wound. Laine gritted her teeth, then felt like a wimp when it didn't hurt much, although she couldn't relax until he began winding on a fresh bandage.

He fastened the bandage with a clip and stood, moving the chair back into place. "When I dried out your things last night, I found a dagger in your bag. Is that the one you cut yourself with?"

Startled, she nodded.

"Mind if I look at it again?"

Kalil's gaze strayed to Laine's hair as she bent and reached for her holdall, which he'd placed beside the bed earlier on in the day. Ever since he'd walked into the room, he'd barely been able to pull his gaze from the mouthwateringly long rope. In the dull light the colour was rich, the texture satiny, so that he longed to reach out and run his fingers through the silky strands.

Gingerly she lifted the dagger out and handed it to him. "It's heavy, not your usual cheese-board accoutrement. I guess in those days size counted."

Her comment surprised another grin out of him. "I don't think that philosophy will ever change."

Her gaze dropped fleetingly, and Kalil stifled a groan. All she'd done was look at his zipper and he was gone. There was no way she could miss his arousal now, but at least that one glance had told him what he needed to know. Laine might have been dreaming about someone else last night, but he had her full attention now.

"This was with it." She handed him a piece of jewelry.

He set the dagger down and took the brooch in his hand, and everything inside him went still.

He had his own unique insights into the past, but he also knew the history of his family—it was long and well preserved. Al Saqr had had a wife who, after he'd died, had borne him a child. Kalil had always thought that if he was able to remember anything from that time, he would remember that relationship, that woman, but he never had. All he had to go on was a gut instinct that whoever she'd been, she was special. He knew her name, the bare details of her background, but that was all he'd ever had—eight-hundred-year-old information that was about as useful as a name, rank and serial number. As hard as he'd tried to make a memory happen, all he'd ever come up with was a frustrating blank. It seemed he could remember his weapons and his name, he could re-member his horse and the drunken artisan who'd made his dagger, but he couldn't remember the woman he'd been in love with when he died.

He turned the brooch over and examined the in-scription on the back. When he saw the initials and the de Vallois crest, he went blank with shock. "This was in Hannah's attic?"

"It was hidden along with the dagger in a secret compartment in a book, which probably explains why both items didn't get sold off by some member of the Ransome family years ago."

She bent back to the bag, and the dark swing of her hair drew his eye again as it slowly unraveled from the thick, loosely wound rope. When she straightened with the book in her hands it spilled silk-ily around her shoulders, partially veiling her face, and déjà vu hit him like a breaking wave, the dizzying sense of time dissolving so strong that the floor seemed to tilt beneath his feet. He swallowed, took a deep breath and tried to get his bearings, but it was like fighting a tidal surge. Her gaze touched on his, jewel-green in the watery light, and his belly clenched. A name ached in the back of his throat.

Laure.

The sharp click of the brooch hitting the floor broke his momentary stasis.

Laure—*Laine*—gave a startled cry and went down on her knees. The brooch was in two pieces; the am-ethyst had popped out of the setting.

She held the two pieces gently cupped in her palm and awkwardly tried to put the brooch back together, but with the bandage impeding her movements, it was an impossible task.

"Leave it," Kalil said hoarsely, taking the brooch from her and setting it down on the bedside table alongside the dagger. "I'll fix it." He'd fixed it before. It was—*had been*—her favourite piece of jewelry.

Laine climbed to her feet and found herself so close to Kalil that she was practically in his arms. The only way she could have gotten so close was if *he* had moved.

His gaze locked with hers, and heat swept through her. She knew he was aroused. She had seen it happen, and the moment had turned her legs to jelly. He hadn't made any attempt to conceal his arousal; in fact, she was certain he had wanted her to know he was turned on, and the knowledge filled her with panic. She had no problem understanding why she wanted him, but she didn't understand why *he* wanted *her.*

His fingers slid through the curtain of her hair, and she froze, transfixed by the caress.

"I need to kiss you."

The rough statement made her mouth go dry. For a split second she wondered if she'd heard wrong, but the heat in his gaze burned away her doubts.

"Let me," he said hoarsely, then lowered his mouth to hers.

His breath shuddered against her lips, the caress more exquisite, more intense, than anything she could have dreamed or imagined. Everything was moving in slow motion, her bones turning to liquid in the steamy humidity of the room. She felt as if she was once again caught in a curious limbo somewhere between dream and reality, held in thrall by the dark intensity of his gaze, the stroke of his hands in her hair, the hunger of his mouth as his lips pressed hers apart and his tongue slid into her mouth.

White-hot intensity shafted through her, so that for dizzying moments all she could do was wind her arms around his neck and hold on. She could smell the wind and rain on him, the warm scent of horse, the clean spicy scent of his hair.

His hands found her bottom and gripped, his fingers digging into her as he lifted her against him and ground the firm swell of his sex into the soft flesh between her legs. Another raw shock of desire went through her, so powerful that she hung blankly in his grip, clinging to his shoulders. He hadn't spoken again, except to mutter her name. She didn't care; she was in the grip of a fever of a different kind. Every part of her responded to Kalil. She wanted him, the emotion so powerful it swamped her.

He lifted his mouth, and a muffled moan rose to her lips.

His gaze locked with hers. "Let me make love to you."

Emotion shuddered through her, threatened to take

her under. Suddenly she didn't care if this was a casual encounter never to be repeated, or if it was something more. It didn't feel casual, and she needed it to happen with an intensity that scared her. "Yes."

He groaned, his arms coming hard around her.

Just as abruptly, he released her, peeled his T-shirt off and let it drop to the floor. With his torso naked and his jeans moulding his long legs, he looked wild and uncivilized, his muscles sleek, his shoulders broad, gleaming copper in the dim light of the room. It flashed through her mind that she was way out of her depth. Then his mouth came down hard on hers, and she was lost. He kissed her for a long time, his mouth hungry, feverish, as if he was starving for her. She felt his hands at her jeans, easing the denim and her panties down to her ankles. She stepped out of the puddle of clothing, and his hands slipped up her bare legs, beneath the tails of her checked shirt to cup her bottom, his palms warm and rough against her skin.

Her head spun as he tumbled her onto the bed. He reared over her, broad and dark in the increasingly gloomy room as he unfastened his jeans, mounted and penetrated her in one smooth movement.

His gaze locked with hers. "I don't have a condom."

She could see the question in his eyes, feel the tautness of his muscles as he fought for control.

Shuddering heat rolled through her, the decision abruptly made. There was a piercing intensity in his gaze, an aching sweetness, that reached inside her, shattering the code she'd lived by all her adult life. What she was doing was wild—impulsive—she'd never had unprotected sex in her life, but she didn't want to stop. Everything was wrong; nothing had ever felt so right.

She arched wildly under the impact of the first heavy thrust and clung to his shoulders, dazed at how quickly he'd entered her and quivering beneath the burning lash of pleasure. He was smooth and hot in-side her, and for long seconds she fought to adjust to the enormous sense of impalement, the knowledge that he was naked inside her.

Her fingers tightened on his shoulders, and he groaned. Lightning played through the room as he began to thrust, holding her gaze as he held her spread beneath him, penetrating her fully each time, sliding in a powerful rhythm that made her twist restlessly beneath him, her hips rising to meet the heavy plunge of his.

Rain spattered on the windows, floated on the hot air, the scent of the storm mingling with the scent of their bodies as the tormenting rhythm continued. She still had her shirt and bra on, the fabric damp and twisted and clinging to her skin.

Denim scraped on her sensitive inner thighs as wave upon wave of tingling heat slammed through her. It was hot, so hot. She couldn't bear it, the heat building inside her, all the air pressed from her lungs.

His mouth found the exposed arch of her throat,

and pleasure poured through her, white-hot and intense, building the pressure even higher, so that tears seeped from her eyes in mute frustration.

His thumbs stroked across her cheeks. "What's wrong?"

"I can't," she said flatly.

His dark gaze was fixed on hers. "What do you mean, can't?"

"I can't...climax. I never have."

Something fierce and primitive flashed in his eyes. "You will this time."

He gripped her wrists and stretched her arms above her head, his voice low and soothing as he held her arched beneath him. He dipped, and his mouth closed over the tight, sensitive bud of her nipple through the layers of her shirt and bra, and she climaxed on a hot shock of pleasure, crying out into the dark, wet afternoon, the sound absorbed by the muffling fall of rain.

A growling purr tore from Kalil's throat as he shoved deep and held himself locked against her so that she felt the pulsing hot flood of his release.

She must have drifted off to sleep, because when she woke, Kalil was moving inside her again, a deep, slow glide that made her senses spin so that she stretched and arched beneath him, basking in the heat that poured from his big body like a lazy cat on a terrace. She had climaxed, and it felt wonderful. *She* felt wonderful...different, as if that moment had unlocked some hidden female part of her. For years she'd thought she was defective in some basic way, but the problem had been simpler than that. She had never made love with anyone who had touched her deeply enough.

The rain had intensified again, a dull drumming in the background, and lightning flickered, splitting the sombre gloom. Moist heat seemed to explode through the room, so that perspiration dewed her skin. The excitement of the electrical storm ran through her body, making her breasts tight, the nipples painfully erect. She felt at once lethargic and sleepy, yet so utterly alive that every nerve ending tingled.

"Kiss me," he murmured.

Framing his face with her hands, she pulled his face to hers. The kiss was long and leisurely and delicious, and delight shivered through her. She had never fully enjoyed kissing before, disliking the intrusion of a male tongue, but now she gloried in it, gloried in the sheer animal pleasure of touching Kalil, learning his scents, his taste.

Eventually he lifted his head to watch her with heavy-lidded eyes. Rain continued to fall, the steady drumming hypnotic. A damp breeze stirred the warm air as he unbuttoned her shirt, pushed the lapels aside and bent to suckle her through the lace of her bra. The lazy thrusting continued, subtly increasing her tension until the hot ache spread through her belly, throbbed in her breasts. Thunder rumbled, and abruptly the room became dimmer as the cloud cover thickened. Another flicker of lightning played through the room.

His heat, the musky scent of his body, rose up,

engulfing her, making her head swim. Sleepily she ran her hands over his shoulders, his back, almost purring with pleasure, loving the feel of him.

The muscles of his back flexed beneath her fingers; his hips moved sharply in response. Her nails sank into his skin at the rougher penetration. He pushed her to the brink of climax again and again, until she was swamped by sensation, every nerve ending acutely sensitive to his slightest touch.

After a period of time he stopped moving and simply held himself deep, his belly tight against hers, the heat building with every pound of her heart until the exquisite tension whiplashed, and she arched.

Kalil said something low and rough as she shivered and clenched around him, the fit so tight that even that movement was restricted.

"Oh, do that," he groaned, and she felt him twitch and spurt deep inside her, his whole body shuddering in her arms.

When next she awoke, the murky gloom of afternoon had deepened into the oppressive heaviness of another rain-filled night. The room was lit by the dim glow of a lamp, the bifold doors had been closed and Kalil was moving about the room drawing the drapes.

In the shadowy gloom, with his hair loose around his shoulders, he looked big and male and exotic, his every movement fluid and catlike. He was different from any man she'd ever known or was ever likely to know, and so utterly alien when compared with Robert, with his hound's-tooth jackets and chiselled English good looks, that her mind kept stalling every time she considered that she had just made love with him.

It was still raining outside, a slow, heavy pattering that increased the steamy heat as Kalil came back to bed. His arm came around her, pulling her snugly into his side as naturally as if they'd shared the same bed for years. With his free hand he reached for the tray on the bedside table, balanced it on his legs and offered her a sandwich filled with ham and thick slices of avocado. As she bit into the sandwich, she realized she was starving.

Between bites he asked her about her job, her house, her family, his interest intense, keeping her talking until they'd finished the makeshift meal. When he left to take the tray downstairs, she realized that she'd told him most of the salient facts of her life but hadn't managed to find out much about him other than the fact that he'd attended school in the States and was now more than content to occupy himself with the horses and the challenge of farming the island.

That was the problem. When he was around she could barely think, let alone reason. He simply overwhelmed her. It was a safe bet that everywhere he went, women swarmed over him, fussing and spoiling and cooing, and that he was so used to the constant feminine attention, he probably hardly noticed it.

She found her shirt, pulled it on and fastened the buttons before using the bathroom. The mirror threw back a reflection that startled her, and for a moment Laine had the unnerving feeling that she was staring at a stranger. Her eyes were sparkling, and her mouth was soft and full, her hair a silky tangle around her face.

For the first time she realized how devoid of emotion her life had been since she'd found out Robert had been unfaithful. She'd simply closed down, not allowing anyone close. The deaths of her parents and then Hannah hadn't helped. She knew she'd pulled inward even further after each funeral. Living in Ransome in her parents' house, peaceful as it was, had isolated her even more.

Kalil had swept into her life and turned it upside down. He'd proved she wasn't weird or lacking. She was a normal, healthy woman, and she had a sex drive. She didn't know how much she could change, but the process had started, and she was determined not to stop.

When Kalil returned, she was already in bed. Mouth dry, she watched as he unfastened his jeans, pushed them down and stepped out of them. His body was smooth and muscular and brown all over, with very little body hair, his genitals heavy but beautifully formed.

When he climbed into bed with her, the full consequences of his nakedness hit her all over again. When she'd made love with him this afternoon, she'd been battered by emotions that were alien, powerful, but now her stomach churned at the risk she'd taken—for them both. She let out a breath. "You could make me pregnant."

"Is that likely?"

"My period ended over a week ago," she said

flatly. "I've always been able to feel my cycle. I ovulated on Friday."

Something hot and bright flared in his dark gaze. His hand tightened on her waist as he gathered her close. "Then it's too late. It's already done."

Pregnant.

Laine felt as if she'd just been hit by a train.

A baby, *Kalil's* baby, probably already forming in her womb.

A sharp sense of certainty filled her. What she'd said to Kalil was true. She knew her body, was sensitive to its every cycle. The chance that she wasn't pregnant was so small that she didn't even consider it.

She tried to imagine what it would be like to have Kalil's child growing in her belly, and a shuddering heat rolled through her. She hardly knew him. Right now she hardly knew herself. It was crazy to want a child. If she got pregnant, her options would be narrowed, and so would his.

"What if I do get pregnant?"

For a moment his expression was blank, as if he hadn't heard; then his gaze snapped to hers, dark and possessive.

"I'll marry you."

Chapter 7

The next time Laine opened her eyes, it was daylight and she was alone. She lay for a moment, listening to the steady howl of the wind, her stomach knotting at the spectacular U-turn her life had just taken, and the decisions she had to make.

Propping herself on one elbow, she checked the bedside clock. It was six-thirty. She yawned and sank back into the warm comfort of the bed; then awareness, along with a solid dose of reality, hit. She jackknifed, jerking the covers back. It wasn't Sunday, as she'd initially thought. Sunday was yesterday. Today was Monday, and she had to go to work.

She showered and dressed, the details of her life gradually piling up. Aside from the library to open, she had to go home and check on Hector. He hadn't been fed since Saturday morning. If he was hungry, he always had the option of moving back with old Mr. Appleby across the street, but all the same, she worried. Hector was stolid, but loyal. Whatever reasoning process went on in his little cat mind, he had chosen to live with her over Harris Appleby. As much as he loved food, she wouldn't put it past Hector to stubbornly refuse to go back to his old home just to get fed. She also had her house to check over for storm damage. When she'd left on Saturday, she hadn't prepared for a cyclone. Not that there was much she could have done, but if a branch had gone through a window, she would have water damage to cope with.

She stopped in the act of buttoning her shirt, abruptly disoriented.

She was worrying about whether or not she had to mop up water, when the most important thing she had to do today was make an appointment to see Janice and see how soon she could have a pregnancy test done.

Her hand strayed to her flat belly.

He had said he would marry her, but she shied away from that. No matter how enticing that fantasy was, no matter how much she might want that to be possible, it just wasn't. They had slept together, period. That didn't make a marriage, no matter how much either of them might want it to be so. She wouldn't allow Kalil, or anyone, to railroad her into a relationship that didn't have a chance of working.

After she'd brushed her hair into some semblance of order, she strolled through the house, looking for Kalil. As she descended the stairs into a spacious, richly furnished foyer, she was overwhelmed by how little she knew about her surroundings—and this man. She'd been in the house since Saturday night, but she'd spent most of that time in bed. Now the utter separation from her normal, everyday life, the strangeness of her situation, hit her all over again. Time had seemed suspended. *Some of the most important rules she'd lived by all her adult life had been suspended.* It was past time to go home.

She wandered through a lounge, a kitchen and family area, and a formal dining room, looking for Kalil or some sign of life. She knew from local gossip that the sheik used a professional cleaning and gardening service, but he obviously didn't have anyone but Kalil living in. Eventually she found an office. A pair of riding boots was stuck under a beautifully crafted kauri desk, and a denim shirt was hooked over the back of the swivel chair, indicating that this was Kalil's office. As she turned to leave, a photograph on the wall caught her eye, and she paused to study it. The photo was a relaxed family portrait of Kalil with a couple who had to be his parents. Beneath this photo was another of Kalil's father, dressed in formal robes.

Laine went still inside. Disconnected bits of information began to fall into place. The size and luxury of Kalil's bedroom and bathroom, his years of travel, his education in the States.

She didn't have to open any drawers or rifle any files; the fax letterhead sitting on the desk blotter, with a note scribbled and signed by the sheik in a strong, flowing hand, told her all she needed to know. The fax had been sent yesterday. The only person who could have signed it was Kalil.

She stared at the thick creamy paper, her mind blank. The man she'd just spent the past thirty-six hours with wasn't a groom or a hired hand. He was the Sheik of Jahir.

Taking a deep breath, Laine retraced her steps back to Kalil's room. Methodically she collected her bag and checked that she hadn't left anything behind; then she walked from the room in the direction opposite the way she'd gone before. Instead of finding the back entrance she was looking for—one that faced *away* from the stables—she ended up in a lounge that opened onto a private enclosed courtyard.

She stopped and tried to get her bearings, but the house was large and sprawling, with wings going in different directions. Numbly she opened doors and kept walking, passing through another huge lounge, then on into a suite of rooms that were fully self-contained, including a gleaming kitchen.

Now that she knew the house belonged to Kalil, the incredible wealth of her surroundings began to register: the art on the walls, the beautifully crafted wood floors strewn with rich Turkish rugs. She found a door to the outside, stepped out and closed it behind her, uncaring that it was still drizzling.

There was a word for what she'd just done. It was *dumb.* Not only had she slept with a younger man she barely knew, she had slept with a sheik who possessed wealth beyond her imagining. Their relationship, if you could call it that, was the mismatch of the century.

She rounded a corner and, despite her determination to go in the opposite direction, found herself staring directly at the stables, which also included a set of garages. Movement registered out of the corner of her eye, and her heart slammed hard in her chest as she caught a glimpse of Kalil. Shrinking back out of sight, she turned on her heel and walked quickly back the way she'd come, only to find that the door she'd closed was now locked.

Closing her eyes, she took a deep breath and counted to ten. To get out of this house she had to either walk past the stables and risk bumping into Kalil, or cut through the thick plantings and find another way out.

It was no contest. She wanted to go home. Alone. She had to think, and she had to have time to pull herself together. In bed, her relationship with Kalil had been simple. He was a man and she was a woman, and against all the odds, for a few hours, they had found something magical, but now she was utterly confused. She didn't know what Kalil wanted, but one thing she was sure about: she wasn't it.

The gardens were covered in a thick layer of bark, which made for easy walking, but every leaf and branch she disturbed dropped water on her, so that she was soaked to the skin within seconds. The garden ended in a wall, which she followed until it butted up against the house and another locked door. Frustrated, she retraced her steps, following the wall in the opposite direction, zigzagging around palms until she heard a horse whinnying and stopped in her tracks. The wall was taking her back to the stable courtyard.

That made sense. Restricting access to the house was one of the first rules of good security, and this house would have very good security. Just because Kalil's home was on an island didn't mean it couldn't be burgled. It was filled with expensive furniture and appliances, not to mention the art on the walls and the exquisite rugs. The Sheik of Jahir would never have to buy copies or cheap imitations of anything; he would buy the originals, first class all the way.

Hitching her bag more securely over her shoulder, she walked the perimeter of the wall and studied the trees. She was getting out of there, and if she had to climb a tree to do it, then that was what she would do.

Minutes later she selected a tree with branches that brushed the top of the thick wall and pulled herself up onto the first branch, gritting her teeth as pain spiked through her hand and twigs caught in her hair.

To reach the wall she had to lean out at a precarious angle and jump.

Throwing her bag over the wall, she took a deep breath and launched herself from the tree branch, landing on her stomach with both elbows hooked over the edge, anchoring her in place. For a moment she simply lay there, getting her breath back; then with a shimmying movement, she levered her legs up onto the ledge and dropped onto the grassy field on the other side.

Minutes later she clambered over a wire fence and began walking through the thick, tussocky grass toward Hannah's house.

The sight of her car parked alongside the house filled her with relief. She didn't know how long it would take Kalil to realize she was gone and come looking for her, but she didn't think he would be far behind. She didn't fit into his life, but that didn't change the way he was or the way he'd react. As mysterious as he was to her, there were some things about Kalil she had instantly recognized. He was strongly male and used to taking charge. Over the space of the past couple of days, he had rescued and cared for and made love to her. They had crammed the equivalent of weeks of courting into a weekend. He wouldn't like it that she'd walked out on him.

She retrieved her keys from her bag, unlocked the car and slipped into the driver's seat, but when she turned the key in the ignition, nothing happened. On a surge of disbelief, she turned the key again. Nothing.

Sitting back in the seat, she stared at the key dangling in the ignition and felt like thumping the steering wheel. How dare her car betray her at a time like this?

She took a measured breath. Think. What could it be? Maybe the rain had blown beneath the bonnet and had soaked the electrics, and it was just a case of waiting for the moisture to dry? But there had been no sound at all when she'd turned the key. The engine was absolutely dead. The starter motor should make a noise, but it hadn't, which meant that the battery was probably flat. She would need a jump start to get the motor turning over and the battery recharging— if it was worth recharging. She'd bought the car new, and it was now five years old. In that time, there had been no major repairs, and she hadn't changed the battery. Chances were that the battery had simply died.

She tried the key one more time, then abandoned the car. The causeway was only a few minutes away if she took the track behind Hannah's house.

When she reached the causeway, the sea was still running high, but the tide was low enough to allow a crossing, despite the fact that occasionally larger waves sent spray dashing across the surface. She hesitated, then started walking as briskly as she could, watching the waves and her footing, because the surface was treacherous with algae. As she reached the other side, the sound of a vehicle registered, and she saw the rural delivery van coming toward her.

Toby Bolton, a widower in his sixties, pulled to a halt beside her and pushed the passenger door open.

"Saw you from my house. Thought I'd see if you needed a lift."

Wearily she climbed into the passenger seat, dumped her holdall on the floor between her feet and pushed wet hair back from her face. Toby would have seen her walking across the causeway from his house, which overlooked most of the town and the island. Not much happened that he didn't personally see.

As Toby slowly reversed and turned the van, a flash of movement on the island caught her eye. Adrenaline pumped, but the movement turned out to be one of the itinerant goats that inhabited the island picking its way down to the rocky, windswept shore.

Toby gave her a speculative look before he put the van in gear and chugged slowly up the hill. "Been staying at Hannah's place? Thought that old house was condemned."

Laine sat back and took a steadying breath, trying to calm her pulse rate. She could lie, but the last time she'd tried that she'd been ten, and she'd been lousy at it. "The roof blew off Hannah's house. I spent the weekend at the sheik's house."

Toby's withered hand slipped on the gear stick. The gears graunched, and the old motor coughed and almost died. Toby looked as if he was on the verge of having a stroke.

Laine closed her eyes and let her head drop back on the cracked vinyl headrest. The whole town would probably have a stroke. An Abernathy had finally done something unexpected.

Hector was waiting for her when she got home. As soon as she unlocked the door, he shot inside like a plump ginger bullet and zeroed in on the fridge.

Laine put her bag on the kitchen table, took out a carton of milk and poured some into a saucer, then shook some kitty bites into his tray. While Hector was tucking in, she rang Ellen and told her she was taking the day off sick; then she rang the auto electrician and arranged to meet him outside her house in ten minutes. When she hung up, she took the phone off the hook, changed out of her wet clothes into fresh jeans and a T-shirt, collected her first-aid box and sat on the edge of the bed to dress her hand, her mind numb as she smeared ointment on the cut, then wound on fresh gauze. The cut actually looked better despite the beating she'd given it today. Dully she noted that the antibiotics Kalil had given her had cleared up the infection. Pity it wasn't that easy to clear up what was wrong with her now. She'd spent the weekend making love with the man she had dreamed and fantasized about, a man she had no hope of holding.

And she'd had to go and fall in love with him.

A tear splashed on her wrist as she fastened off the gauze, then another. Sniffing, she rummaged in her drawer for a handkerchief, blew her nose and wiped her eyes, but the tears kept trickling down her cheeks. All she wanted to do was lie down on the bed and have a good cry, but she didn't have time. If she stayed here, Kalil would find her, and she wasn't ready for a confrontation.

Her heart squeezed tight as she locked the house and went to wait for the auto electrician's van on the sidewalk. She didn't want to go back to the island so soon, but life didn't make allowances for a bruised heart. She had to get her car before the tide turned, and, if it was possible, she had to retrieve Hannah's journals from the house.

Kalil checked the library. The grey-haired lady at the desk told him that Laine was off sick today, but when he asked for her address, she eyed his long hair with fascinated horror and refused to give it to him, citing the Privacy Act. Kalil thanked her and strode across the road to the Town and Country.

Silas Baker's eyes narrowed at his request, as if he was contemplating withholding the information. Kalil eyed him flatly. His account wasn't a small one, and he was likely to spend a lot more. He wasn't above applying a little pressure—not ethical, maybe, but the hell with ethics; he needed to find Laine—*now*.

When Silas found out he was the sheik, he caved. "She lives down on Timms Street, just off Broadway. There aren't any numbers. The house is white, with a green roof and postbox. A big ginger cat usually sits outside her place. Can't miss him."

Kalil took the first left into Timms Street and cruised slowly down. The street was filled with old established properties with large trees and picket fences. There was a large ginger cat sitting in the middle of the road outside a colonial-style white house with elegant verandahs wrapped around two sides, and rambling gardens. He swerved around the cat and pulled into the drive.

The house looked closed and empty, and when he pounded on the door, no one answered. He walked around the house and peered in windows. Apparently Laine wasn't at work and she wasn't at home.

Kalil swore beneath his breath. Unless she had left town entirely, the only other possible place she could be was on the island, collecting her car. She had probably left for the island while he was talking to Silas. He must have missed her by a matter of minutes.

Aside from the fact that the roof was missing from Hannah's house, and that the entire structure had shifted off its piles, moving a few inches to one side, the house looked eerily normal from the front. Out back it was a different story. The kitchen lean-to had slumped, all the windows were shattered and pieces of the roof were scattered over the back lawn and in amongst the trees.

The front door was hanging off its hinges, and the hallway itself was soaked, the floor littered with plaster. The sitting room was an even bigger mess. Broken glass and plaster littered the floor, and the old rotted drapes still hanging over the front bow window flapped in the breeze. The ceiling had been extensively water damaged and was sagging. In places the rafters were exposed, and the iron chandelier had dropped a few inches and hung at a precarious angle, shifting and turning with every gust of wind. Laine gave the chandelier a wide berth as she quickly walked around the edges of the room to retrieve Hannah's journals, which were still sitting in a pile beside the armchair.

As she carefully gathered the fragile, sodden notebooks, a faint noise registered above the steady roar of the waves and the wind.

Kalil was standing in the doorway.

"Have you got a death wish?" he said quietly as he walked toward her, his gaze moving around the room, studying the damage. A heavy gust hit the house, and the curtains flapped wildly. "I should have known you'd—"

"*No!*" Horror filled her as the chandelier rotated at a drunken angle directly above Kalil's head. There was no time to explain, no time to do anything but launch herself at Kalil and hope she was fast enough. She hit him full in the chest. His arms wrapped around her as they fell, and he somehow managed to roll so that his back hit the floor and she ended up sprawled over his chest. A split second later the heavy iron chandelier speared into the wood floor in a flurry of plaster. The ornamental spikes stabbed clear through the hardwood, missing them both by inches.

Seconds later they were both outside.

Laine leaned against her car, her legs still shaky.

Kalil eyed her flatly. "Are you crazy, walking into a house that's on the verge of total collapse?"

"In case you hadn't noticed, the house is still standing, despite a cyclone, and I was only in there for a few seconds getting Hannah's journals. *I'm* not the crazy one. I didn't walk under that chandelier."

"Not the crazy one," he repeated in a soft, even tone, and a shiver coursed down her spine. "Lady, I ought to put you over my knee."

"Just try it," she muttered, shoving strands of hair back from her face. "See what you get."

"A fight?"

The odd tone in his voice had her meeting his gaze warily.

"As it happens," he continued, "I'm looking for a fight. Why did you run out on me?"

"You're a sheik."

"You're a librarian."

She wrapped her arms around her waist in an instinctive defensive gesture, and also to hide the fact that her hands were shaking. She was probably as white as a ghost, to boot. When she'd realized the chandelier was about to fall on Kalil, cliché or not, she'd actually felt all the blood drain from her face. "I'm glad we agree on something."

"We agreed on a lot yesterday. And the day before."

Heat flushed her cheeks. "We had sex."

His hand rested on the car roof behind her. "Don't piss me off," he said silkily.

"I'm thirty-two," she snapped.

"And I'm twenty-eight. The statistics for sex and longevity are all in our favour."

She gritted her teeth. "You can't seriously want me."

"Feels pretty serious to me. What do you suggest I do about it? Go and have *sex* with someone else?"

Laine felt herself going white again, and he swore beneath his breath.

"You asked for that. For your information, I have never had casual sex with anyone. The last woman I made love to was my wife, and that was over five years ago, just before she started on chemo."

Laine squared her jaw against a surge of hope. She wanted this fantasy to be true, wanted it so much it hurt. "I've been trying to figure out why you want me," she said doggedly. "Aside from the fact that you're a sheik, you're four years younger than me. I'm a divorced librarian, and the only male who's shown any interest in me in the last two years is a cat."

"You own that big ginger cat that sits on the road outside your house?"

She blinked. "You've been to my house?"

"I was there a few minutes ago."

Her heart began to pound so hard she was having trouble breathing. She had known Kalil would come after her. Part of her panic when she'd been trying to find her way out of his enclosed fortress of a house had been rooted in an instinctive recognition of that fact. Even so, the swiftness and efficiency of his pursuit stunned her. She had assumed that when he found she wasn't at work or at home, he'd back off and that their next meeting would be more than likely accidental, and buffered by the distance of time and embarrassment. "Technically, the neighbour owns Hector. He just moved in on me."

"The cat's got taste."

His other hand came to rest on the roof of her car behind her head, so that she was effectively corralled. The heat and scent of his body wrapped her, cutting out the cool bite of the wind. "Why did you come after me?"

"How about the fact that I'm in love with you."

She blinked, struggling to absorb his words. She'd dreamed about Kalil—wrenching dreams that had had her waking in tears. He'd rescued her, and she'd spent the weekend in bed with him. She had no problem admitting she was in love with him, but she couldn't see how he could possibly be in love with her. "Don't say things you can't mean."

"I haven't said one thing I don't mean. And there's more. Whether or not you believe any of it is your choice, but you'll damn well listen." He began talking, his voice deep, flat, almost completely devoid of emotion as he chronicled events in his childhood and from another lifetime, places and objects he'd recognized.

As Laine listened to the spare, harsh narrative, fragments of dreams surfaced like bright pieces of flotsam, blending seamlessly into the barbaric vignette of life and death, of blood spilled and love lost, sending a chill skimming down her spine. What he was saying was impossible, and yet she could ''see'' him, different and yet the same, *feel* the dreams as if they were actual memories. The sun, hot, searingly bright. Dust in her mouth, stinging her eyes, the wild, lonely cry of a falcon. Loss and grief so intense her belly contracted and all the air was squeezed from her lungs.

She didn't realize she was crying until his hands cupped her neck and his thumbs brushed tears from her cheeks.

He was silent for a moment. ''When I picked up the dagger you'd found, I had that same sense of recognition I'd felt for the sword when I was a child, and when you handed me that brooch, I got another jolt.'' A shudder went through him. His gaze locked with hers, fierce and bright. ''*I remembered you, Laine. I finally remembered you.* I was already falling in love with you. Remembering kicked me right over the edge. In 1192, that brooch belonged to you. Your initials and your family's crest are carved into the back of it. Your name was Laure de Vallois, and you were married to Al Saqr. I don't care that it was eight hundred years ago, it feels like yesterday. I was Al Saqr, Laine, and you were mine. You were married to *me.*''

His fingers slid through her hair. "The night you were ill, you had a dream. You spoke in Arabic."

"I don't know any Arabic." She shook her head. "I did dream...." And the dream had been like the others: more vivid, powerful. She shook her head again at the sheer impossibility that what seemed to be happening could actually *be*. Everything she'd been taught told her that what Kalil had just explained wasn't possible, yet everything inside her cried out that it was more than possible. "I've had the same dream more than once. The man in the dream..." She closed her eyes briefly. "He looked like you, but you can't be him." She stopped, swallowing. Tears were sliding down her cheeks again, and suddenly she didn't care what was rational and what wasn't. The grief she'd felt was *real*, and still so raw that the horrifying battle she'd dreamed could have happened yesterday. "You *died*." She touched his chest, half expecting the terrible wound to open up. "If the dreams are real, then I didn't save you. I had the chance, and I—"

"Shh," he said soothingly. He unbuttoned his shirt, exposing his chest. He touched a point midway on the breastbone. "That's where the dagger went in. It's a hell of a place to stab anyone, because the bone and cartilage are so thick." His mouth curved in a grim smile. "Sometimes it aches there, but there's no wound now."

The wind gusted, blowing his hair into a rough tangle about his broad shoulders. He looked wild, barbaric, yet his dark eyes were so soft she felt as if she could melt straight into them. Dreams or reality, she could almost taste the wild sweetness of how it had been between them, the intolerable need that had pulled at her both then and now. But the stark, uncompromising hunger of that love scared her. She was used to the quiet, grey world of scholars and libraries, of weeks, months, years to study and work, to plan and decide. "You were married."

"So were you." His black gaze burned into hers. "And if you were married to your ex-husband now, it wouldn't make one bit of difference. I'd take you from him."

It was odd that it took that flat male statement to convince her. For the first time in days she felt completely calm. Why would she want to run, when this was what she'd been waiting for all her life? She was in love, head over heels in love, and the man she wanted wanted her enough to obliterate anyone and anything that stood between them.

She blinked to clear the moisture from her eyes. With that one blunt statement she had seen him—not in any mysterious way, but simply as a man. Whether he was spurring a war stallion into battle, loading sacks of feed onto a trailer or taking her temperature, she *knew* him. He was direct and ruthless, and so soft beneath all that machismo that just looking at him did strange things to her stomach. She no longer cared if he was Al Saqr, a sheik or a ranch hand—he was Kalil, and she wanted him. The clean angles and planes of his face came into sharper focus. "Yes," she said bluntly.

"Yes, what?" he demanded, and she realized she'd pushed him to his limit. He might be a modern man, living in a space-age world with jets and computers and fax machines, but his instincts were still firmly rooted back in the twelfth century. If she refused him, he would likely toss her over his shoulder and carry her away regardless. Last week, that thought would have scared her; now she felt an almost feline satisfaction that she could get that far under his skin. Falling in love with Kalil had kicked her out of the rut she'd dug herself into, and despite the fact that she was about to shackle herself to a man who had challenge stamped into every cell of his body, a heady sense of freedom soared through her veins.

She lifted her hand to his chest and pressed her palm against the place where the dagger had pierced him, gritting her teeth against the whispering echo of grief. "I'll marry you."

His stillness was disconcerting, his gaze fixed on her but eerily distant, so that for a moment she wondered if he'd heard; then he muttered something low and rough beneath his breath.

The unexpected familiarity of the phrase sent a jolt of emotion through her so powerful that for an endless moment time dissolved and there was no past, no future, only the moment, and it seemed to go on forever.

All the blood drained from her face. "What did you say?"

His gaze was stark, arrested, and for the barest second the gulf between them opened up again, as cold as time, as powerful as eternity. His hand closed over hers, pressing her palm more fully into his chest so that she could feel the pounding of his heart, and the sense of separation evaporated in the living warmth of his touch.

"Mon coeur," he repeated softly, voice hoarse, tears glittering in his eyes. A primal little shiver slid down her spine. "It's been so long."

Epilogue

Five months later

"I've found it," Kalil said quietly.

Laine put down the peeling knife and went to peer over his shoulder, her stomach turning over as it always did when she was near him. Kalil had been studying the genealogy of her family in the Ransome family Bible, which she'd taken down from the shelves for the express purpose of recording their marriage to complete the record for the current generation.

He pulled her onto his lap, his arms warm as they cradled her and the faint bulge that was the baby they were expecting in four months' time.

He pointed to a faded entry near the beginning of the genealogy. Amalie Marie de Vallois had married a Ransome back in 1739, before the Ransomes had emigrated to New Zealand.

A tingling chill went up her spine as she reread the Bible entry. The final piece of the puzzle had just fallen into place. She'd done extensive research on Kalil's family and the de Vallois family in an effort to find some kind of link that would explain why her aunt had had the dagger and the brooch in her keeping, but the scant remnants of information she'd managed to uncover hadn't cast any light on the mystery.

She knew that Laure de Vallois had borne Al Saqr one child and had managed to keep him alive through the final years of the Crusades. The remnants of the sheikdom had made it to the island of Jahir, and it was the shipping wealth that Laure had brought to the marriage that had formed the basis for the sheikdom to be reestablished after the years of fighting and levies had broken the back of the family's wealth. There had been no information of a personal nature about Laure's family, other than that she had been one of several children in the extremely wealthy and powerful de Vallois family.

This entry in itself wasn't conclusive, but it was enough for Laine.

"Laure de Vallois was my ancestor."

She swallowed, the remembered grief from the dreams still so intense it made her ache inside. "If only Al Saqr—" She stopped. Her mind still tripped over the fact that she and Kalil had lived and died before, that the dreams she'd experienced weren't dreams, they were memories. "If only he'd lived."

"He's alive now."

She eyed him flatly. "I won't let you die this time." This concept she had no trouble with. She had her man, and she was keeping him.

"Don't worry, I'm planning on being a wizened-up little old man this time. No more messing around with knives." His hand curved warmly around her nape, and he grinned lazily. "I'm even careful crossing the road these days. Got a lot to live for."

She thumped him on the chest. "Don't joke about it. Sometimes…"

"I know." He clasped her hand and smoothed her fingers open, careful of the still-tender skin around her scar, and pressed her palm to his chest so that she could feel the rapid slam of his heart. His gaze burned into hers, abruptly fierce. "It's finished. We've come full circle, back to a new beginning. We live for *now,* not the past."

Her eyes narrowed. "Does that mean you're giving up fencing?"

He ducked his head and kissed her neck, but she caught the edge of his grin.

"You're not," she accused, not bothering to hide her outrage, after all the assurances he'd given her. "You still like it. You're still *him.* You still want to fight."

"Mon coeur," he complained, his voice muffled as

he nuzzled her hair. "I'm a married man now. I can get all my fighting done at home."

She hit him on the shoulder, and he complained some more. She was forever beating him, which went against his dignity as a sheik, and to add insult to injury, she never called him her lord in bed the way he wanted her to, and she didn't say she loved him often enough.

Somehow her hair got undone, and so did his, and it was such a wild mess over them both that she didn't see what he was doing with her shirt until it was too late, and then she had absolutely no will to resist, anyway.

Other things happened that had no right to happen next to an open Bible…. The casserole burned…and the potatoes never did get cooked.

Hector sat stolidly in the kitchen, watching the fridge and complaining loudly, and Laine had the fragmented thought that she was going to have to get used to complaining males, because the ultrasound she'd had last week had revealed that the baby was a very definite boy.

There was a minor crisis when the oven started to smoke, but Kalil managed to put the fire out before it did too much damage. Despite being naked and having to work around Hector's unmoving bulk, he handled the minor disaster and the prospect of buying a new stove with a philosophical shrug. After all, what could you expect when your wife abandoned preparations for dinner to make love to her husband?

He wasn't about to complain; he'd never been happier. He'd waited over eight hundred years for this kind of bedlam to come into his life.

It was kismet.

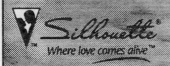

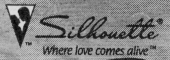